A winter snowstorm on a desolate highway. Amanda and her daughter were not alone.

The other car was slowing down even more now, making Amanda slow down as well. Her speed dropped down from twenty miles an hour to fifteen to ten, and then the gray car pulled into the center of the road and stopped.

"Why did he stop?" Ashley asked. "You think he's looking for a motel, too? Maybe he's lost."

"I don't know," Amanda said, feeling more uneasy by the moment.

"Oh, look," the girl said, pointing. "He's from Massachusetts, too. Maybe that's why he stopped."

Amanda felt an icy lump of fear growing inside. . . . There'd been a gray car behind her most of the day. Now one had caught up with her and forced her to stop, one with Massachusetts plates.

"Mom, what . . . ?" Ashley's question trailed off because the gray car's door had opened and a man was stepping out.

"Mom!" the girl exclaimed, grabbing Amanda's arm. "It's him, the guy who tried to get me after school. . . .".

TENDER PREY

S.W. BRADFORD

JOVE BOOKS, NEW YORK

To Sharon Novotne and Bill O'Keefe

TENDER PREY

A Jove Book / published by arrangement with
the author

PRINTING HISTORY
Jove edition / November 1990

ISBN: 0-515-10421-3

Jove Books are published by The Berkley Publishing Group,
200 Madison Avenue, New York, New York 10016.
The name "JOVE" and the "J" logo
are trademarks belonging to Jove Publications, Inc.

PRINTED IN THE UNITED STATES OF AMERICA

10 9 8 7 6 5 4 3 2 1

PROLOGUE

THE man who opened the door was wearing a ski mask.

The motel was a brick *U*, one of those independent operations where the owners lived on the premises and where you could spend the night for less than half of what it would cost at a big chain. The accommodations were neither luxurious nor seedy. No pool, no playground for the kids, no restaurant, but no cockroaches, either. The place was located on Route 9, midway between Boston and the western Massachusetts city of New Shipton.

The man in the ski mask glanced nervously around the asphalt parking area, apparently making sure no one was out there watching; then he stepped back from the doorway, motioning for them to come in.

"This is Dick Kilmer, my cameraman," Amanda Price said as the man in the ski mask closed the door.

Kilmer set down the two cases he was carrying. One contained his video camera, the other lighting equipment. He immediately began removing his gear, setting it up.

"You don't need the ski mask," Amanda said. "Like I told you, we'll electronically distort your face and your voice. You've seen how it's done. Your face will be a bunch of little squares."

"He'd see me," the man said, looking at Kilmer. "So would the guy who did the electronic distortion. This way's safer."

"You just want to go with the ski mask, or you want your face distorted too?"

"Both," the man said. "These people find out who I am, I'm dead. Period. You understand that?"

"Nobody'll learn who you are. You have my word on it."

"I'm only doing this because I want to help put a stop to what's going on in New Shipton. I don't want it bad enough to die for it, though." His blue eyes peered out at her from behind the ski mask, driving home the message.

"I understand," she said.

Dick Kilmer had placed the camera on a tripod. Now he was setting up a pair of lights, which stood about seven feet high on lightweight aluminum stands. The cameraman was in his mid-twenties, tall and lean, with thick brown hair and eyes that were an unusual shade of dark blue. He was a hunk who had probably slept with half the women working at the TV station. Amanda was not among his conquests, however. The politics of working in a TV news department were complicated enough without getting into sexual entanglements with your coworkers.

"Ready whenever you are," Kilmer said.

"Where you want us?" Amanda asked.

"How about him sitting on the edge of the bed and you facing him in that chair?"

They moved into the positions Kilmer had suggested, and he clipped a small microphone to the guy's shirt, then handed another one to Amanda, which she attached to her dress. The cameraman asked them both to say a few words, checking the audio level, then he said, "All set."

"Anything in that picture that would identify this motel?" the guy in the ski mask asked.

Kilmer said, "The background's just the wall, and that'll be out of focus."

The man in the ski mask nodded, Kilmer started shooting, and Amanda said, "Tell me about New Shipton. Tell me what goes on there."

"Where do you want me to start?" the guy asked. "The bribes and the kickbacks? Or the murders?"

"Let's start with William Steen, the guy who wanted to build the restaurant."

"Yeah, Mr. Steen. Came in from the Midwest, saying he'd bought the Massachusetts franchise for this chain of steak houses and he was going to build one in New Shipton. He didn't know how things were done in New Shipton and he got into trouble. He bought a piece of land on Berkshire Avenue that was zoned for commercial use, applied for a building permit, and got refused. A restaurant would require a zoning variance, which would cost two thousand bucks, a thousand to the chairman of the zoning commission and a thousand to the mayor. The guy paid once he figured out that he had no choice.

"He had his permit now, so he hired a contractor. Only the foreman showed up. To get the construction unions out there, there were more people who had to be paid off. Steen paid them off and got his workers. But he was getting madder by the moment.

"His next problems came when all his restaurant equipment arrived and was delivered to the site. It was stolen that night, every last piece of it. He went to the cops, and they said they hadn't been informed that there was anything there that needed special protection, so what did he expect? He was beginning to get the picture of the way things work in New Shipton, so he went to see the police chief and said he had some stuff that needed special protection. I don't know just how much it cost him, but he had to pay to have his missing stuff recovered, as well as the regular fee for protection. It was the chief's way of making his point, making sure Steen understood the way things worked."

"What happened then?" Amanda asked.

"They pushed Steen too far. He'd got his restaurant all built, but it wasn't hooked up to city utilities—water and sewer and all that. Which meant old Steen was going to have to pay another bribe. He went to see the utilities commissioner, but he refused to pay the five hundred the guy asked for. He said he'd been tape-recording the sessions he'd had with the police chief and the other public officials he'd been paying off. He said he had those tapes in his safe-deposit box and he was going to take them to the state police if people in New Shipton didn't start treating him right."

"We'll get back to Steen," Amanda said. "First, let's sort out who all these people are. Can you give me their names?"

"Sure." He named nearly a dozen people, including the police chief, the utilities commissioner, the chairman of the zoning commission, and the mayor.

"Which one actually runs everything? Who's in charge?"

"None of them. The guy in charge is Edward Casperson. He owns the town and everybody in it. There's Casperson Street, Casperson Lumber Company, Casperson Construction, Casperson Pharmacy. The biggest building in town is the Casperson Building. There's even a Casperson Elementary School."

"And he gets a piece of all the action?"

"All of it."

"It sounds like he's wealthy. Why does he need all these underhanded dealings?"

"How do you think he *got* wealthy? The Casperson family is like the Mafia of New Shipton."

"Let's get back to Mr. Steen, the guy who wanted to build the restaurant. What happened to him?"

"First, before they could do anything to him, they had to locate the tapes, but that didn't turn out to be a problem, because they were right there where he said they'd be, in his safe-deposit box at the New Shipton Bank of Commerce."

"They took them out of his safe-deposit box? How could they do that?"

"Casperson owns the bank."

"What happened after they had the tape recordings?"

"They killed him."

"How?"

"He was coming out of his motel room one night and got

mugged. Seems the mugger stabbed him with a long, thin knife that went up under his ribs and into his heart. One thrust. Isn't that something, a street mugger killing a guy like that?"

"Sounds more like the work of a professional hit man."

"Does, doesn't it?"

"Cops catch the guy?"

"Never got a single lead. But then the detective assigned to the case only spent an hour working on it, just enough time to type up an initial report."

Amanda took him through it again, nailing everything down, getting more names, dates, details; everything the man in the ski mask could give her without saying so much that he'd give himself away. And he told her about another murder, a guy named Wilcox, who, like Steen, had decided to fight rather than pay up.

"Have you heard about how people down in Latin America sometimes just disappear when they oppose one of those military dictatorships?" the man in the ski mask asked. "Well, that's what happened to this guy. He just vanished one day. His body's at the bottom of Ashmere Lake. North end. Check it, you'll see."

He went on, telling how a fifty-dollar bribe could get a traffic citation forgotten, a hundred dollars if it was for drunk driving—explaining how you could avoid being punished for any crime, even murder, if you had the money to pay.

"They're all part of the system," he said, "the cops, the judges, everybody."

"They're all crooked? Every last cop? Every last judge?"

"Of course. Casperson decides who gets to be a judge— just like he picks the police chief and the mayor."

"Aren't there elections? Can't the people vote these guys out?"

The man in the ski mask snorted. "Everybody in town's got what you'd call a vested interest in the system."

"The citizens of New Shipton *want* things this way?"

"A lot of them do. Some don't, but voting's sure not going to do them any good."

"Why not?"

"Who do you think counts the ballots?"

"Casperson's people," Amanda said.

"You got it. City employees do the counting. City clerk certifies the results. They could post them before election day if they wanted to. The numbers have all been decided ahead of time."

"Sounds like a wonderful place to live."

"You got a piece of the action, it's a great place to live."

"Why are you doing this?" Amanda asked. "Why are you taking the chance?"

The man was silent for a few moments; then he said, "If nobody speaks up, it'll go on forever. A hundred years from now Casperson's descendants will still be running the town, still making it a cesspool."

When they'd finished shooting the interview, Kilmer put his equipment back into its metal cases. The man was still sitting there, still wearing the ski mask when they left the motel.

"That's some heavy-duty shit," Kilmer said as they were heading back toward Boston.

The photographer was driving the station's unmarked news car, the one they used when they were being sneaky. It was a gray December day, two weeks before Christmas. A few snowflakes hit the windshield and promptly melted. The road was clear. New England was still awaiting its first major snowstorm of the season, which would not come today. The sky was just sort of dreary-looking; it lacked that white, threatening cast that meant a really heavy snowfall was in the offing.

"That dude in the ski mask was talking some heavy-duty shit," Kilmer said again. "You believe him?"

"As far as I know, it's all true," she said. "I first talked to the guy two weeks ago, and since then I've been doing a lot of checking. I think I've looked over every public record

in the New Shipton City Hall and read every back issue of
the *New Shipton Chronicle*. Sometimes you have to read
between the lines, but it all checks out."

"Man, oh, man," Kilmer said. "You got yourself one
hell of a story."

Amanda nodded. She recalled how she'd started looking
into it just on the basis of rumors, the unspecific, unproven
things people said about New Shipton. Things such as the
ready availability of hookers and drugs—even more open
than in New York, more like some Third World country
than America. Hints that there were places in town where
you could gamble in back rooms. Suggestions that you
could illegally dump hazardous wastes there if your drivers
carried enough cash with them. Stories, rumors, gossip. But
it had been enough for Amanda to sell the idea to her news
director.

At first she'd accomplished nothing. No one in New
Shipton would tell her anything. They'd talk, like the
Chamber of Commerce guy who wanted to tell her all about
the bright future New Shipton was looking at, about how it
was such a fine place for new industry to locate. But no one
would say word one about anything sordid going on in the
community.

And then a man had phoned her at the TV station,
refusing to give his name. He told her he knew she'd been
poking around New Shipton, asking questions but getting
nowhere. Would she like to hear the truth about New
Shipton? he asked. Amanda said she would, and he told her
where you could find gambling and prostitution and drugs
and who ran the operations, who paid off whom. And he
told her about the murders of Steen and Wilcox, the first
she'd heard about anyone being killed. The information, if
it checked out, was dynamite, and Amanda wrote it all
down.

Then she took a chance; she told him she couldn't use
information from anonymous sources, that they'd have to
meet face-to-face. Amanda promised that no one would

learn his identity from her, even if a judge threw her in jail and left her there. The man said no and hung up. An hour later he called back and reluctantly agreed, saying the risk to himself would be worth it if it would help end the corruption that had turned New Shipton into a cesspool.

They met at a restaurant in Framingham two days later. The things he told her on the phone had checked out. Steen, for example, had indeed been murdered by a "mugger," who'd stabbed him in the heart. And Wilcox had indeed disappeared. As Amanda had explained to Kilmer, the truth was often hidden in between the lines of official documents and newspaper accounts. Amanda knew she might well be involved in the biggest story of her journalistic career.

At the restaurant the man told her still more things, including his name. When she asked him to go on camera, his jaw dropped and he looked at her as though she were a madwoman. But Amanda persisted, promising him that his voice and face would be distorted, that no one could ever learn his identity from seeing him on television. No one but Amanda and her cameraman would know who he was. After an hour of pleading and cajoling and reasoning, she talked him into it by convincing him how much more effective the presentation would be with him telling what he knew in his own words. The more effective her report, she'd implied, the more likely it was to get action from the authorities.

And today he'd surprised her by wearing the ski mask, so that not even her cameraman would see his face. So that only one person knew his identity instead of two.

"I'm going to go to the state police," Amanda said to Kilmer. "I have to talk them into dragging Ashmere Lake for that body."

"They're going to want to know your source."

"That's the one thing I can't tell them."

"They're going to be pissed."

"Probably. But I bet they'll drag the lake."

"How you figure that?"

"They'll look awfully stupid if they ignore me and then one day Wilcox's body comes floating up, attached to the end of somebody's fishing line."

Kilmer thought it over. "You're probably right. But they're still going to be pissed."

ONE

"THAT many?" Amanda asked, astonished.

She was sitting in the office of Bob Miller, her news director. He was one of those men who went in for almost anything athletic—jogging, swimming, tennis, skiing—and it showed. He was lean and muscular and just sort of glowed with vitality and good health. His blond hair was carefully styled to look casual, and a lock or two usually hung over his forehead, as if he were a middle-aged Beaver Cleaver. He was sitting at his desk, holding up some sheets of paper on which his secretary had typed the names of numerous organizations.

"You're kidding," Amanda said.

"No," Miller replied. "Elaine looked them all up. Every one of these organizations has awards for investigative reporting. We're sending a copy of your New Shipton series to all of them."

"The videotape alone's going to cost a fortune." It was a silly thing to say. Network-affiliated stations in major markets—even medium-sized markets—made money hand over fist and usually spent it with near total abandon, buying everything from helicopters to satellite-communications trucks that could send live reports back from anywhere on the planet.

Miller dismissed her comment with a shrug. "I think you're going to win most of these awards. Then we'll promote the hell out of it." He grinned. Miller's philosophy was to promote the hell out of yourself, make yourself look so good that you dazzled the station's owners along with the

11

viewers, dazzled them so much that if the ratings fell a point or two, they'd think it was a mistake.

"What makes you so sure I'll win?" Amanda asked.

"You kidding? A special grand jury's been empaneled to investigate a dozen public officials for crimes ranging from extortion to murder. And there are exclusive pictures of the state cops pulling that body out of the water, exactly where your informant said it would be. It's the best investigative reporting that's been done around here in a hell of a long time. The other stations and the papers are eating their hearts out."

"We were lucky on the Wilcox body," Amanda said. "Another few days and that lake would have been suitable for ice skating. Wouldn't have found him till spring."

Again Miller shrugged. He wasn't a man to be concerned about could-have-beens.

Amanda's report had been aired in ten parts, a major segment of the late news for two weeks. It had been a tremendous success. The station's general manager had called her in to congratulate her. People wrote the station to praise her efforts, stopped her on the street to tell her what a great job she'd done. And most rewarding of all, even other journalists—both the print and electronic varieties— had complimented her for doing such a splendid job.

Amanda had worked long and hard on the New Shipton story. For weeks she'd gone in early and gotten home late, often giving up her weekends as well. At times she'd worried that her twelve-year-old daughter, Ashley, would forget what she looked like. But it was over now, and Amanda was relieved. She had mixed feelings about the praise she was getting. A part of her was a little embarrassed. But another part was soaking it all up, floating along on it, enjoying the hell out of it.

"I know I've said it before," Miller said, "but I'm going to say it one more time. It was a hell of a job."

And as she had nearly every other time he'd said it, Amanda felt herself blush. It was strange how compliments could be so rewarding and disconcerting at the same time. Still, there was only one appropriate way to respond to one, no matter how many times it was repeated. "Thanks," she said modestly.

"Hey," Miller said, as if it had just dawned on him, "it's Friday evening. It's the weekend. Go. Get out of here. Relax. Enjoy yourself for a couple of days."

"Consider me gone," Amanda said.

Leaving the news director's office, she stepped into the newsroom. Despite the high-tech aspects of the operation, the room looked as newsrooms had since they were invented; a huge space filled with desks. In the background was the constant crackle of police communications, which local news operations everywhere monitored so they could be aware of a newsworthy event the moment it occurred: "Ten four, Adam Sixteen . . . need a ten twenty-eight on Vermont plate Sam Lincoln Ida . . . signal twenty-one subject at 1416 East Adamley Loop." Mixed in with the cop talk was the soft clicking of computer-terminal keys. Typewriters were rapidly becoming a thing of the past, it seemed. Nowadays the script for the newscasts was typed directly into a computer, which displayed it on the Tele-PrompTer.

Amanda's blue Ford Mustang was in the station parking lot. After brushing a light dusting of snow off the windows she headed home. It was about seven, and the evening rush was over. Still, the traffic was fairly heavy. People coming into town to celebrate because it was Friday night, others getting away for the weekend, Amanda supposed.

It had been an unusually severe winter throughout the Northeast, with both snowfall amounts and low temperatures setting records. The first storm had hit a few days before Christmas, and the snow it had deposited never melted. It was now February, and the snowbanks lining the streets had grown into dirty white mountains.

It was seven-thirty when she pulled into her space in the high-rise apartment building's underground parking area.

As she rode the elevator to the sixth floor Amanda realized how exhausted she was. Although a week had passed since her last report in the New Shipton series had aired, she still hadn't recovered from the weeks of long hours and hard work. Stepping out of the elevator, she resolved to spend the entire weekend at home, doing nothing more demanding than watching television or reading.

"Hi, Mom," Ashley said as Amanda entered the apartment. The girl took her coat and gloves and hat, and Amanda collapsed on the couch.

"You look beat, Mom," Ashley said, putting her mother's coat in the closet.

"I probably look better than I feel."

"I don't know," the girl said. "You *look* awful."

"Gee, you really know how to cheer a person up."

The girl laughed. "I'm sorry. I didn't mean it the way it sounded. I just meant that you look really bushed."

Amanda nodded tiredly.

"Dinner'll be ready in about five minutes. All I have to do is pop it into the microwave. Leftovers okay?"

"In my state you could probably feed me artificially flavored soybean loaf and I'd never notice."

Ashley cocked her head. "You're close. Leftover meat loaf."

Amanda kicked her shoes off as Ashley whirled around and headed for the kitchen. Suddenly the warm, prickly sensation of love washed over Amanda, and she realized for the hundredth—thousandth? millionth?—time how lucky she was to have Ashley. Because of her job, she neglected her daughter terribly, and Ashley never complained. The girl cleaned, cooked, did the laundry, made decent grades in school, never got into trouble. Ashley was more than her child; she was her closest friend, the one person on whom she could always depend.

"Everything's in the micro," Ashley said, sitting down beside her on the couch.

"What would I do without you?" Amanda asked, patting the girl on the leg.

"Ugh! Don't even think about it. Without me to keep things running right, your life would be a disaster."

Amanda gave her a squeeze. "You're probably right."

And she wondered whether she depended too much on the girl. Ashley was, after all, only twelve. She should be out doing kid stuff, going to see movies with her friends, going on Girl Scout outings, whatever. Instead she was keeping house for her mother.

"You happy living the way we do?" Amanda asked.

"Huh?"

"Are you happy?"

"Sure. Why wouldn't I be?"

"Just checking," Amanda said, and dropped the subject, not wanting to get into it right now.

The girl had inherited her mother's looks. Both were tall and slender, with long legs, shiny dark hair, and large green eyes. The time would come when Ashley would walk into a room and not a man in it would fail to notice her. At the moment, though, she was in that gangly stage between childhood and adolescence, her arms and legs and feet growing faster than the rest of her. Her breasts were beginning to develop, an event the girl didn't seem to know how to deal with. At times she'd slip on a sweater, look at her changing profile in the mirror, and seem pleased with what she saw. At other times she seemed a little embarrassed about the whole thing. Amanda tried to recall how she'd reacted to the change from childhood to womanhood and found that she was unable to remember. It seemed ages ago, eons, epochs. Amanda had to remind herself that she was thirty-five; she only *felt* eighty.

In the kitchen the microwave began to beep softly, and Ashley said, "Dinner's ready."

They ate in silence at the kitchen table. Amanda was too tired to carry on a conversation. She found herself worrying about Ashley again. The girl spent a lot of time taking care of herself. She was too old to need day care or a baby-sitter but too young to be entirely self-reliant. Still, Ashley had adapted without difficulty to being a latchkey kid, seeming almost to thrive on the independence and responsibility.

At least when Amanda had been working late on the New Shipton story, Ashley had been able to spend the evenings with Mrs. O'Donnell across the hall. She was a nice old woman who'd lost her husband a couple of years ago. She and Ashley got along famously, the child easing the woman's loneliness while Mrs. O'Donnell provided companionship and adult supervision.

Amanda had divorced Ashley's father seven years ago, when the girl was five. Although divorce was always tough on a kid, Ashley had bounced back remarkably well. Apparently living with her mother and occasionally visiting her father seemed normal to her, and she never questioned it.

Dinner was almost over when Ashley looked at her mom and said, "Are you going to need me for anything tomorrow?"

"Sounds like you've got some plans of your own," Amanda replied.

"Well . . . Kristin's having a birthday party tomorrow."

"Of course you can go. Do we need to get her a present?"

"Yeah."

"Okay, we can do it tomorrow morning."

The girl nodded. There was something about her manner that made it clear there was more to be discussed. Amanda waited.

"It's a slumber party," Ashley said at last.

"Okay."

Ashley looked at her, puzzled. "Okay that you understand it's a slumber party, or okay that I can go?"

"Both."

"No kidding?"

"No kidding."

"Hey, great! I thought I'd probably have to talk you into it."

"I went to slumber parties when I was a kid. Girls always have slumber parties. It'll do you good to get out and be with people your own age. You spend too much time cooped up here in the apartment by yourself."

The girl took a moment to think that over; then she said, "In that case, can I have a slumber party here on my birthday?"

Amanda pictured the apartment full of giggling twelve-year-olds, eating cookies and potato chips and chattering until dawn. "We'll see," she said.

Ashley seemed entirely satisfied with that answer, apparently having learned that a *we'll see* could almost always be turned into a *yes* with only a minimal amount of effort on her part.

The next afternoon Amanda took Ashley to K mart, where she bought Kristin's birthday present, a record album. It was by a group Amanda had never heard of, and it wasn't really even a record. Records, it seemed, had been replaced by compact discs that reproduced what was recorded on them flawlessly and cost considerably more than the old black platters of her day had.

As they were leaving the store Amanda recalled the music she'd listened to when she was a teenager, when a record album had cost about five bucks—less if you found one on sale. "You ever hear of Three Dog Night?" she asked.

"Who?" her daughter asked, looking up at her blankly.

"Never mind."

Kristin, whose parents were both doctors, lived in one of those places that had been gentrified. Although it still looked a little like a slummy brick row house on the outside, the Volvos and Porsches and BMWs parked along the street made it clear that there was nothing at all seedy about the insides of these places. She pictured a tasteful mixture of antiques and things from Conran's, minor paintings by major artists—maybe one of the Wyeths or Chagall—along with shiny new floors and sinks and cabinets and bathroom fixtures. But seeing no available parking spaces, Amanda didn't go inside to see how reality conformed to the things she'd pictured. Warning Ashley to be on her best behavior, she let the girl out in front of the building and drove on.

Glancing in the rearview mirror, Amanda watched her daughter walk across the sidewalk and into the building, carrying her small suitcase and Kristin's birthday present. The scene made her feel melancholy. In another month and a half Ashley would turn thirteen, officially a teenager. She was already in her first year of junior high. The next step would be high school, then college. Someday Ashley would walk away carrying a suitcase and leave for good, not just for a sleepless night of giggling and snacking. The image left Amanda feeling empty and terribly alone.

Cheer up, she told herself. Ashley will be back in the morning. The day she leaves for good is still many years away.

Ahead was a traffic signal, where the street on which she was driving intersected with a main artery. Amanda stopped, waited for the light to turn green, and when it did, she impulsively turned right, headed for her favorite shopping mall. She had decided to get some use out of all those credit cards she carried, splurge a little, buy some new things for Ashley and herself.

"Uh, excuse me," the woman said, looking a little embarrassed. She was about twenty-two, a carroty redhead whose face was awash in freckles. "But are you Amanda J. Price?"

"Yes," Amanda said, smiling. She was used to this. People were always glancing surreptitiously at her, thinking they recognized her, sometimes pointing at her and whispering to their companions. It went along with being on TV. At first the attention had left her both flattered and disconcerted, but now she pretty much took it for granted. She was, she supposed, a very minor celebrity.

Amanda and the woman were standing in front of a shoe store on the mall's lower level. Looking more embarrassed by the moment, the woman said, "Uh, that was really a great report you did on New Shipton. When we elect people, we have to trust them—you know what I mean? And when they do things like that . . . well, I just hope they send the whole pile of them to prison for a very long time."

"It could happen," Amanda said.

The woman hesitated, then said, "Uh, would it be possible for me to ask you for your autograph?" She blushed so brightly that her freckles nearly disappeared. "Nor for me. For my little sister. She, uh, she collects autographs, and I'm sure she'd love to have yours."

"Sure," Amanda said, and the woman handed her a small spiral notebook. "What's her name?"

"Linda."

Putting her packages on a bench, Amanda wrote:

Linda,
  Here's wishing you all the best.

                    Amanda J. Price

Thanking her, the woman hurried away and Amanda continued her shopping. It was dark when she finished, and the mall was ready to close. Amanda groaned, thinking about the huge bills she'd run up on her credit cards. For herself, Amanda had purchased two dresses, a blazer, a pullover sweater, a pair of inexpensive earrings, and four pairs of panty hose. For Ashley, she had bought a pair of jeans, a skirt, a sweater vest, and a blouse. Amanda hoped her daughter would approve; the girl had reached the difficult-to-buy-for stage, in which style was something only understood by her peers and anything selected by parents was suspect.

Carrying shopping bags from four different stores, Amanda stepped from the heated mall into the crisp, clear February evening. She had to watch her step as she made her way across the mall's asphalt parking area. The temperature was plummeting, and the spots that had been salty, sandy slush earlier in the day were now slick ice.

Because it was Saturday, the mall had been crowded when she arrived, and she'd been forced to leave her car in the hinterlands of the parking area. Now the lot was practically deserted. Her Mustang was grouped with four or five other cars, all of them surrounded by a huge expanse of empty asphalt.

As she neared the car she turned, startled, thinking she'd heard footsteps coming from behind her, getting closer. She saw nothing but the frozen asphalt, endless shadows dotted with pools of yellow illumination from lights mounted atop tall metal poles. Something icy that had nothing to do with the cold night slithered through Amanda's insides, and she shivered, suddenly feeling exposed and vulnerable. She hurried toward her car.

The Mustang was parked beside a station wagon and bumper-to-bumper with a rusty Japanese compact. Unable to unlock the car while carrying so many shopping bags, Amanda set her purchases on the car's hood. She was digging in her purse for her keys when a strong hand grabbed her by the shoulder, spun her around, and propelled her toward a white car two spaces away.

"You make one peep and I'll give you more pain than you can even imagine," a man's voice said behind her. And from the cold, flat way he said it, Amanda feared he was quite capable of carrying out his threat.

He pushed her forward so forcefully that she collided with the side of the white car. Quickly opening the door, he started shoving her inside, and suddenly Amanda didn't care about his threat to hurt her, because if he got her into the car, he was going to hurt her anyway, maybe even kill her.

Wriggling out of his grasp, she screamed, clawing at his eyes, trying to hurt him any way she could. She got her first look at him then, a tall, wiry man with a long, pale face and eyes that stared at her unemotionally, almost lifelessly, as if she were being attacked by a corpse.

"Help me!" she screamed.

The man slapped her hard. For a moment little golden lights danced before her eyes, and then she felt herself being turned around, pushed into the car.

"Help!" she screamed again. "Please!"

"Hey," a man's voice demanded. "What's going on here?"

"Nothing that concerns you," Amanda's attacker said.

There were two of them, big, broad-shouldered guys who looked like they'd spent their lives working construction. One was fair-skinned, very Irish-looking. The other was black.

"Help me," Amanda said. "Please help me."

"What's going on here?" the white guy asked. He was the one who'd spoken the first time.

"None of your business," Amanda's attacker said.

"She's calling for help. I think that makes it my business."

"She's my wife, you asshole. This is private, between me and my wife."

"No!" Amanda screamed. "I've never seen him before. He's . . . he's kidnapping me!"

"Don't pay any attention to her," her assailant said. "We'll get home, get it settled, and everything will be okay."

"Hey, I know her," the black guy said, speaking for the first time. "She's that lady on TV."

"Yeah," the other one said. "You're right. Amanda what's-her-name."

For a few seconds they all stood there, staring at each other. Abruptly the white guy grabbed Amanda's attacker and pulled him away from the car. She scrambled to safety.

Her rescuer was holding the guy by the front of his jacket, looking at him menacingly.

"I don't like assholes like you," he said. "So you just stand there nice and still while we get this thing straightened out."

Despite the size of the beefy man holding him, Amanda's attacker gave him a jab in the gut that knocked him backward. Instantly he turned and brought his knee into the black man's midsection, doubling him over. Then, so fast that it could have been an act performed by a magician, he was holding a gun. The white man, surprised but unhurt by the jab he'd received, was stepping in to aid his companion, but the sight of the gun stopped him as surely as if he'd been poleaxed.

Amanda kept backing away. She wasn't getting in the car with the man, gun or no gun. If he shot her, he shot her; it was a chance she was willing to take.

But the man seemed more concerned with her rescuers than he was with her. "Back away," he told them. "Now."

They complied. The blow to his midsection had taken the fight out of the black guy, and the Irish-looking one was staring at the gun as if mesmerized by it. The man climbed into the car, started the engine, and sped away. For an instant Amanda was afraid he'd try to run her down, but he drove straight to the nearest exit and then he was gone.

For a few moments Amanda and her rescuers simply stood there, staring at each other. Amanda was trembling, her heart thumping like a steam locomotive on a long straightaway. She had no idea why the man had attacked her, tried to abduct her, and questions for which she had no answers churned in her head. Was she a random selection, or had he picked her because she was on TV? Who the hell was he, this man with the zombie eyes who carried a gun and could handle a pair of good-sized men with ease? And then there was the most frightening question of all: What would he have done to her?

Amanda saw an image of herself lying in the snow,

bloody and dead. She forced it from her mind. She was breathing in short, little nervous breaths, the way you breathe when you've very nearly been scared to death, and she realized she had just experienced the most terrifying moment of her life.

"Jesus," the white guy said. "He had a *gun*. The crazy son of a bitch could have blown us away, all of us."

The black guy, still not looking too good, stepped over to Amanda, taking her arm to steady her. "You okay?" he asked.

"Yes," Amanda said, her shaky voice revealing that she really wasn't okay at all. "Are you?"

"I'll be all right," he said.

They stood there, no one seeming to know what to do. Finally Amanda said, "Did anyone get his license number?"

The two men exchanged glances. No one had.

Two

Her daughter looked bleary-eyed but happy when Amanda picked her up the next morning.

"How was the slumber party?" Amanda asked as she pulled away from Kristin's gentrified row house.

"Didn't get much sleep."

"That's not surprising. Actually I never could figure out why they call them slumber parties. It would be more honest to call them stay-up-all-night-and-talk parties."

The girl thought it over, then said, "Yeah, but if we called them that, our parents would never let us have any of them."

Amanda laughed.

She waited until they were home to talk about last night. "Come and sit here with me," she said, patting the cushion beside her on the couch.

"Uh-oh," Ashley said, complying. "This means we're going to have a heavy talk about something, right?"

"Oh, not real heavy. It's just that something happened to me last night, and I need to tell you about it."

She had considered not telling Ashley about it at all and rejected the idea. Although an attack on a local TV reporter wasn't big news, it was interesting enough to make the papers—a few inches in section C or D probably, but the story would come out. And Amanda wanted her daughter to hear it from her.

"First of all," Amanda said, "I wasn't hurt, and everything's fine. But last night as I was leaving the mall, a man grabbed me and tried to pull me into his car."

Ashley was staring at her in wide-eyed, stunned silence.

"Two men came along and rescued me. The guy who attacked me pulled a gun on them and got away. Nobody was hurt."

"Wow," Ashley said, clearly shaken. "Did you call the police?"

"Yes. An officer came and took a report, but I don't think they're likely to catch him. Nobody thought to get his license number."

"What . . . what do you think he wanted?" the girl asked.

Amanda had been afraid her daughter would ask her that. But then, in a way, it was probably a good thing she had. It was something she and Ashley should talk about.

Amanda drew in a slow breath, said, "There are people who are . . . well, mentally disturbed. They like to hurt people. Or maybe they don't like it exactly, but feel compelled to do it. For some reason they're usually men, and the people they hurt are often women and children."

The girl considered that. "You mean, like child molesters?"

"Yes. And there are men who like to abduct women and girls and . . . and do things to them. Bad things." Amanda frowned, reflecting on her words. She didn't want to sound as if she were talking down to the girl.

"Sometimes they kill them," Ashley said, understanding. "I've heard about it on the news."

Ashley, of course, was an avid viewer of TV news, one of the few kids who could turn on the set each evening and see her own mom. And in so doing, she saw other things as well—awful, sick, disturbing things.

Suddenly the girl's eyes widened even further, and she seemed to pale. "Mom, do you think that's what . . ." Her words trailed off.

"I don't know what the man wanted to do to me," she said. "Fortunately some nice people came to my rescue."

Ashley nodded, but behind the girl's wide green eyes thoughts swirled. Amanda hoped Ashley wasn't envisioning what might have occurred had the two men not shown up last night.

"The lesson to be learned from all this is to be careful," Amanda said. "Most people are nice and caring and kind. Most people are good. But there are a few out there who aren't. The reason I got into trouble last night was because I wasn't careful. Do you know what I did wrong?"

Ashley shook her head.

"I left my car at the far end of the parking area, then waited until after dark to leave. I should have left earlier, in daylight, when there were more people around."

"You shouldn't have to do that," Amanda's daughter said. "You should be able to leave when you want. It isn't fair."

"No, it's not fair. But it's common sense. And when you stop to think about it, leaving a few minutes early isn't much of a price to pay for being safe."

Ashley stared at her, listening intently, her expression dead serious.

"It's like not accepting rides from strangers or not letting them into the house when you're here alone. It's just good sense. What I'm trying to say, honey, is that you shouldn't be afraid just because there are some bad people out there. You shouldn't let it worry you. But there are a few things we have to do, just to be on the safe side. Easy things. Mostly it's just a matter of being careful. Understand?"

"Uh-huh."

"And if anyone should ever bother you, I want you to do just what I did last night. Scream like hell."

The girl looked a little surprised. "Did you scream?"

"You bet your sweet bippy I did,"

"My what?"

"Bippy."

"What's a bippy?"

"You know, I don't have the foggiest idea." She fluffed the girl's hair.

A faint smile peeked through the worry on Ashley's face.

Apparently she was considering all the possibilities, trying to figure out what a bippy might be.

"Hey," Amanda said, "I bought you some things yesterday. Want to see them?"

"Yeah," the girl said, perking up.

"I bought myself some things too. Should we give each other a fashion show?"

"Okay."

"Your stuff's in your bedroom. Come on, let's go."

They hurried to their bedrooms to change.

After the fashion show Amanda took a nap. She hadn't slept much last night, because every time she'd started drifting off, she'd seen the man with the corpselike eyes, felt his strong, irresistible grip, felt herself being forced into the white car. And every time he'd just about succeeded in kidnapping her, her eyes had popped open, for she'd known that this time no help would arrive.

And as the night wore on, the dream had changed, presenting her with ever more macabre creations of her unconscious mind. Though unable to remember all of them, one was crystal-clear, embedded in her memory as if her brain had videotaped it. In that dream the man had been a zombie, the rest of him as lifeless as his eyes. His flesh had been dark and putrifying, hanging in rotten strings from the bones that showed through in places. His eyes had been worse than just lifeless; they'd been empty black holes out of which worms crawled. He'd smelled like rotten meat. And when he'd touched her, his flesh had been squishy.

Her nap was not interrupted by nightmares.

When Amanda awoke, she sat on the edge of the bed, staring groggily at the clock on the bed table. It was two-twelve. She'd been asleep for three hours. After a few moments the grogginess began to lift, and Amanda felt better for having slept a little. She found Ashley in the living room, sound asleep on the couch, while wrestlers threw each other around on the TV set. Clearly the show had come on after Ashley dozed off, for she would never watch such a thing. She was into sitcoms and MTV, not sports—especially not wrestling.

Amanda stood over the sleeping form of her daughter, studying her. Her dark hair—the same color as Amanda's—was piled up on her head, thick and shiny and healthy-looking. Amanda had been told often that she was pretty, but Ashley might well go beyond just pretty. If she continued to develop as she was, she would be beautiful.

Amanda's eyes filled with tears. Ashley was a great kid, and that wasn't just a mother's biased analysis—at least Amanda didn't think it was. Her daughter had every quality she—or any parent—could hope for. Ashley was honest, kind, helpful, intelligent, and didn't mind performing tasks a lot of kids despised, such as dishwashing, cleaning, running errands. No, Ashley wasn't perfect. She had a stubborn streak, and her grades would fall if she took a dislike to a particular teacher. And she absolutely loved loud, screechy rock and roll music that made Amanda cringe as if she were hearing a fingernail squeaking on a blackboard, except that the music was louder—*much* louder.

Still, Amanda's complaints were few. She was proud of a number of things she'd done in her life—moving from a station in Omaha to a major market like Boston, the work she did on the New Shipton story—but she was proudest of all of the job she had done as a single parent.

"You're okay, kid," she said softly to the sleeping girl.

Then she switched off the TV set just as a wrestler was about to leap off the ropes and onto the fallen form of his adversary. She stretched, trying to rid herself of the last traces of sleep, and walked to the window, looked out on Boston from six stories up. It wasn't an impressive view for a luxury high rise, mainly other tall, boxy buildings like the one in which she lived. She could see neither the harbor nor the Charles River nor Boston Common. She couldn't even see the Prudential or John Hancock towers, because her apartment faced the wrong way.

The roofs of the lower buildings were covered with snow—the roofs of taller ones, too, but she couldn't see those—as were the vacant lots and parks and any other open spaces. The streets were all lined with snow piled up by the plows. Amanda had never seen a winter this severe—not in New England, anyway. She had lived through some pretty spectacular blizzards in Omaha, but they were usually followed by periods of dryer, warmer weather. This was the first winter she'd experienced that held an entire region in such a tenacious grip, week after week, month after month.

Amanda's gaze dropped to the street below. Only one car moved along it on this wintry Sunday afternoon—a small brown van, one of those with the angled front end that made it seem less boxy. The driver was looking out the window, looking up toward her.

At her.

Amanda sucked in her breath, because she was staring into the lifeless eyes of the man who'd attacked her last night at the mall. She stepped back from the window, fear encircling her stomach like a hangman's noose, tightening, squeezing.

For a moment Amanda just stood there, listening to the silence of her apartment. Dick Kilmer, the cameraman, said no room was ever truly silent. There was always some ambient noise—the distant hum of heating or air-conditioning equipment, the sounds that drifted in from other rooms and from outside, the whir of clock mechanisms. Room tone, he called it, this silence that wasn't silent.

Finally Amanda stepped back to the window and looked down. The van was gone. Another car came down the street, and as Amanda watched it she realized there was no way she could have looked into anyone's eyes from six stories up. Her mind had been playing tricks on her; that was all. Perhaps down in the distant reaches of her consciousness she was still terrified because of what had happened, still not able to come to terms with it. So she'd imagined it was the same man, imagined he was looking up at her.

And then a new thought occurred to her. What if what happened at the mall hadn't been a chance encounter at all? What if he'd followed her there? Was he watching her, even now, waiting for another chance to strike?

Amanda shook her head. He was a psycho who attacked women randomly. He'd spotted her at the mall, maybe recognizing her from TV, maybe not, and because of whatever twisted notions made him act, he'd tried to grab her. She had to believe that, for if she didn't, then she was stuck with something much more frightening.

She was being stalked.

By someone who would try again.

Amanda found herself unable to sleep again that night. But instead of having recurring nightmares, she lay in bed with her eyes closed, her mind darting here and there, dredging up lost snippets of conversation, minor happenings from childhood or college or previous jobs, meaningless bits of trivia that popped from her subconscious like bubbles from a simmering stew. Though nonthreatening and inconsequential, they kept her awake as effectively as a truckload of caffeine.

Amanda got up on Monday morning feeling wrung out. While Ashley ate cereal for breakfast Amanda stared bleary-eyed at her coffee cup until it was time to go. On her way to the station she dropped Ashley off at school.

Amanda was assigned to do a piece on the stalemated contract negotiations between the Boston police union and the city. The cops were presently working without a contract, and the more militant among them were talking strike. She spent most of the day rounding up people she needed to talk to and getting the tape shot. It was mid-afternoon by the time she made it into the editing room to assemble her report with the assistance of Liam Flaherty, one of the videotape editors.

The editing station had two monitors. On the one on the left, a burly Boston policeman was saying striking violated his sense of duty, but the city wasn't leaving him any choice, because it wasn't negotiating in good faith.

"Cut it where he says 'Nothin' else I can do,'" Amanda said. "Then go to general shots of cops doing cop stuff for my voiceover, then to the stand-up close."

"Can do," Flaherty said, and began pushing buttons on his editing machine. He was an extremely fair-skinned Irishman whose nose peeled at the first hint of a sunny summer day. He was about six-three and as thin as a piece of spaghetti, and he was a whiz at tape editing. Amanda watched as his fingers danced nimbly over the buttons on his machine.

"Amanda in here?"

Turning around, she saw the round face of Ned Asherton, the assignment editor, in the doorway. He said, "You got a phone call. Line four."

Amanda went into the newsroom and took the call at her desk.

"Mom, it's me." As soon as she heard her daughter's voice, Amanda knew something was wrong. "Somebody broke into the apartment," Ashley said. "It's a mess. Everything's all turned over and everything."

Amanda felt a shiver travel through her. Your home was a private, personal place, and for someone to violate it seemed a little like rape. "You're not in the apartment, are you?"

"No. I took one look inside and ran over here to Mrs. O'Donnell's."

"You did just right," Amanda said. "Did you call the police?"

"Yeah. I was going to call you first, but Mrs. O'Donnell said I should call the police first, so I did."

"I'll be there as quick as I can," Amanda said. "You stay with Mrs. O'Donnell until the police get there."

Ashley promised she would, and Amanda hurried to Bob

Miller's office to let him know she had an emergency, had to leave.

"Where are you on the police piece?" the news director asked.

"Flaherty has everything he needs to finish it," she said.

He told her to go, and a few moments later Amanda was on her way home, dreading what she'd find when she got there.

Ashley's description had been accurate. The place was a mess. Furniture had been overturned, clothes pulled from hangers and drawers, papers and books strewn about, potted plants smashed. A uniformed police officer was there when Amanda arrived, a big-boned blond woman who kept making notations on a clipboard as Amanda answered her questions. Ashley stood off to the side, letting her mom handle the situation.

"That's the only thing that was taken," the officer asked, "a portable tape player from your daughter's room?"

"Yes," Amanda said. "And frankly I'm confused. Why go to all the trouble to break in here, then just take a sixty-dollar tape player?" She pointed at the stereo TV set. "That's worth nearly a thousand dollars."

"Too much for a lone thief to carry," the cop said. "This was probably the work of a drug addict. They break in, grab whatever they can carry that can be unloaded for a few bucks, and get out."

"But why all the destruction? What's the point?"

"People like that are crazy. You never for sure know why they do anything. Sometimes I think they do stuff like this because they're jealous. They see a nice place like this, the way you live, and then they think of how they live, constantly trying to survive from one fix to the next. Makes 'em mad."

Amanda shook her head. "It must be awful to live like that."

"Don't feel sorry for 'em," the cop said. "Nobody forced

'em to put that needle in their arm the first time. They chose to be scum."

Although Amanda thought that was a rather simplistic view of a complicated problem, the cop did have a point. The world was full of not very nice people. It also seemed to her that she was having more than her share of trouble with them lately.

"Can you catch whoever did this?" Ashley asked, speaking up for the first time.

"We'll get 'em," the police officer answered. "Probably won't ever be able to charge 'em with this particular break-in, but we'll get 'em for something. They always wind up with us sooner or later."

The child stared at her, digesting that, fitting it into what she knew of how things worked in the world.

"This is the first break-in I know of in this building," Amanda said. "Is crime in this neighborhood getting worse?"

The police officer shook her head. "There's no place that won't get hit sooner or later. You need a better lock on the door. The one you had was a little better than the ones that can be opened with a credit card, but not much. One quick push with a crowbar and he was in, didn't even make enough noise for the neighbors to notice. You need to call a locksmith, get something solid installed."

Amanda said she'd do that.

After the police officer left, Amanda and Ashley began cleaning up the mess. The destruction wasn't as bad as it had seemed at first. Although Amanda's clothes had been scattered all over the place, none of them had been cut or torn. And Ashley's clothes hadn't been touched. The intruder had smashed some potted plants but spared the stereo TV set. And although furniture had been turned over, nothing was broken or slashed. As she went about hanging up clothes and righting furniture, Amanda sensed that there was some purpose to all this that was eluding her, that she was missing something that was right here for her to see.

But that was nonsense. What other purpose could a burglar have except to steal?

Ashley helped her right the couch, then Amanda said, "You see the phone book?"

"Over there," the girl said, pointing toward an armchair.

"Get the Yellow Pages and find a locksmith. Maybe there's still time to get one out here before we have to pay double or quadruple time or whatever they get after five o'clock."

It took six calls to find one who could come today at all, and he showed up at seven, smiling because of all the money he was going to make.

For the third night in a row Amanda was unable to sleep. And now that she looked back on it, she hadn't slept soundly in months. While working on the New Shipton series she'd often lain awake, her mind churning with each new fact, each step that was taking her closer and closer to the biggest story of her career. Being irritable, nervous, and constantly exhausted had become her norm. She had to relax, get some sleep; otherwise she'd soon be a nervous wreck, snapping at Ashley, being bitchy with her coworkers, running on coffee and nervous energy. It wasn't healthy to live like that.

And here she was, wide awake again. When she arrived home today and saw for herself what had occurred at the apartment, Amanda had been relieved to discover that nothing extremely valuable had been taken and that the destruction looked a lot worse than it actually was. But now she found herself thinking about it: Ashley's phone call, the overturned furniture, the scattered papers and clothes swirling around in her head like debris sucked into a whirlwind.

She opened her eyes, hoping to chase away the images, and found herself staring at the ceiling, a dull rectangle barely illuminated by the city's brightness seeping in through the window. When she was a little girl in Omaha, she'd lain in bed at night and watched the shadows move and shift as cars passed or the breeze stirred the trees, the patterns sometimes looking like horses or dogs or other harmless things, and sometimes turning into scary monsters.

But here on the sixth floor her night was unaffected by things like trees and cars, and the ceiling's dim rectangle was static. She was up here in the sky, above all that. And at the moment it seemed a very lonely place to be.

She heard the whir of the elevator as it rose to the eighth or ninth floor, and then the building was silent.

Why had the burglar chosen her apartment? This was a building in which people were usually coming and going. The residents were engineers and accountants and insurance agents, people who worried about their big-screen TV sets and home computers and who were quick to call the cops. The sight of a sleazy-looking drug addict would have people all over the building rushing to dial 911. Not a good place to burglarize from a safety standpoint, but on the other hand, it was probably like being turned loose in Bloomingdale's from the standpoint of all the goodies that were available for the taking.

And yet the person who broke into her apartment had taken the risks involved, walking away with nothing but a sixty-dollar tape player. It didn't make sense.

But then, if the blond cop was right about it being the work of a drug addict, this was a person whose brain cells had been pretty well pickled by poppy juice. Maybe he was no longer able to think straight. Maybe the lure of all the goodies was just too much to pass up.

So out of all the apartments in the building, why hers? Why go all the way to the sixth floor? The elevator ride made it more likely that he'd be noticed, put him far away from an exit through which he could escape. Any burglar with any sense, it seemed to her, would go for a ground-floor apartment. True, the higher up you went, the higher the rent, which meant the upper reaches of the building were where the wealthier tenants lived. So why didn't the burglar go on to the floors above hers? Why stop on six?

She pictured some down-and-out character getting into the elevator and just punching a button at random. Maybe, but the image didn't sit right somehow. Something was wrong with it.

And then something occurred to her that made her sit bolt upright. It was a whole series of interconnected things that led to a terrifying conclusion. The burglar had pulled all her clothes out of *her* dresser and closet, but not Ashley's. The small desk in the corner of the living room had been thoroughly rifled. It was the source of the papers that had been strewn about. The rest of what was done was meaningless, merely an attempt to cover up the intruder's true purpose. He had been looking for something.

Amanda turned the idea around a few times, finding she was comfortable with it, that it seemed to fit. But what was he looking for? For whatever he could find, she decided. He'd gone through her pockets, through her papers, which meant he was looking for information. And there was only one thing she had done lately that could cause someone to go to that much trouble.

The New Shipton series.

People could be indicted, charged with murder. That was certainly reason enough to search her apartment. And this conclusion brought her to an even more frightening one.

The break-in and the attempt to abduct her were related.

That sent an icy nugget of pure terror sliding down Amanda's spine. If they'd tried to grab her once, they could try again. She wasn't even safe in her apartment; today's events had proven that. Even her new super-heavy-duty door lock didn't make her feel particularly safe. Besides, she was vulnerable in the elevator, driving to work, even while she was out covering stories. The icy nugget was in her stomach now, felt as if it were freezing her vital organs.

And then a new thought occurred to her, one so terrifying that she shuddered, emitting a high-pitched gasp that was almost a squeak. This new fear could be summed up in one word: Ashley. What if they tried to get to her through Ashley?

Suddenly, knowing it was foolish, knowing her daughter was all right, Amanda got out of bed and hurried across the short hallway to the open door of Ashley's room. Standing in the doorway, Amanda saw a lump under the covers, heard the girl's regular breathing. Ashley muttered something unintelligible and rolled over, wiggling herself farther down under the blankets so that only the top of her head was showing. A mass of dark hair, the same color as her mother's.

Amanda stood there for a minute or two, just savoring the knowledge that her daughter was here, safe, deep in the innocent sleep only a child could enjoy. The guy at the mall was just a psycho, Amanda told herself, a sick person who saw a lone woman and tried to take advantage of the opportunity. Really, when she came right down to it, she had no proof that it was anything else. And the break-in was just what the cop said it was, the work of an addict desperate for a fix who took some of his frustrations out on her apartment. Any connection between the two events was pure speculation, based on the most tenuous logic, held together by the weakest of threads.

The corrupt New Shipton officials were being investigated by a special grand jury. They were, to use one of Ashley's expressions, in deep doo-doo. Messing around with the reporter who broke the scandal would only make things worse. Anyone connected with the New Shipton scandal would want to avoid her at all cost.

Amanda went back to bed and spent the rest of the night convincing herself of that.

THREE

ASHLEY'S last class of the day was language arts. She sat in the third row from the door, in the middle of the room. Mrs. Scholl, the teacher, was writing something on the blackboard, but Ashley wasn't paying much attention. Absently she wondered why they were called blackboards. In her seven and a half years of school, she'd seen green ones and brown ones but never a black one.

But this thought merely flicked through her consciousness and was gone. What was really on her mind was the way her mom had behaved this morning.

Looking nervous and worried, her mother had said, "I don't want you to walk home from school today like you usually do. Is there anyone you can get a ride with?"

"How come you want me to get a ride with somebody?"

"Never mind that," her mother had snapped. "Just answer the question."

"I can get a ride with Matt Lansky. His mom picks him up every day, and he lives just down the block."

"Are you sure it's okay if you ride with him?"

"Yeah. He's asked me lots of times."

"How come you never ride home with him?"

"He's a creep."

Ashley's mom had sighed. "How do you usually come into the building?"

"Through the parking area. It's easier to walk down the ramp than to go around to the front of the building."

"Today I want you to have Matt Lanksy's mom let you off at the main entrance, okay?"

"Do you think someone's trying to . . . to get us or

something like that?" Ashley had asked, searching her mother's face.

"It's like I told you the other day. It pays to be careful, and that's all we're doing, being careful. All right?"

Although Ashley had thought there was a lot more to it than just being careful, she had nodded.

"When you get home, go to Mrs. O'Donnell's and wait for me there."

"I'd rather come home," Ashley had protested. "Mrs. O'Donnell's a nice lady, but she always watches boring religious stuff on TV in the afternoon."

"Take your books. Do some studying."

Now, sitting in class, Ashley was feeling increasingly uneasy about all this. Someone had attacked her mom. Someone had broken into their apartment. Did someone want to hurt them? She turned it around in her mind, trying to understand why anyone would wish them harm. The only answer she could come up with was that it might have something to do with her mother's being a TV reporter. The things journalists did made people mad sometimes.

Her mom's evasiveness particularly troubled her, for it meant whatever was going on was so serious her mother didn't want to tell her about it. Although a lot of kids didn't communicate with their parents, Ashley had never had that problem. She and her mom were always open and honest with each other. This evening she was going to make her mother explain what was happening. The way Ashley figured it, she had a right to know. The truth certainly couldn't scare her any more than not knowing was scaring her.

And then a new idea occurred to her. She was a child of divorced parents. She'd seen on the news how divorced parents were always trying to steal the kids from each other. Was her mom afraid her dad was going to try to snatch her?

Ashley immediately dismissed the notion. As usual she was going out to California to spend a few weeks with her dad this summer. All he'd have to do would be to wait a few months and she'd come to him on an airplane, no hassles, no cloak-and-dagger stuff. Besides, whenever she was at her dad's place, the situation was always a little uncomfortable. She and Jo-Ann, her dad's new wife, never seemed to know how to deal with each other. Although she missed her dad when she left California, coming back home to her mom was always a relief.

Ashley pushed these thoughts away. She didn't like thinking about the divorce. Although she'd long since adapted to it, she'd never forgotten the nights of lying in bed, crying her five-year-old's heart out when she'd been told that her mom and dad were splitting up.

Feeling a gentle tap on her knee, Ashley looked down to see Megan, the girl who sat in front of her, pushing a piece of paper at her. Ashley took it and, keeping it in her lap so the teacher wouldn't see it, read:

> FOR MELANIE PARKER
> PASS IT ON
> PRIVATE

Ashley passed it on, and at that precise moment Mrs. Scholl called her name. The girl looked up, certain she'd been spotted handing the note across the aisle to Shannon Kennedy, but everything was okay. The teacher wasn't looking at her sternly.

"What are the two elements you must have to form a sentence?" Mrs. Scholl always talked like that, sort of rigidly. She was a tall, broad, severe-looking woman who wore her hair in a bun.

"A subject and a predicate," Ashley answered.

"Very good, Ashley. I wasn't sure any of you knew that, not after looking at the papers you handed in yesterday. I thought you'd somehow all managed to get to the seventh grade without knowing what a sentence was." She gave the class a look of utter disgust. "Ashley, give me the simplest sentence you can devise."

"I do," the girl replied.

"Sounds like she's getting married," someone a few rows away said, and several kids snickered.

Mrs. Scholl silenced them with a withering look. "I do," she said, repeating Ashley's sentence. She wrote the words on the blackboard. "Please note—" She was interrupted by the bell.

Instantly kids were scrambling for the door. It was the last class of the day, and they wanted *out*, away from school, away from language arts, away from Mrs. Scholl.

"Hold it!" the teacher bellowed, and everyone froze. "Now then, if you all don't want to spend another half hour here, learning more about sentences, you can file slowly and quietly out of the room."

They did. And once they were in the hall, they went berserk, running to their lockers, throwing in books, slamming the locker doors, hurrying for the exit. Ashley was jostled by a boy with curly red hair, and she gave him a disgusted look he didn't see. It was the boys who made all the commotion, and Ashley found the majority of them revolting. Sometimes she found it hard to believe that she would ever even talk to one, much less fall in love with one and marry him. That the boys in her school could ever grow up and become decent human beings was almost unthinkable. They pulled your hair, threw snowballs at you, said stupid smart-mouthed things to you. And there was one, a real slimeball named Jeremy, who kept bumping into her and "accidentally" brushing against her breasts. He was so repulsive that Ashley shuddered just thinking about him.

She looked around for Matt Lansky and didn't see him. He was probably already out of the building, which was emptying rapidly. She had her first class of the day with him, and she'd asked him for a ride home, as her mom had commanded. Matt had said no problem, meet him outside, he'd have his mom wait for her. Ashley put her language-arts book into her locker, took out those she'd need for tonight's homework, and put on her coat; then, closing her locker, she left the building.

As she strolled between the snowbanks that lined the walk leading to the street, Ashley looked for the green car Matt Lanksy's mom drove. She saw station wagons pulling away, big cars, little cars, and lumbering yellow school buses, but she saw no sign of Matt Lansky. Turning around, she looked back toward the brick school building, seeing lots of familiar faces, none of which belonged to Matt. Had he forgotten?

She looked back toward the street just as a snowball sailed past her nose. A creepy boy named Jimmy Rance looked at her as if to say, "What you gonna do about it?" Then he turned his back to her and slouched away. How could any self-respecting girl ever grow up and marry one of them? Ashley asked herself disgustedly.

"Hi, Ash." It was Tyne Collins, a petite blond girl who had so many braces on her teeth, she displayed a pound and a half of metal every time she smiled. Some of the boys called her Jaws, after the character in the James Bond movie, and Ashley thought they were cruel. Tyne was very nice.

"Hi," Ashley said. "You seen Matt Lansky?"

"He went home sick during third period."

"Uh-oh. I was supposed to ride home with him."

"We were in history class, and he just sort of turned green, told Mr. Campbell that he was going to throw up. He never made it to the boys' room. He threw up in the hall. They took him to the nurse's office, and she sent him home."

"What was wrong with him?"

"I don't know. What are you going to do for a ride?"

Ashley tried to figure out whether there was anyone else she could get a ride home with and decided there wasn't. "I'll just walk like I usually do, I guess. It's only a few blocks."

"Can't you ride the school bus?"

Ashley shook her head. "I live too close to the school. They won't let me use the bus."

"I wouldn't feel too bad about that," Tyne said. "It's a zoo on the one I ride. They yell and scream and steal your books, throw stuff at each other, shove you around. And then there's that boy, Timmy something-or-other, who fills up those things like balloons with water and then throws them."

"What things?"

"You know." Tyne blushed. "They're used for sex."

Ashley nodded. She knew what they were, but she was unable to remember what they were called. Beige-colored balloonlike things. You were supposed to use them so you wouldn't get AIDS. Tyne said she had to go and hurried off to her waiting school bus. There were fewer kids around now. Ashley took one last look around to see whether there was anyone she could get a ride with, decided there wasn't, and started walking.

At the street she turned left, moving past a line of school buses. The neighborhood was a mixture of new and old, modern high rises like the one in which she lived and old buildings made of brick or stone. Actually the whole city seemed to be like that, places that looked ancient all mixed up with shiny new ones.

A snowbank separated her from the street. In a month or so it would start to melt and get all dirty and yucky-looking. Snow always seemed so pure when it fell, but it never stayed that way very long.

A brown car rolled up beside her, stopping slowly, as if it were going to park. There were signs along here that said NO PARKING 7 A.M. TO 7 P.M.; they were right there for the guy in the car to see, so if he got a ticket, it was his own fault.

But the car didn't stop; it kept rolling, staying alongside Ashley. She eyed it warily, uncertain what was happening.

Rolling down the window, the driver said, "Excuse me, are you Ashley?"

She stopped and turned to face him, not sure whether to

confirm her identity. He had a long, sort of bony face and thin hair. And there was something funny about his eyes, like the lusterless look she'd seen in the eyes of a squirrel that had been run over by a car. Ashley decided to keep on walking. If she ignored the man, he might go away.

But he didn't go away. The car rolled along beside her. "Don't be afraid, Ashley. Your mom said for me to give you a lift home."

She slowed a little, considering that. Could her mom know that Matt Lansky had gone home sick? Maybe Matt's mom had called her and she'd sent this man to pick her up. That explanation made a lot of sense to Ashley, and she stopped, turning to face the man again. There was a cut in the snowbank about five feet from her. The man had pulled up to it and stopped. Deciding it was okay, Ashley headed for the opening in the snowbank.

Never accept a ride from a stranger.

Her mother's words sounded so loud inside Ashley's head that her mom could have been standing right there on the sidewalk, yelling at her. Ashley stopped, stared at the man, vacillating, uncertain what to do.

"What's the matter?" the man asked. "I told you your mom sent me."

"What's her name?" Ashley asked, her voice sounding weak, making it plain how unsure she was about how to deal with this situation.

"Amanda. I work at the TV station with her."

"How did she know I needed a ride?"

"She just said you needed one and asked me to pick you up. She was on her way out to cover a story. She didn't have much time to explain anything."

Ashley just stood there, recalling what her mother had said about being careful. Everything the man said seemed reasonable. Matt's mom could have called her mom, who could have asked this man to pick her up so she wouldn't walk home from school. Her not walking home from school had seemed real important to her mother this morning. And if her mom had sent this man, and if Ashley refused to get in the car, she was going to be in heavy-duty trouble. Knee-deep in doo-doo.

On the other hand, getting into that car wasn't being *careful*. And that's what decided it. That and a gut feeling that was sort of like the feeling she got when she was a little girl in Omaha and her ball had rolled under the front porch. She'd refused to reach into the blackness under that porch because she didn't know what might be lurking there. She might reach right into a spiderweb, might put her hand right *on* a black widow. Maybe cockroaches would scuttle over her flesh. Or centipedes. Or worse things. Who knew what lived under that wooden porch?

And that's how she felt about getting into the car. Who knew what might be waiting for her in there? If her mom yelled at her, she'd just say she was being careful—as she'd been told to be.

Ashley backed up a step. "Thank you for your offer," she said, trying to sound grown-up and polite. "But I don't know you, and I can't accept a ride from a stranger."

She started walking again, and the car rolled alongside her. The man said, "But your mother sent me. Amanda Price, your mom. She'll be mad at both of us if I let you walk home."

But Ashley had made her decision and she was sticking by it. She kept walking, looking straight ahead.

The brown car kept pace with her.

Ashley ignored it. Go away, she thought. Just go away. And then, as if the driver had been reading her thoughts, he sped up, leaving her behind. Ashley was on the verge of breathing a big sigh of relief when she realized the man had stopped at the end of the block. He was getting out of the car, coming toward her.

Ashley froze. For a moment she didn't know what to do, and then she realized that she needed the help of an adult. She was just a kid, and she was into something here a kid wasn't equipped to handle. Looking around, she saw no one, no one except the thin man with the strange eyes who was still walking toward her. He was smiling, moving slowly, unthreateningly. To Ashley he looked like some predatory beast in a wildlife film, stalking its prey. She bolted.

Ashley dashed back toward the school, seeing nothing ahead of her but empty sidewalk, no sign of anyone to whom she could turn for assistance. Glancing behind her, she saw the man coming after her, gaining on her.

She cut into the cleared walk leading to a brick building, running as hard as she could, frantically searching for someone—anyone—who could help her. There was still no one in sight.

Get inside, her frantic mind was telling her, where there'll be people. But she found herself between two buildings, still following the cleared walk. Looking to both sides, she saw no doors, only rows of windows looking at her like indifferent glassy eyes, and they seemed to be saying, *We don't care if the man gets you, little girl. Don't give the slightest, tiniest damn one way or the other.*

Ashley wanted to cry for help, but she was uncertain whether anyone was around to hear her. Besides, she had no breath for yelling; she needed it all for running. She started to glance over her shoulder, to see if the man was still behind her, still closing the gap, but before she could do so, her foot hit an icy spot on the cement walk and Ashley was slipping. Her schoolbooks went flying, disappearing into the snow. Her arms windmilling, she fought for balance, thinking she was going to fall for sure, and the man would get her, drag her back to the car while the rows of glassy eyes looked on, unconcerned.

And the man was there. Ashley heard his footsteps, his labored breathing, almost within an arm's length, almost close enough to grab her.

And then he cried out.

Ashley turned, watching as he hit the icy spot, his feet slipping out from under him, and then he was sliding off the walk and into the snowbank. And Ashley was running again, following the walk wherever it led. Seeing another shiny spot, which meant more ice, she leapt over it, forcing her tired legs to keep running. Suddenly, a high snowbank appeared ahead of her. She had reached a street. There was no cut in the bank, so she scrambled over it, looking back as she went over the top. The man was coming after her again.

She ran blindly into the slushy street, almost hoping she'd run in front of a car, forcing the driver to jam on his brakes. At least it would be someone who could help her.

The street was deserted.

Ashley rushed across it, angling toward the closest cut in the snowbank. When she reached it, she heard the man's feet splatting and splashing in the slush, once more getting closer.

Ashley knew she was running out of strength. If she didn't find help quickly, she would be staggering and wobbling and so badly out of breath that all she could do would be collapse wherever she happened to be and pant. And the man would have her. That thought gave her renewed strength, which she funneled to her legs, forcing them to pump. Harder. Faster.

She was on another sidewalk now, and it was as deserted as the last one had been. Then she saw something, a sign of hope. It was one of those helping-hand symbols they'd told her about in school. The symbols identified places where kids could go for help. Turning so sharply that she nearly fell, Ashley rushed up the steps to a brick row house, barely stopping herself in time to avoid crashing into the aluminum storm door. The helping-hand symbol was in its glass upper portion. Ashley pounded on the door and pressed the buzzer at the same time. Looking behind her, she saw the man. He was in front of the house next door, running hard, coming to get her. Forgetting the buzzer, Ashley used both her fists to pound on the aluminum door.

The man was coming up the walk.

Pulling open the storm door, Ashley began pounding on the wooden door behind it, but that made less noise, was less likely to attract attention. Knowing the man's hands would be on her in a fraction of a second, she sucked in what little breath she had left, planning to let it out in one piercing scream for help, but the door opened and Ashley stumbled forward into the house. As the door closed behind her there were three solid sounding clunks, the bolts of heavy-duty locks sliding into place.

Ashley found herself looking at an elderly woman whose white hair was piled on her head in a bun. She was wearing a floral-patterned apron and looked the way grandmothers always did in TV commercials. "What's going on here?" the woman asked, looking at Ashley with kindly blue eyes.

But before the girl could answer, there was violent pounding on the door. Ashley stared at it, knowing that despite the three locks it was only a piece of wood, a couple of inches thick at the most, and she backed away from it, shuddering, her heart pounding, her lungs still desperately sucking in air.

"Hey!" the man yelled. "Open up!"

Pulling Ashley to her and gently holding her, the woman said, "It's all right, child. That door's solid. He can't get in here."

"He . . . he . . ." Ashley was still shivering, and she seemed unable to find the words to tell the woman what was happening.

"Hey, come on!" the man yelled. "That's my daughter. She ran away from home."

The woman looked at Ashley questioningly, and Ashley shook her head. "He . . . he's a stranger," the girl said. "He tried to . . . to make me get in his car."

"Hey, inside the house!" the man hollered. "Let me in so we can talk this over. Ashley's angry and upset because she just learned that we're getting a divorce."

Ashley shook her head violently. "He . . . he's lying."

She looked into her rescuer's blue eyes, hoping and praying the woman believed her.

"I'm calling the police," the woman said to the man. "If you've nothing to hide, then you won't mind waiting for them."

There was a moment's silence; then the man said, "Yeah, okay. But can I wait inside? It's cold out here."

Again Ashley shook her head, throwing her arms around the woman and holding her to prevent her from moving to the door.

"I'm sorry," the woman said. "But you'll have to wait outside."

There was no response from the man.

"Come on," the woman said to Ashley. "Let's go call the police."

She led the girl into a small kitchen filled with the odor of the freshly baked chocolate-chip cookies that were cooling on wire racks on the counter. The woman gently pushed the girl into a chair at the kitchen table, then picked up the wall-mounted phone and called the police.

When she finished, she joined Ashley at the table. "Would you like a cookie?" the woman asked.

Ashley shook her head. Ordinarily she would have been delighted to get her hands on a freshly made chocolate-chip cookie, but she was too terrified to think about food at the moment.

"What's your name?" the woman asked.

"Ashley. Ashley Price."

"How did that man know your name?"

"I . . . I don't know. I never saw him before."

"My name's Lucille Bridges," the woman said. She patted the girl's hand. "Everything's going to be all right. The police will be here in a few moments."

Ashley had been trying to hold back her tears. She was twelve, almost thirteen, and she didn't want to start bawling like a little kid. Still, despite her best efforts, a tear slid down her cheek, then another.

"I . . . I lost all my books," she said. And then tears came in earnest. Lucille Bridges held her as she sobbed.

Amanda sat with Ashley on the couch. She remembered getting her daughter's phone call at the station, but everything after that was a jumble: running out of the newsroom; driving like a madwoman through a blur of buildings, pedestrians, taxis, buses, traffic signals; locating the Helping Hand house and hurrying inside; hugging Ashley while holding back hot tears of relief; answering the questions put to her by a Boston cop.

Although Amanda had calmed down now, she didn't want to let Ashley out of her sight, and she kept hugging her, holding her. The TV set was on, one of the sitcoms Ashley liked so much. Amanda had been trying to lose herself in it, but the jokes were inane, the laughter fake, the dialogue phony.

Ashley's description left little doubt that the man who'd chased her was the same man who'd tried to force Amanda into a white car at the mall. Tall and thin with strangely vacant eyes. The eyes were the giveaway. Remembering them sent something cold and clammy slithering around inside Amanda's stomach.

She didn't think it was Ashley the man was interested in. It was her. Ashley was only a means of getting to her. But then that was all speculation, guesswork based on what she knew, and she understood very little of what she knew. All this was beyond her. She'd never dealt with a situation like this before. It was like something out of one of the B horror films Ashley liked to watch on TV. Things like this didn't happen in real life.

Real life was politicking on the job, backstabbing and infighting, getting ulcers, being late to work, your kid flunking English, maybe—if the gods were really pissed at you—getting mugged on a dark street. Real life could involve your bank going under, the IRS auditing you, your teenage daughter asking for birth-control pills when the only guy she's seeing is a Neanderthal with green hair and an IQ around that of a grasshopper. Real life could mean getting fired, getting slapped by someone's old girlfriend, finding a scary lump in your breast.

But not this. Not some guy with the skill of James Bond and the attitude of Jack the Ripper who wanted to abduct you and your daughter, and . . . and what? She didn't know what he'd do. Despite her efforts to suppress them, terrifying words swirled in her mind, words like rape, torture, disfigure, kill. . . .

"Mom, you okay?" Ashley asked.

Amanda realized she was shivering. "Yeah," she said. "I'm okay. How about you?"

"I'm all right. I was scared at first, but once I got inside and I realized Mrs. Bridges wasn't going to let him in, everything was okay."

Amanda studied her and was amazed at how calm Ashley was. She was safe now, and to her that was all that mattered, Amanda supposed. To a child, what *could* have happened wasn't nearly so terrifying as it was to an adult. Kids lived for the moment, unconcerned with the next week or even the next day—unless it was Christmas or the last day of school or the day the family left for a vacation to Disneyland. Feeling the fear that undulated in her belly, Amanda wished things could be so simple for her.

"I'm not sending you to school tomorrow," Amanda said. "I'm going to ask Mrs. O'Donnell if you can stay with her."

"Why? You think he'll . . . he'll come back?" Worry appeared on Ashley's face. Apparently the notion that he might try again hadn't occurred to her.

"I just don't want to take any chances."

"Would he? Come back, I mean? Wouldn't he be afraid of getting caught?"

"Honey, I don't think he'll come back. It's just . . . well, like I said, we're just being careful."

Not looking entirely convinced, Ashley nodded. Amanda

had no idea what she was going to do. She couldn't keep her daughter out of school forever. But how could she send her back? The man would try again; she had no doubt about that. He'd tried to grab her, then Ashley, and he'd broken into the apartment. There was a purpose behind what he was doing, and that purpose still existed. He'd be back.

How was Amanda going to protect herself and Ashley? She didn't know.

While talking to the police at Mrs. Bridges's house, Amanda had explained about the attempt to kidnap her at the mall and the break-in. The cop had written it all down, offering no assistance. "If anything happens again, call us," he'd said. Big help. By then she or Ashley could be dead.

Ashley chuckled at the sitcom. It was okay for a twelve-year-old to chuckle, but the responsibilities of this thing were Amanda's. She was the adult, the one who couldn't afford to chuckle, the one who had to cope— somehow. And the best she could do was keep Ashley out of school. How long before the man decided to try to find her? How long before he found out that she often stayed with Mrs. O'Donnell? If she kept Ashley out of school, she'd have to find someplace other than Mrs. O'Donnell's, watch to make sure she wasn't followed when she picked her daughter up and left her off.

But where was safe? Where could she leave Ashley? She could think of nowhere in Boston.

The phone rang, making Amanda jump. It was cordless, and at the moment it was on the arm of the couch. Amanda picked it up, said hello.

"Amanda Price?" a man asked.

"Yes, who's this?"

"Me. I don't want to say my name over the phone."

"You mean—"

"Don't say my name."

"I wasn't. And I know who you are." It was the man whose face and voice had been distorted when he appeared in her series of reports on New Shipton, the man who had told her what she needed to know, made the story possible.

"They're after you," he said.

"Who?"

"Who the hell do you think?"

"Casperson, the people in New Shipton?"

"Yeah. Get away. Get out of town."

"But—"

"There ain't no but. They find you, you're dead. Period."

"But I—"

"You really think you can hide from them? Or that the cops will protect you? The guys they'll send after you will find you no matter where you hide, no matter how many cops you have protecting you—if you're lucky enough to have any police protection, which isn't real likely."

"What . . . what can I do?"

"I told you. Get out of town. Use cash, no credit cards or checks, because those can be traced. Remember, these guys may be thugs to you, but here they're the establishment— the cops and the banks and all the rest of it. They got all the connections they need to find you unless you're very careful."

"But I can't just—"

"Listen, don't give me that shit. You can do what you gotta do. Or are you more worried about your job and all that than you are about staying alive?"

"Of course not, but—"

"There you go again with that 'but' shit. You got a family, they can wind up dead too. And if they get you, I'll wind up dead as well."

"You don't have to worry about that. I'd never—"

"The hell you wouldn't. They say talk or I'll cut up your kid and you'll talk. They say talk or watch your skin being peeled off, you'll talk. Do you understand?"

"They wouldn't—"

"They would, and you know it. Get out of Boston. Run, lady. Run for your fucking life."

The line went dead.

FOUR

"I'M scared," Amanda said. "More scared than I've ever been in my life."

She was sitting in the office of Bob Miller, her news director. It was the day after Ashley's narrow escape, the day after she'd been warned to get out of town. She'd just finished telling Miller everything that had happened.

"The man who tried to kidnap Ashley is the same man who tried to grab me," Amanda said. "I'm sure of it." Thinking about that man, who was so capable of defending himself against a larger opponent and who could make a gun pop into his hand with the skill of a stage magician, made her shudder.

"I might have been followed when I drove to work this morning," Amanda said. "A gray car got behind me right after I left the apartment and stayed there until I got here."

"But why would the New Shipton people attack you now?" Miller asked, frowning. "The series has already been run. The grand jury's already investigating."

"I don't know." Maybe she did know, but at the moment it wasn't worth discussing. The only thing that mattered was keeping Ashley and her alive.

Bob Miller leaned back in his desk chair, the furrows in his brow deepening. "Maybe I can get you police protection. I've got some pretty good contacts in the Department."

"Ashley too?"

"I'll try."

"No, it won't work. The cops don't have enough spare manpower to protect us both twenty-four hours a day."

"Let me try, Amanda. I've got some pretty good contacts, I really do. There's a deputy-chief I've got some IOU's with."

"Bob, the cops are talking strike."

He looked at her helplessly, saying nothing. It went without saying that she wouldn't get any protection if the Department went on strike.

"I have to get away," Amanda said. "Away from Boston."

"But—"

"Look," she said, cutting him off, "the next time this guy goes after Ashley, she may not be so lucky. We're talking about a guy who carries a gun and can physically handle two guys who could break him in half." She waved her hand in a circular motion, designed to show she didn't know what—her frustration, she supposed.

"We can put you up somewhere, get you a hotel room or something, hide you out."

She shook her head. "All he'd have to do would be to follow me from work, follow Ashley from school."

Miller sighed. "Then how can I help you?"

"I told you. I have to get away from Boston."

"You want to take some vacation days? You certainly deserve them after all the hours you put in on the New Shipton series."

"No. I want an extended leave of absence."

"For how long?"

"Until I'm ready to come back."

Miller was silent for a few moments, thinking it over. "You'd be letting this . . . this thug chase you away from your job, your home, everything."

Amanda nodded. "Okay, I'm a coward."

"I didn't mean it like that."

"I'm sorry, Bob. I know you didn't. Look, I'm a nervous wreck, I'm exhausted, and I need a rest. Maybe if it was just me, I'd take a week's vacation, get some sun down in Florida. But it's not just me. I've got a twelve-year-old daughter to think about."

"Could she stay with your ex-husband?"

"No," Amanda said flatly.

"I mean, under the circumstances . . ." He trailed off.

"It's nothing to do with the divorce or custody of Ashley or anything like that. It's just that it's not good enough. How much trouble do you think this guy would have finding out that I'm divorced and where Ashley's father lives?"

"Not much, I guess."

"And if this guy really wants something from me, grabbing Ashley is the best way to get it."

"Maybe you should take a few days off, relax, think things over."

"I stayed up all last night thinking it over. Here's the situation I'm in. Ashley's staying with the woman who lives across the hall because I'm afraid to send her to school. This morning I went out on my first assignment, a follow-up on the police strike story. I started to interview the mayor, and all of a sudden I just started shaking, and I couldn't think of a single question to ask him. He was looking at me like I was some kind of weirdo, like maybe he shouldn't be standing too close to me. How the hell can I go on like this?"

"I can see why you're upset, but to leave town, to run away . . . well, I think you might be overreacting."

"I'm not quitting my job or giving up my apartment. I just want a leave of absence. Bob, listen, all this has been . . . the best word I can think of is 'methodical.' The guy who grabbed me at the mall was no amateur, not just some psycho who gets his kicks hurting women. He'd been *sent* by someone. Then came the break-in at my apartment, with nothing of much value taken, but all my clothes and papers had been gone through. Then right after that, the same guy who tried to grab me tries to grab Ashley. This is not the work of some flako who sees me on TV and decides I remind him of all the women who ever hurt him or whatever."

She leaned forward, fixing her eyes on his. "This is

serious, heavy-duty stuff I'm into here. The New Shipton people murder anyone who gets in their way. We already know they killed Wilcox and Steen. Who knows how many other people they've killed. We're talking about some very nasty people here, all right?"

The news director sighed. "If you really want to get away this badly, there's no way I could refuse you a leave of absence."

"Thanks, Bob. I really appreciate it, I really do."

"Where will you go?"

"I don't know."

"Do you have enough money? The general manager would never approve a paid leave of absence, but I might be able to arrange some kind of an advance. Also, I suggested to him once that it might be a good idea to give you a bonus for all your work on the New Shipton series. He didn't say no. Maybe if I hit him up on it again . . ."

Amanda forced a small smile. "I won't say anything to discourage you from getting me a bonus, but I'm okay moneywise. My mother had an iron-clad rule about saving a portion of whatever we made. I guess she passed the habit along to me, because I do the same thing. I should have all I need in my savings account."

"When do you want to start your leave of absence?"

"Today. Right now. As soon as I leave your office."

He studied her in silence a moment, then said, "Be careful, Amanda. I'll miss you."

"Thanks," she said again, and a tear trickled down her cheek. Wiping it away, she stood to leave.

"Call me as soon as you get where you're going, so I'll know you're okay."

"I will."

"For sure?" he asked, looking at her sternly.

"Promise."

Amanda left the office, both her insides and her thoughts a big churning muddle. She felt as if she'd shatter should anyone so much as touch her. But she walked through the newsroom largely unnoticed. When she reached the parking lot, Amanda slipped behind the wheel of her car, rested her head on the steering wheel, and sobbed.

"We're just . . . going?" Ashley asked, looking bewildered.

Amanda had stopped at Mrs. O'Donnell's apartment to get the girl. They were in their own apartment now, sitting on the couch while Amanda explained what she had in mind.

"We're going to get away for a while, go spend the rest of the winter somewhere warm." She opened the road atlas resting on her lap. "Now, where would you like to go? Florida? Arizona? California?"

The girl was silent for a long moment, then she looked at her mother, her green eyes filled with worry. "Is this because of that man who tried to get us?"

All sorts of reassuring lies floated through Amanda's mind, lies about it being time for a vacation or getting away from the cold New England winter or her boss rewarding her with unexpected time off. Though still a child, Ashley was old enough to see through flimsy pretexts. And she *deserved* the truth. She was as deeply involved in whatever was going on as Amanda was. And in every bit as much danger.

So Amanda told her daughter the truth, repeating everything she'd told Bob Miller, and when she was done, Ashley's expression seemed to say, *Thanks for being honest with me, Mom. Thanks for not treating me like a kid.*

Amanda gave her a reassuring hug. "It's not always best to run away from your problems," she said. "But we're not exactly running away. Remember what I said about being careful? Well, that's what we're doing, being careful."

Ashley pulled the atlas over until it was on both their laps. "I wouldn't mind seeing Disney World or Disneyland," she said.

"Let's think about it," Amanda said. "We've got to pack,

go to the post office, go to the bank—and a whole lot of other things I probably haven't thought of yet. Let's try to get everything done today so we'll be ready to leave first thing in the morning. By that time we'll have decided where we want to go."

"Okay. What should we do first?"

"Let's go to the bank and the post office and anywhere else we have to go. We can pack this evening."

As they stood up, Ashley abruptly hugged her. "It'll be okay, Mom. Maybe it's not really a vacation, but we can make like it is."

"You bet," Amanda said with a cheerfulness she didn't feel at all.

Amanda told the post office to hold her mail until instructed otherwise. At Ashley's school, Amanda said her daughter would be away for an unspecified period because of a family emergency, offering no further details. The school secretary gave her forms to fill out. Amanda left the questions about where she could be reached and how long she'd be gone blank, over the secretary's objections. Everything went smoothly until they got to the bank.

Most of Amanda's savings were in certificates of deposit, and the bank had the option of requiring thirty days' written notice for early withdrawal. The bank had decided to exercise its option, which left Amanda with the contents of her checking account. A few hundred dollars.

She left the bank, furious that it was preventing her from getting her own money. She had to pay interest penalties for taking her money out of the CDs. Wasn't that enough? She resolved to change banks when she got back.

Got back? She didn't have enough money to *go*, unless she used her credit cards, which she couldn't do because of the trail she'd leave. As she and Ashley drove back to the apartment Amanda constantly checked the rearview mirror to make sure no one was following them. It was getting to be automatic, and Amanda wondered whether she'd always do it, even after the danger had passed.

And when would that be? A month from now? Two months? A year? When would life return to normal, be safe again? Amanda wondered whether she was being foolish to run. Maybe the thing to do was to stay put, fight.

Get out of Boston, her informant had warned.

Run, lady. Run for your fucking life.

Recalling his voice, the intensity of his warning, made a chill slide down her spine. And some inner part of herself, some gut-level feeling, told her that running was the only thing she could do, that the danger was very real, very close, and that the time for escaping it was growing shorter by the moment.

They say talk or I'll cut up your kid. . . . They say talk or watch your skin being peeled off. . . .

Amanda shuddered. Running was the right thing to do. Running was the *only* thing to do. If she was short on money, so be it. She'd use the credit cards if she had to—move on as soon as she charged something, be many miles away by the time the credit-card company received the bill. It might be risky, but it was less risky than staying here.

Amanda checked the rearview mirror, seeing no familiar cars. Which didn't mean they weren't there, of course. She was an amateur at this sort of thing. Fooling her would be easy.

She glanced at Ashley, seeing not only herself in terms of physical resemblance but also the part of herself that would go on after Amanda Price was gone, carrying her genes into future generations, her immortality. She loved this child, more than she could explain in words, and she had to do whatever she could to protect her.

Talk or I'll cut up your kid. . . .

Amanda squeezed her eyes closed, trying to shut out the vision that had just popped into her head. Then she remembered she was driving and opened them again. Amanda pulled into the underground parking area, watching every shadow, every car. Getting out of her Mustang, she dropped to the grease-stained floor, peering under the parked vehicles for a pair of feet that would mean someone was watching, waiting. She saw no one.

Ashley was staring at her, wide-eyed. "Mom . . ." But she let whatever she'd meant to say trail off.

"Come on," Amanda said. "Let's get into the elevator." The car arrived, the doors opened, and no one pounced on them. As they rode up to the sixth floor Amanda said, "I'm afraid we don't have the money to go to Disneyland right now. Maybe we can go in a month or so, after we get our money, but for now I think we'd better pinch our pennies."

"Are we still leaving . . . right now?"

"Yes."

"Where are we going?"

"I don't know."

Amanda had Ashley wait at Mrs. O'Donnell's while she checked to make sure no one was waiting inside their apartment. No one was. She got Ashley, then collapsed on the couch, her nerves shot.

Ashley joined her, picking up the road atlas. "Mom, if we're going, we'd better figure out where."

"Someplace motel rooms are cheap and plentiful this time of year."

"Where's that?"

Amanda was saved from having to answer that by the phone. It was sitting beside Ashley on the couch. Figuring it wasn't for her, the girl handed it to her mother, extending the antenna as she did so.

"Amanda, it's me—Bob. Have you decided where you're going yet?"

"No, not yet."

"Well, I've got an idea, if you're interested. Uh, before coming here, I was at a station in Minneapolis, and while I was there I bought a cabin up in the northern part of the state. That's one of the big things if you live in the Twin

Cities. You've got to have a summer cabin up north. Anyway, I still own the place. Simply never got around to selling it. If you need a place to go, it's yours as long as you need it."

"A cabin? In northern Minnesota?" Amanda realized she'd sounded incredulous, and she hoped Miller hadn't taken offense. He was only trying to help.

"It's suitable for year-round living. It's really a small house. It's heated, well insulated, has all the appliances, and the road to it is plowed during the winter."

"I . . . I don't know what to say."

"Say yes. You'll be living rent-free, and I'll be the only person who knows where you are. And think about this too. You'll be in a place no one would ever dream of looking for you."

Although Amanda could think of reasons for saying no, they were all outweighed by the reasons for accepting Miller's offer. She had enough money to get somewhere but not enough to spend very many nights in motels. She'd have to use her credit cards.

Amanda explained all this to Miller. "You've really helped me out, Bob. I'm truly grateful."

"Just glad I could help. When are you leaving?"

"In the morning."

"Stop by the station and I'll give you the keys to the place and a map showing you how to get there."

He fell silent, so Amanda thought the conversation was over. She said, "Thanks again, Bob. I—"

"I think it's pretty clear what they want from you," he said.

"The name."

"Yes."

"They want to make an example of him," Amanda said. "Demonstrate what happens to people who talk."

"That, and make sure he doesn't tell what he knows to the grand jury."

"That too," Amanda said.

"Do you think you should tell me who it was, in case . . . well, just in case."

Amanda knew what he meant. In case something happened to her. "No," she said. "I promised not to tell anyone."

"Under these circumstances . . ."

"The circumstances don't matter. I promised."

"A promise is a promise, right?"

"Yes. A promise is a promise."

When she ended the conversation, she found her daughter looking at her curiously. Amanda said, "Ashley, how'd you like to spend some time in northern Minnesota?"

"In February?" The girl looked astonished.

Amanda explained Bob Miller's offer, and Ashley agreed that under the circumstances it was too good to pass up.

"How long will we have to stay there?" the girl asked.

"I don't know."

"Any chance we'll make it to Disneyland?"

"Hon, right now I don't know what's going to happen. Let's wait and see, okay? I promise that we'll get there someday."

"Mom's honor?" Ashley said, smiling.

And Amanda realized that—at this moment, anyway—Ashley was being the adult. She was trying to lighten things up, take some of the tension out of the room.

Amanda held up her hand, as if taking the oath in a courtroom. "Mom's honor," she said, and they hugged each other.

The next morning they left Boston. Amanda took the Massachusetts Turnpike only as far as Interstate 84, where she headed south into Connecticut—not because this was necessarily the best way to go but because she didn't want to go anywhere near the western part of Massachusetts, where New Shipton was located.

Before leaving Boston, they'd stopped by the station to get the keys and map from Bob Miller. The news director

said he'd checked with Greg Houghton, the station's mete-
orologist, who'd told him there was a snowstorm moving in
from the west, but unless it slowed and intensified, it should
move slowly northward into Canada, posing no problems
for Amanda and Ashley.

"I'm the only one who knows where you're going,"
Miller had said. "I haven't even told my wife." Then he'd
studied her a moment, the concern in his eyes obvious. "Be
careful," he said. "Phone me after you get there so I'll
know you're okay."

"Thank you, Bob," she said, her eyes moist. They'd
looked at each other a moment, then she'd thrown her arms
around him and hugged him.

Leaving Boston, Amanda had checked the rearview
constantly. As far as she could determine, no one was
tailing them. She and Ashley were leaving Hartford, heading for New Britain and Waterbury, when the first big
snowflakes fell.

"You think it's going to snow hard?" Ashley asked
nervously.

"It's not supposed to," Amanda replied.

But looking at the white sky, she wasn't so sure. Greg
Houghton's forecast had been that the storm would move
into Canada *unless* it slowed and began to intensify. As she
stared through the windshield at those big flakes it sure
looked as if it might be intensifying to Amanda.

"If it gets too bad, we'll just find a motel and hole up till
it's over," Amanda said.

"There's New Mexico," Ashley said, pointing to the
red-and-yellow license plate on the station wagon that had
just passed them. To pass the time she'd been keeping track
of license tags, noting each new state she saw.

The New Mexico driver was going fast, and the station
wagon quickly disappeared. Amanda automatically checked
the rearview mirror. There was a gray car behind her, so far
back that it was barely a dot in the mirror. She had noticed
the car before, but then there was nothing unusual about

another vehicle going in the same direction at the same speed on an interstate highway. Amanda decided to keep an eye on it, but for now there was probably nothing to worry about.

"Alaska!" Ashley said excitedly, spotting another license plate. "I bet he won't have any trouble driving in the snow."

"Not if he's from Alaska," Amanda agreed. But then Amanda was no novice at driving in snow herself, having grown up in Nebraska, where the howling north wind could drive the white stuff into mammoth drifts. And her career had taken her from a station in Omaha to one in Milwaukee and then on to Boston. She'd never lived anywhere but snowy places.

The snow began to fall more heavily, then abruptly slacked off. Amanda checked the rearview mirror. Although there was still a gray car behind her, she wasn't sure it was the same one. It might be lighter gray than the one she'd seen before. Ashley pointed out a South Carolina license plate.

The day seemed to brighten somewhat, and Amanda saw a small patch of blue sky to the south. Maybe Greg Houghton had been right, after all.

Ashley seemed to have stopped spotting new license plates, and they drove in silence, each thinking her own thoughts. Amanda found herself recalling her marriage to Ashley's father. Like her, Tom was from Omaha, a salesman at the TV station at which she worked. Something about his easygoing nature had attracted her to him—or that's how she saw it at the time. Looking back at it, maybe she'd married Tom because he seemed unthreatening—unlike some of the more aggressive men she'd met. But then she'd been twenty-two, still living in her hometown, not terribly experienced.

Too late she discovered that Tom's easygoing nature was just the outward manifestation of his insecurity. He'd gotten the position at the station because his uncle had some pull with people who mattered, but he hadn't been good enough to keep the job. He was fired about six months after Ashley was born. Then he managed to get a job selling time at a top-forty radio station and eventually lost that position too. He lost more jobs as time went on. Meanwhile Amanda's career was going quite well. She was getting raises all along, and even offers from other stations. Suffering from a wounded ego, Tom had sought solace in a liquor bottle, drowning himself in booze and self-pity. He wouldn't talk to her; he wouldn't seek help.

Finally Amanda had given him an ultimatum: "Get yourself together or I'm filing for a divorce." That had stunned him. And Amanda would never forget what happened next.

They were in the living room of their house in Omaha, Tom on the couch, Amanda standing. He rose slowly, his eyes turning wild. "You want me to be tough, is that right?"

"I want you to get help. I want you to stop drinking. I want you to be able to hold a job."

He shook his head. "You want me to be tough, like a lot of the guys I know. Well, I can be just as tough as they are."

Advancing on her so quickly that she didn't have a chance to react, he hit her. Startled, Amanda had staggered backward, sitting down hard on the floor.

She filed for divorce the next day.

Amanda had a friend who was a battered wife. She had promised herself that if a man ever hit her, even once, she would leave him instantly. She would never be like Peggy, who kept going back for more, letting the son of a bitch tell her it was her fault that he hit her, for misbehaving, when she knew it would make him mad.

Tom instantly reverted to his old self, begging her to forgive him. When she'd refused, he meekly went along with whatever she wanted in the divorce settlement. They'd divided up the property evenly. Amanda got custody of Ashley. She kept her married name because that was Ashley's name, and she didn't want to go through the confusion of a mother being called one thing while her daughter was called another. The alternative would be to change Ashley's last name, and that would have been just one more thing for a little girl to cope with, on top of the divorce of her parents.

Shortly after that she got a better-paying job in Milwaukee, a bigger market and a step up. Tom eventually moved to California, where he was now the manager of a shoe store. Both his job and his second marriage were lasting. Apparently he and Amanda were both better off without each other.

Since her first experience with it Amanda had steered clear of marriage. She had no trouble attracting men. She'd slept with some, had short-term relationships with a couple, but when things started getting too serious, she always brought them to an end. Was she now scared of marriage, the way she'd once been afraid of aggressive men? Once burned, so never again? It wasn't a real good attitude, but then maybe she simply hadn't met the right guy. Amanda made herself stop thinking about these things. This really wasn't the right time to start analyzing and evaluating her life.

"Nebraska!" Ashley exclaimed, finally seeing a new license plate. "Our home state."

"It's where we were both born," Amanda said, "but I think we have to call Massachusetts home now."

Ashley shrugged, the point clearly of little importance to her.

The patch of blue had vanished as quickly as it had appeared, and the sky had taken on the color of weathered aluminum. A few snowflakes were beginning to fall, small ones this time. They hit the windshield, melting and trickling down the glass. Amanda set the wipers on intermittent, so that every few moments the blades would sweep away the slowly accumulating moisture.

Turning on the radio, Amanda said, "I think we'd better try to find a weather forecast."

There was nothing but static on the Boston frequency to

which it was tuned, so she switched it to the search mode, let it find a station on its own. It stopped on one playing big band music.

"Yuck!" Ashley protested. "Can't we find a better station than that?"

"Put it on any station you like. I just want one with a weather forecast."

Ashley fooled with the radio until she had a strong signal coming in from a station playing rock and roll. Ugh! Amanda thought, but kept her feelings to herself. They crossed into New York.

The station faded before giving a weather report, and Ashley quickly managed to find another one playing rock and roll. To Amanda it sounded even worse than the last one, some guy screaming unintelligibly. She'd understood the lyrics easily enough when she was a teenager, and Amanda wondered whether the music had changed or she had.

The snow was falling harder now.

Amanda switched the wipers from intermittent to slow.

Finally the screechy electric guitars and incomprehensible words stopped, and the announcer said, "The weather bureau has issued a winter storm watch for eastern Ohio and western Pennsylvania. The conditions are right for a severe winter storm to develop in that area. If it develops, it'll arrive in southern New York State and northern New Jersey late this afternoon. Sounds like a good day to curl up with your radio. Stay tuned to Z-Rock, and we'll keep you up to date on the weather, while we play the best rock on the East Coast."

This was followed by three commercials and more music that pleased Ashley and gave Amanda a headache. She checked the rearview mirror. She didn't see the gray car.

The snow was steady but not heavy enough to stick to the road. Amanda kept going. She was a long way from Ohio or western Pennsylvania. It was still early in the afternoon, too soon to stop as long as the road surface remained in good condition.

"Texas," Ashley said, noting the plate on a Pontiac that had just passed them.

They drove on, the snowfall increasing and decreasing but never getting quite bad enough to make Amanda start looking for a motel. Z-Rock faded out, and Ashley, taking pity on her mother, found a station that was playing oldies—stuff from the fifties and sixties. Buddy Holly sang "Peggy Sue," followed by the Beatles doing "I Wanna Hold Your Hand." Amanda understood every word.

It was about four o'clock when the announcer said, "This just in from the weather service. A winter storm warning has been issued for the entire state of Pennsylvania. Snow and blowing snow can be expected statewide by evening, with accumulations of six to eight inches likely in most areas."

Amanda and Ashley crossed the Delaware River. They were in Pennsylvania.

FIVE

THE snow was coming down more heavily by the moment, swirling around between the snowbanks lining the highway, sticking in some places, blowing away in others. The storm had hit with the suddenness of a hammer blow. The aluminum sky darkened, a gust of wind hit the car like a cannonade, nearly pushing it into the other lane, and then the snow was coming down with a vengeance, the visibility diminishing to almost nothing, forcing drivers to slow down, switch on their headlights.

"We'll stop at the first motel we come to," Amanda said.

Ashley watched the road nervously and said nothing. A gust of wind buffeted the car.

Finally they saw a neon sign ahead, its red letters growing out of the falling snow like a mirage. It read, MOTEL. Amanda got off at the exit, followed the access road toward the glowing red letters. And when she finally reached the sign, she saw the smaller letters below the big ones, letters that spelled out NO VACANCY.

"We have to keep going until we find somewhere to stay," Amanda said as she headed back toward the interstate.

Traffic on the highway was thinning rapidly. The patches of sticking snow were growing larger, meeting in some places. On the radio, Del Shannon was singing "Runaway." When the song ended, the announcer informed his listeners that the Pennsylvania state police had issued a bulletin discouraging travel throughout the state. Because of the storm, night was coming early, the grayness in which they

71

were engulfed getting darker by the moment, closing in on them.

It took twenty minutes to reach the next motel, and by the time they got there the snow was starting to pack on the highway, making it slippery. The motel's NO VACANCY sign was lit, but Amanda pulled up to the office, anyway. Inside she found a dumpy blond woman with her hair in tight little curls.

"No vacancies," the woman said.

"I've got a little girl with me," Amanda said. "The storm's getting worse."

The woman looked sympathetic, but she said, "I'm all filled up. The last room I had, two cars got here at the same time, and the people agreed to share it. There were five of them in all, so I guess some of them are sleeping on the floor."

"Where's the closest place I might be able to find a room?"

"You gotta get off the interstate. Which way you headed?"

"West."

"Next exit's only two miles. It's a state highway. Go south. There's some small towns not too far away, and most of them have motels. The people on the interstate don't know about them, so you can probably find a room."

It was fully dark when Amanda returned to the car. The tires spun a couple of times as she and Ashley drove up the ramp leading to the interstate, but they made it. The highway itself was almost deserted now. Amanda saw no cars ahead of her and only one set of headlights behind her. The tire tracks in the snow left by other vehicles were rapidly being covered over by the falling snow. The Ford's headlights turned the scene in front of them into a hypnotic dance of thousands upon thousands of white dots.

"Shouldn't we have reached the exit by now?" Ashley asked nervously. She was peering through the windshield, as if she could make the overpass appear by sheer force of will.

"It's taking us a long time to get there because we have to go so slowly," Amanda said. She was going thirty-five. Any faster and the car started to feel unstable, as if it were a skittish animal over which she had practically no control.

Finally a sign announcing the next exit appeared in front of them, and then the exit itself. Amanda went down the ramp slowly so she wouldn't start sliding. The oldies station was still coming in, Peter, Paul and Mary singing "Blowin' in the Wind." It faded out as Amanda headed south on the state highway.

There was a single set of faint tire tracks in the snow, heading in the same direction Amanda was. After she'd been on the road about five minutes, the tracks disappeared altogether. Snowbanks about three feet high lined the two-lane highway. The snow had been pushed just to the edge of the road, barely leaving enough room for two cars to pass. Ashley tried to find a new station on the radio. She tuned in a preacher telling people to give themselves to Jesus—the first step being to make a contribution to the preacher's ministry—then a station running a call-in talk show, people discussing their most intimate problems with some guy who offered instant advice.

"Is it okay to turn it off, Mom?"

Amanda said that would be just fine with her.

Glancing in the rearview mirror, Amanda saw headlights behind her. It was comforting to know she wasn't alone. If she lost control of the car and slid into the snowbank or something like that, there'd be someone close behind her who could help.

On the other hand, at the rate the car was catching up to her, it seemed more likely that the other driver would be the one sliding off the road and needing her help. The car rolled up behind her, its headlights filling her rearview mirror with their intense glare, and then it was pulling out to pass. To give it room, Amanda pulled as close to the snowbank as she dared, thinking this turkey had to be an absolute idiot to be driving like that.

The car was a midsized gray four-door. It glided past her without incident, the driver even taking the trouble to signal his intention to return to the right lane. The man driving it was the only person in the car. As soon as he was in front of her, he began slowing down.

"What's that guy doing?" Ashley asked anxiously.

"Must have finally figured out he was going too fast for these conditions."

The car was slowing down even more now, forcing Amanda to slow down as well. Her speed dropped from twenty miles an hour to fifteen to ten, and then the gray car pulled into the center of the road and stopped.

"Why did he stop?" Ashley asked. "You think he's looking for a motel too? Maybe he's lost."

"I don't know," Amanda said, feeling more uneasy by the moment.

"Oh, look," the girl said, pointing. "He's from Massachusetts too. Maybe that's why he stopped."

Amanda felt an icy lump of fear growing inside her, getting bigger by the moment. There'd been a gray car behind her most of the day. Now one had caught up with her and forced her to stop, one with Massachusetts plates.

"Mom, what . . . ?" Ashley's question trailed off because the gray car's door had opened and a man was stepping out.

"Mom!" the girl exclaimed, grabbing Amanda's arm. "It's him, the guy who tried to get me after school."

Amanda also recognized the tall man who had emerged from the car. She'd met him in the parking lot of the mall, when he'd tried to abduct her. The incident flashed into her memory, and she was again looking into his dull, lifeless eyes. The image vanished. The man was standing there by the open door of his car, looking at her, knowing she couldn't get past him, knowing she'd probably skid into the snowbank if she tried to turn around quickly. Amanda saw one chance, and she took it.

"Try to remember his license-plate number," she said. She wasn't sure why she'd said that. Maybe to make Ashley think they were going to get out of this. Maybe because no one had gotten the license-plate number of the man's car when he'd tried to grab her at the mall.

Amanda stepped on the gas.

The Ford's tires spun, the car sliding to the side, and then it was rolling forward, picking up speed. Realizing what was happening, the man pulled out a gun, started to aim it, but he was too late. Tilting dangerously as its left wheels rode up on the snowbank, the Ford sped through the space between the snowbank and the gray car, the man jumping back inside just as Amanda's car tore his door off, flipping it in the air. There was a loud screech as the two cars scraped against each other, and then the Ford was on the road again, sliding. Amanda corrected for the skid, easing up on the gas. The car straightened. Amanda gave it some gas again, trying to pick up as much speed as possible, expecting that at any moment the back window would be shattered by a bullet. But no shots were fired.

Looking in the rearview mirror, Amanda saw the gray car's headlights, swinging from side to side as it slipped in the snow. Then they steadied. The man was coming after her in his now doorless car. Amanda sped up until the car felt as if it were floating, out of control, at the mercy of the wind, snowflakes flying by like a barrage of white bullets. Even so, the gray car was gaining on her.

Ashley was looking from the windshield to the back window as if she didn't know which scared her the most, the speed at which they were traveling or the man in the gray car. Its headlights were about ten car lengths behind them now. Amanda moved into the center of the road. If she could keep the man from getting in front of her, there'd be nothing he could do, and eventually they'd come to a town, where she could get help.

The gray car was about twenty feet behind them now, still closing fast.

"Mom! He's going to ram us!"

It might have been what he had in mind, but he never managed to do it, because when he'd closed to within five feet of them, he lost control on the slick surface, his headlights swinging away to the left. Amanda watched in the rearview as the gray car spun around twice, then slid into the snowbank, its headlights disappearing.

"He wrecked! He wrecked!" Ashley squealed.

Amanda slowed until she was sure she had control of the car. The road behind her continued to be dark. And then lights appeared ahead of her, the lights of a town. They passed a billboard advertising a restaurant—BILL'S COUNTRY KITCHEN, JUST LIKE MAMMA'S HOME COOKIN'—and then street lamps appeared, followed by a sign that read TRAVELERS INN MOTEL, and beneath that in smaller letters VACANCY.

Amanda pulled up to the office. She could call the police from here.

"We found the gray car," the state trooper told her the next morning. "It matched the license-plate number your daughter gave me last night, not that there was much doubt about it being the right car, missing a door the way it was and having Massachusetts tags."

Like state policemen everywhere, he was a big, solid-looking guy, six-one or six-two, a man who could handle difficult situations without help, which could often be twenty or thirty miles away. He'd knocked on the door of Amanda's hotel room a moment ago, saying he wanted to fill her in. Now he was sitting in the room's only chair while Amanda and her daughter sat on the bed.

"His car plowed right through the snowbank and went off the road into deep snow," the officer said. "It'll take a wrecker to pull it out."

Amanda nodded. Last night she'd lain awake, sure that

every shadow that passed the window, every car door that slammed, every rattle of the plumbing was the man with the corpselike eyes coming to get her. Even now she wondered whether he was in another room at the motel, watching, waiting for her to leave so he could resume his pursuit.

As if reading her thoughts, the state cop said, "We checked all the motels in town, and no one showed up on foot—no one matching his description showed up at all."

"Where could he have gone?" Amanda asked.

The officer shrugged. "No telling. Hitched a ride with someone, maybe. There's farms around. He could have spent the night in a barn—woulda been cold, but I guess he could have done it. We're still keeping an eye out for him, but there's no way of knowing whether he's still in the area."

"Did you check the license-plate number to see who the car belonged to?" Ashley asked.

"Massachusetts says the car was stolen."

Amanda wasn't surprised. Their adversary seemed the sort who would use a stolen car. She was also willing to bet that the Pennsylvania authorities weren't going to find him. He was a professional.

"You told me last night about being attacked by this man back in Massachusetts, and I'd like you to go over that again, if you wouldn't mind."

Amanda and Ashley told their stories. When they were finished, the cop said, "And this guy's after you because of a story you did."

"Yes. There can't be any doubt, not after the phone call I received."

"Why didn't you stay in Boston, let the police there take care of the situation?" He was studying her closely, a slight frown on his face.

"Because the police in Boston couldn't protect both me and my daughter twenty-four hours a day."

"You ask them?"

"I didn't have to ask them. I know they don't have that

kind of manpower. And I know that if these people really want to get me, they'll get me. Unless I go where they can't find me. It's the only way my daughter and I can be safe."

"Judging from what happened last night, it hasn't worked too well."

"No," Amanda said.

"So what are you going to do now?"

"I don't know," Amanda said truthfully. She needed to call Bob Miller, talk things over with him, see what he thought. She'd been trying to figure out what to do all night, and the only conclusion she'd come up with was that she was too confused and frightened to think straight.

"When you get ready to leave," the police officer said, "you can give me a call if you want. I'll escort you a ways, make sure no one's following you."

"Thank you," Amanda said, suddenly feeling relieved. She'd been worried about what might happen when she left.

The state policeman nodded. "Your car's pretty badly scraped on the right side, but it looks drivable. Your insurance company's probably going to want a copy of the report. Tell them to get in touch with our district office in Scranton."

Amanda said she'd do that.

After the state policeman left, she called Bob Miller and told him what had happened.

"Jesus!" he said. "I'm glad you're all right. You sure it's the same guy?"

"Positive. Both Ashley and I recognized him immediately."

"Wow. That was quite a piece of driving you did, going up on that snowbank like that. Sounds like James Bond."

"You'd be surprised what you can do when you think someone's about to . . ." Glancing at Ashley, she let her words trail off.

"Guy must have followed you all the way from Boston, just waiting for his chance."

"Yeah," she said, and drew in a slow breath. "Bob, what am I going to do?"

The news director was silent for a few moments, apparently thinking about it. Finally he said, "Keep going, Amanda. There's no way this guy can know your destination. I mean, if you look at a map, you could be headed for Illinois or Colorado or California or just about anyplace. Just make sure you're not being followed. Double back a couple of times, make sure no one has to turn around to stay behind you. It shouldn't be that hard to do. Then once you're sure you don't have a tail, head for Minnesota. You'll be safe once you get there. He'll never find you."

Amanda considered that, then said, "Yeah, you're right. The state policeman said he'd escort me out of town, make sure I'm not being followed. That's probably even better than all that doubling back you were talking about."

"So you're going on?"

"The only alternative's to go back to Boston, and I don't see what that would accomplish. Ashley and I would be as vulnerable as we were before we left."

They talked for another few moments then the news director said, "Call me as soon as you get there."

Amanda promised she would.

She and Ashley ate breakfast in a little restaurant a block down the street from the motel. No one followed them. The tall man with strange eyes was not among the café's customers. After they ate, Amanda called the state police from a gas station. The officer met them about fifteen minutes later.

"You decide what you're going to do?" he asked, leaning down so he could see her through the window of her car.

"I'm going on," she said.

"To Minnesota?"

"Yes."

The officer frowned. "I don't know anything about the situation in this New Shipton place, but if the local police are involved, they might request a copy of my report on this incident—maybe claim interest in the stolen car with the Massachusetts plates. Just to be on the safe side, I won't put anything about Minnesota in my report."

"Thank you," Amanda said, a little unnerved. There were so many ways for the people in New Shipton to learn things. She'd never considered that a Pennsylvania police report could get into their hands. She was an amateur at things like this, in way over her head. This time she'd been lucky, but luck wasn't something you could rely on. She had to think things through more carefully. Her and Ashley's survival depended on it.

"You heading west on the interstate?" the policeman asked.

"Yes."

"Okay. I'll tag along behind you for a while, make sure nobody's following you."

Amanda and Ashley drove out of town with the state trooper behind them. The storm was over. Although the sky was still a little gray, it was brightening, and there was some blue to the west. The snowplows had been through; the road was clear.

Amanda and Ashley drove silently, each thinking her own thoughts, each of them still a little shaken by what had happened. Last night, when they were finally inside the motel and safe, Amanda and her daughter had sat on the bed, looking at each other, and Amanda thought they were going to have a good cry, hold each other, let go of some of the tension. But it hadn't happened, maybe because neither of them thought it was over yet.

The state policeman dropped back out of sight when they reached the interstate. Amanda drove for nearly ten miles before the trooper caught up with her, motioning for her to pull off onto the shoulder and stop. He pulled in behind them and walked up to Amanda's side of the car. She rolled down her window.

"There's no one trailing you," he said.

"How can you be sure?" Ashley asked him.

He bent down a little lower so he could look at her. "Because I know what to look for."

"I, uh, I didn't mean . . ." Not sure what to say, the girl let her words trail off.

"No problem," the trooper said. "I understand that you're kinda scared. But you can take my word for it, there's no one there. Even if they're using more than one car, I'd have spotted them. Honest."

Amanda thanked the policeman for his help. He tailed them for another quarter of mile or so, and then Amanda looked into the rearview mirror and he was gone. It had been reassuring having a protector, a guardian angel. His absence made Amanda feel vulnerable and helpless. She drove on, heading west.

Dexter Buchanan slipped several quarters into the pay phone outside a gas station on Interstate 84. He could have called collect or used his AT&T credit card, but either of those methods would have left a record of the call, something Dexter Buchanan did not want to do. He listened as the long-distance service's equipment quickly sought out the right electronic pathways and made connections.

He'd nearly had the woman last night. The maneuver she'd pulled—riding halfway up on the snowbank and tearing the door off his car—had taken him completely by surprise. Even so, he'd come close to getting her a few moments later, in his then doorless car. But the babe had known how to drive in snow, and Buchanan had been forced to take some chances to catch up with her. Luck had turned against him at the last moment, when he'd lost control, spinning out, then sliding through the snowbank and off the road, the car tilting and turning and bouncing. His seat belt had kept him from being tossed through the open space where the door had been, which could well have proven fatal. As it was, he was unhurt, although the car wasn't going anywhere until a wrecker pulled it out.

The thought that he might have been killed in the accident didn't bother Dexter Buchanan. Nor was he angry because the woman had gotten away. Dexter Buchanan did not show emotions, not even to himself.

AT&T made the last connection, and there was a moment of silence before the phone rang in New Shipton.

"Casperson," the man in Massachusetts said.

"Buchanan. I lost her." He didn't bother telling his boss how he'd lost her, or how he'd made his way into the nearby small town and stolen a station wagon from a used-car lot. Such information was extraneous.

"Shit!" the man in Massachusetts said. "Anyway you can pick up her trail?"

"No."

"Fuck!" the man in Massachusetts shouted furiously.

Buchanan was unconcerned. What happened, happened. If his present employer didn't like his work, he'd seek employment elsewhere. He had good mob contacts in Boston and New York, and skills that were always in demand.

"Where are you?"

"Pennsylvania."

"Where in Pennsylvania?" the man in Massachusetts asked, his rage just below the surface.

"East of Scranton."

"Go to Boston. Someone there has to know where she's going."

"I'm on my way," Buchanan said, and hung up.

He left the stolen station wagon at a truck stop and got a ride with a trucker hauling produce from California.

Six

EXHAUSTED, Amanda and Ashley reached northern Minnesota three and a half days after leaving Boston. Although there hadn't been any more snowstorms, the roads were often icy or slushy, conditions that made driving slow and nerve-racking. Adding to the stress was the knowledge that somewhere out there was a man with zombielike eyes who almost certainly still wanted to find them. Thinking about that kept Amanda awake at night, watching the shadows on motel-room walls.

But now, driving through the snow-covered woods in northern Minnesota, Amanda felt the tension begin to melt away. They'd made it. The man had no way of knowing where they'd gone; he couldn't find them here.

"Okay," Ashley said, studying Bob Miller's map. "There should be a whole bunch of mailboxes on the left, and the first one should say J. Heikkinen."

"Let's hope J. Heikkinen hasn't sold the place to someone else. We'll never figure out where to turn."

"There are some mailboxes," Ashley said. "Slow down."

The first one read J. Heikkinen in neat, hand-painted red letters, and Ashley said, "Turn left."

Amanda did so. "Now what?"

"Go two and three-tenths miles. The place will be on the left. It says here that it's a white bungalow with a blue roof and that it's right on a lake."

The road they were following was lined with snowbanks so high it was like driving along the bottom of a narrow canyon. The sun shining on the snow made everything seem bright and pristine and good. A squirrel crossed the road in front of them, scampering up to the top of the snowbank, where it sat up on its haunches and surveyed its surroundings for a moment before disappearing into the woods.

"I bet it's nice here in the summer," Ashley said.

"The fall colors are probably as pretty as they are in New England," Amanda said.

They drove in silence for a while; then Ashley said, "How far have we gone since we turned?"

"Two miles even. We're almost there."

But when they'd gone two and three tenths miles, Amanda saw nothing except the unbroken snowbank and the leafless trees that seemed to stretch off into the distance forever. They passed a man driving a small tractor with a scoop on the front, the only vehicle they'd encountered on the road. Amanda had gone a full four miles before she stopped the car, saying, "Either we missed it or Bob's directions are wrong."

"You think he made a mistake?" Ashley asked.

"It's more likely that we missed it. Two-point-three miles is being pretty precise. It's not like he was just guessing."

Amanda turned around, which took a little maneuvering in the narrow space between snowbanks, and headed back the way they had come. They'd gone not quite a mile and three quarters when they came upon the man with the tractor again. He was using the machine to clear away part of the snowbank. Amanda stopped the car.

"Let's ask him for directions," she said, getting out of the car. Ashley got out too.

Spotting them, the man shut off the tractor and climbed down from it. It was hard to tell much about him, because all Amanda could see of his face was a pair of blue eyes, a nose, and a mouth, the rest hidden by the hood of his blue parka.

"Excuse me," Amanda said, "I'm looking for a cabin that belongs to Bob Miller. Can you tell me where it is?"

"You can't get at it."

"Why not?"

"Because I haven't finished cutting through this snow-bank to the driveway yet. That's why not."

"You mean, this is his place here?"

"If you move to your left a little and look through the tree trunks, you'll see something red. That's the chimney."

"I see it," Ashley said. And then Amanda did too.

The man proffered a mitten-enclosed hand. "I'm John Heikkinen," he said. "Bob called me and asked if I'd plow out the driveway for you. I didn't get around to it till today, and I was afraid you might get ahead of me. I take it you're Amanda Price."

"Yes," she said, shaking the man's hand. She introduced Ashley, and Heikkinen shook the girl's hand too. "I'm certainly grateful to you for doing this," Amanda said. "What do I owe you?"

"Nothin'."

"But I can't—"

"Why can't you?"

"It wouldn't be right."

"Sure it would. If you knew how much fun I have operating this thing, you'd charge me instead of it being the other way around. My wife says if it was up to me, I'd clear all the roads in the county by myself and put the snowplow operators out of work."

Amanda told him again how much she appreciated it, and Heikkinen went back to making a cut in the snowbank. When he'd finished that, he plowed the driveway, then helped them carry in their things, after which he turned on the oil furnace and checked to make sure all the appliances were operating properly. The electricity was on and the phone was working.

"Bob took care of all that," Heikkinen said. "Phoned the power company and the telephone company from Massachusetts. Oil tank's half full. It should last you for a while."

He'd pushed the hood of his parka back, and Amanda finally got a look at his face. He was in his mid-sixties, bald with a gray fringe, and he smiled with teeth too perfect to be the ones he was born with.

"Come on," he said. "Let's go switch on the pump for the well." It was out back in a little structure that looked like an insulated doghouse. Heikkinen flipped a switch and an electric motor came to life. "This is the reset button. If you find yourself without water, just hit that. If that doesn't work, check the fuse." He pointed to the pump's small fuse box. There were extra fuses on top of it.

Back inside, Heikkinen turned on the kitchen tap. Horrid-looking brown water squirted out. "It'll clear up in a few minutes," he said. "Just let it run."

For the umpteenth time Amanda thanked him for his help.

When he was getting ready to leave, he said, "Wife will be by later on with something for you to eat. Don't imagine you brought any food with you, and the store's a five-mile drive."

"What a cool guy," Ashley said after he'd gone. It wasn't the way Amanda would have put it, but she certainly agreed with the sentiment. Another "cool guy" was Bob Miller. She had no idea how she'd ever repay him.

Feeling drained, Amanda sat down on a small uphol-stered chair in the living room. Looking equally tired, Ashley sat in a recliner, leaned it back. The house—to Amanda it seemed much too nice to be called a cabin—had two small bedrooms, a bathroom that had a tub with a shower enclosure, and a kitchen that was large enough to hold a picnic-type table and benches that could seat six, if you didn't mind bumping elbows every now and then. The place had polished hardwood floors throughout, made with wide planks that gave it a rustic look. The furnishings were decent but not fancy, the type of stuff a young married couple might have just starting out, hand-me-downs from uncles and aunts and parents. Completely mismatched but with some life left in them.

The living-room walls were made of diagonal, Vnotched, tongue-and-groove pine that had been varnished but not stained. One wall was dominated by a massive stone fireplace. Amanda had spotted a snow-covered lump out by the well pump that looked like a woodpile. Maybe tomorrow she could drag in some of the wood and make a fire.

Mrs. Heikkinen showed up about five o'clock with a carton of foil-covered containers. Introducing herself as Barbara, she set all the containers on the counter, saying that they were all ovenproof, so everything could be heated up without a problem. She was a short woman about the same age as her husband, and like him, she was blue-eyed and gray-haired. Her hair was straight and fairly short, a no-nonsense style that could be made presentable with a few strokes of a comb. When she smiled, it was clear that her flawless teeth probably spent the night in a glass, beside those of her husband.

"This one contains green beans," she said, pointing at one of the containers. "This is boiled bagies." She pronounced it "beg-ies." "This is Jell-O salad. Be careful not to put that one in the oven. Uh, let's see. Oh, yes, this is leftover pot roast with potatoes and gravy. I'm sorry it had to be leftovers, but I didn't get time to make anything from scratch."

Amanda said she didn't mind.

"What are beg-ies?" Ashley asked.

"Rutabagas. Around here everybody just calls them bagies."

Mrs. Heikkinen explained that rutabagas were sort of a local delicacy, along with walleye pike, beer-batter fried smelt, and certain Scandinavian dishes such as *lutefisk* and *lefse*—cod treated with lye and a flat potato bread that resembled flour tortillas. Mrs. Heikkinen enjoyed talking.

She explained that this was a summer vacation area for people from the Twin Cities. The place was loaded with summer cabins and campsites, but not many people lived here year-round. In fact, you couldn't live here year-round in a lot of the cabins, which were uninsulated and unheated, except for fireplaces. Most of the few permanent residents owned businesses, many of which were strictly summertime operations. She and her husband, for example, rented boats and sold bait and fishing equipment. That, combined with John's pension from the Duluth, Missabe, and Iron Range Railway, was enough to see them through.

The nearest town was Fiddlehead Lake, five miles away. Mrs. Heikkinen said the name came from all the fiddlehead ferns that grew in the area. There was also Fiddlehead Lake, the lake—as opposed to the town. Bob Miller's cabin was about fifty feet from it, although this time of year the lake was nothing but a slab of ice, of course.

"Fiddlehead—we hardly ever use the whole name—is pretty small, but it has everything you need. There's a grocery store, a pharmacy, and a hardware store that's sort of like an old-time general store. It's been featured in a couple of those magazines about living in the country. It's also the post office, so that's where you'll have to go if you want to mail any packages or buy stamps. If you want anything major, a new television or whatever, you'll have to drive to Hibbing, about forty-five miles from here."

Amanda thought someone well known had come from Hibbing, but she was unable to remember who.

"With most of the cabins vacant this time of year," Barbara Heikkinen said, "John and I are your closest neighbors. We live a mile and a half farther down the road, a big A-frame on the right. You can't miss it. If you need anything, just give us a call or drop on by. Most people drive by. This is the time of the winter when you start getting cabin fever, and people will do almost anything to get out of the house for some purpose other than shoveling snow."

Mrs. Heikkinen said the containers in which she'd brought the food could be returned anytime; she had no pressing need for them. After she left, Ashley said, "They're really nice, aren't they?" She seemed amazed.

Amanda agreed. It occurred to her that the girl had never

known anything but city life. People in Boston and Milwaukee had never showed up with good cheer and good food when she and Ashley moved into an apartment. Even in Omaha, where they'd lived in an actual house, the neighbors had warmed up to them slowly, cautiously.

By the time they'd finished unpacking, the heater had finally succeeded in taking the chill out of the house. The place had a dusty, unused odor about it, which Amanda assumed would disappear after a while. The sun had long since set, so she put the food Mrs. Heikkinen had brought in the oven to warm. She missed her microwave, which would have done the job in half the time. Ashley joined her, and together they waited for their dinner to be ready. The aroma of pot roast was filling the kitchen.

Fortunately, since Amanda hadn't thought to bring such items, the place came complete with a handful of mismatched stainless-steel silverware, a few basic cooking utensils, and some well-used plastic plates. Despite the utilitarian accoutrements, the meal looked like a sit-down Sunday dinner when it was served. Ashley dug in with unrestrained enthusiasm until she got to the rutabagas.

"Yuk," she said, making a face. "What's this stuff?"

"That's what Mrs. Heikkinen called bagies."

"Tastes like turnips."

"I think they're related."

The girl stared at the whitish vegetable as if someone had just put a heap of arsenic on her plate. Although Amanda didn't like the bagies any more than her daughter did, she ate them, anyway, because she hated the thought of throwing them out after Mrs. Heikkinen had been kind enough to bring them their supper.

When Ashley had finished, the rutabagas untouched on her plate, she looked at her mother and said, "I feel . . ." She was wrestling with how to put it. "I think we're going to be okay now."

"Me too," Amanda said.

For a few moments they just looked at each other. Ashley

seemed tired and relieved, the way you appeared after you'd exhausted yourself trying to accomplish something and managed to get it done. Amanda supposed she looked the same way to Ashley.

"Come on," she said, "let's get the dishes washed."

Dexter Buchanan was sitting at the bar nursing a beer. It was a quiet establishment, dimly lit, the jukebox turned down low enough so it wouldn't interfere with conversation. This was the sort of place you came to unwind, shoot the breeze with your companions, maybe even grope your date a little, your hand hidden beneath the table at one of the booths. You could buy beer by the pitcher, pizza by the slice; a bowl of pretzels was fifty cents. Buchanan liked the place. He didn't care for raucous bars, where the customers made fools of themselves, got into fights, played music so loud that it made your brain rattle.

This was where employees of one of the Boston TV stations came after the eleven o'clock news.

At the moment Buchanan was keeping an eye on four people at one of the tables. He recognized one of them as a reporter from the TV station, and since they'd all come in together, he assumed they all worked there. Uncertain how he was going to work it, Buchanan relaxed, nursed his beer, and waited. If it didn't seem right tonight, he'd hold off till tomorrow or the night after. Casperon was in a big hurry to get the job done, but that didn't concern Buchanan. Patience was what mattered in this sort of thing, waiting for the right moment.

"You ready for another?" the bartender asked. He was a bald guy with thick hair on the backs of his hands.

"In a little while," Buchanan said, and the bartender gave him a look that seemed to imply the wear and tear on the stool was costing more than he was making off a guy who took an hour to finish a beer. Buchanan ignored him, and the bartender busied himself washing glasses.

Buchanan didn't care much for drinking. Part of it was

probably because his father had been a drunk. But most of it was because he didn't like the way alcohol made you feel, the sort of smiley, lethargic sensation that let you know your reactions, both physical and mental, were below par. Drugs of any kind stole some of your control, which was something Buchanan didn't care to give up.

There were a few things in life Buchanan enjoyed. Very few. But they were unlike the activities that gave most people pleasure. The joys of good food, good booze, good companions, and good sex were unknown to him. Dexter Buchanan was a loner. And the thing that gave him the most pleasure was hurting people.

As he watched the four men Buchanan observed that three of them were drinking beer and the other one was on his third mixed drink. The guy consuming the mixed drinks probably represented Buchanan's best chance. He was a skinny man with wavy blond hair, small hands, thin wrists. He looked barely strong enough to lift the drinks he was tossing down. He wasn't wearing a suit and tie like the others at the table, which meant his job didn't involve being on the air. The four of them were talking about something, but Buchanan was unable to make out what.

About forty-five minutes after they arrived, the three men in suits got up and left. The skinny guy remained behind, signaled the barmaid for another drink. This was the break Buchanan had been waiting for. He walked over to where the man was sitting.

"Excuse me," he said, looking a little embarrassed. "You with the TV station?"

The guy looked up, vaguely puzzled. "Yeah," he said.

"I thought you might be," Buchanan said. "I recognized the guy who was with you—the reporter."

"Sam Jamison?"

"Yeah, that's him. It must be exciting to do that kind of work, always being at the scene of what's happening and everything."

"I wouldn't know. I'm a technical director."

"What's that? Listen, would you mind some company? I'd be happy to buy you a drink. I never met anybody worked at a TV station before."

"Sure," the guy said indifferently. "Have a seat."

The barmaid showed up with the man's drink. She was a tall, thin redhead, practically flat-chested. "Something for you?" she asked, looking at Buchanan.

"Another draft." He paid for both drinks. Then, smiling warmly, Buchanan said, "Name's Chuck Davenport. What's yours?"

The man identified himself as Huntley Cooper and went on to explain that a technical director was the guy who punched the buttons during the newscast, switching from camera one to camera three, going to videotape, live Minicam, whatever.

"Sounds exciting," Buchanan said.

"It's a little nerve-racking sometimes. I don't know about exciting."

"What's nerve-racking about it?"

"Director says, 'Take two,' and you screw up and roll the videotape, the show can go to hell in a hurry. There you are, live, trying to unscramble everything and get the show back on track. It's a nightmare. Sometimes you have to bail out into a commercial, because there's simply nothing else for you to do."

Cooper's speech was becoming slurred, and Buchanan figured it was about time to move into the areas he was interested in. "You got guys there twenty-four hours a day, so you can get pictures if anything big happens?"

Cooper shook his head. "Used to, back in the days when TV news first discovered film. It was all what we called spot news back then. You know, blood and guts— shootings, stabbings, car wrecks, and all that. We don't concentrate on that like we used to. I guess somebody finally figured out that you could film thirty stabbings a day if you felt like it. It wasn't really news." He gulped half his drink. "Anyway, management finally decided it was too expensive to keep a crew on all night for what they were getting out of it."

Buchanan nodded. "Well, you guys do one heck of a job. I was really impressed with that series of reports on New Shipton."

"That was something, wasn't it? Must be nothing but hoods, the whole town."

Buchanan tried to put on the dismayed expression of a hardworking, honest citizen. "That guy who blew the whistle must have some set of balls to come forward the way he did."

Cooper agreed.

"How'd you make his face into little squares like that?"

"Computer. We've got computers now that can do anything to the picture, generate any kind of graphics. It's actually kind of amazing when you figure that it wasn't that many years ago that to super something on the screen we had to physically put white letters on a black background and shoot it with a separate studio camera."

Not wanting a lesson in the advancements in electronics, Buchanan said, "You ever see him, the mystery man?"

"The guy in Amanda Price's series? Naw, nobody ever saw him but Amanda and Dick."

Cooper's glass was empty, so Buchanan flagged down the barmaid and ordered him another drink. "Who's Dick, the manager of the station or something like that?"

That made Cooper chuckle. "Danielson's a jerk-off. He doesn't know shit about covering news stories. All he knows how to do is give speeches at the Kiwanis Club. How the media serves the community, that sort of crap."

"Wait a minute now," Buchanan said. "I'm getting confused. You mean Dick gives speeches?"

Cooper shook his head. "No, Dick's never made a speech in his life. He's too busy dinging broads. It's his hobby."

"The station manager dings broads?"

"No, no, no. Let's start again. The general manager is Rex Danielson. I doubt he's ever dinged a broad in his life.

Dick Kilmer is Amanda's cameraman. He's the one dings the broads."

"So Amanda Price and Dick Kilmer are the only ones who ever saw the mystery man."

"You got it."

Cooper's drink arrived. Buchanan insisted on paying for it, saying, "It's been a while since I saw Amanda. She get a better offer somewhere?"

"I don't know where she is. Nobody seems to know. You ask Bob, he'll just say she needed some time off. I don't even know if *he* knows where she is."

Buchanan laughed. "Now I'm getting confused again. Who the hell's Bob?"

Cooper had already polished off half his fresh drink. His eyes were getting a blank, distant look. "Bob Miller," he said, pronouncing it "Bawb Millah." The booze was making his Boston accent thicker. He stared at Buchanan, apparently trying to figure out whether he'd communicated anything, then he added, "Da news directah."

Buchanan left a few minutes later, having ascertained everything he'd set out to discover. He was pleased with the way things were going. This job was complicated, challenging. He likened it to stalking game. But then, reconsidering that analogy, he decided it was more like a complicated contest. He was matching wits with the man who, image and voice distorted, had appeared in Amanda Price's report. That man, who'd broken the code of silence, was the prize. And Buchanan found himself getting into the thing, liking the game, for the complexities of it would make killing the traitor that much more enjoyable.

Still sitting in the bar, Huntley Cooper stared at his empty glass. That guy who'd bought him the drinks had seemed like a pretty decent fellow. If he ran into the man again, he'd have to buy him a few. Something odd about the guy's eyes, though. Cooper tried to figure out exactly what it was about the man's eyes, but his bourbon-logged brain simply wasn't up to the task.

As he weaved his way out of the bar Cooper wondered whether he'd even remember tonight when he was sober again. The guy he'd been drinking with could walk up and say hi, and Cooper might not recognize him. It had happened before. This was probably the first day of what would be a three- or four-day binge, after which Cooper supposed he'd sheepishly go back to his AA group and admit what he'd done. A wave of guilt rushed over him. Cooper did his best to ignore it.

He hailed three cabs before one finally stopped for him.

SEVEN

THE morning after they arrived at Bob Miller's Minnesota cabin, Amanda and Ashley went into town for groceries. Fiddlehead Lake was a collection of wooden buildings lining the highway. It had a lone cross street, which ended in both directions a short distance from the highway. There were no traffic signals, not even an amber flasher, no stop signs, no parking meters. In fact, the list of things it didn't have would have been truly impressive had anyone bothered to make one up. No bank, for instance. On the other hand, it probably had no muggers or burglars or drug addicts roaming the streets, either. Fiddlehead, Amanda decided, was like everything else in life. You gave up some things, you gained others.

"This is the town?" Ashley asked, her tone making it clear she wasn't exactly overwhelmed.

"This is it."

The piles of snow on both sides of the street were Guinness record size. In the cities in which Amanda had lived, the snow was hauled away when it piled up to the point where it was clogging the downtown streets and sidewalks. Here they clearly just kept adding to the piles, which had spilled out into the street, making it so narrow, there was barely room for two cars to pass. This did not deter people from parking on the street, and driving on it was like maneuvering your way through an obstacle course.

It was clear and sunny, the air bitingly cold. The high, according to the Hibbing radio station Ashley had tuned in on the car radio, was predicted to be about fifteen. Mrs. Heikkinen had said there were days when the temperature got up to thirty-one or thirty-two, and days—especially in January—when it only got *up* to twenty below.

The first stop was the general store/post office to mail the letter Amanda had written to her bank in Boston, asking for three thousand dollars from her CDs, to be sent to her in a cashier's check. For an address she used General Delivery, Fiddlehead Lake, Minnesota. She figured it was safe to do so, since it would be practically impossible for anyone to learn her whereabouts from the bank.

Carlson's General Store looked like a cross between a rustic New England antique shop and Ace Hardware. Mixed in with the power tools and snowblowers and pipe fittings were old crocks, calico lampshades, cracker barrels, oil lamps, and enameled coffeepots, most of which were blue with white flecks. The place was dimly lit, and the worn wood floor gave slightly and creaked under Amanda's weight. Bells had tinkled when she opened the door. Near the center of the store a fire burned in a big wood stove.

A counter ran along one wall. It held the cash register, and behind it were numerous cubbyholes and an official government sign identifying the premises as a U.S. Post Office. Also behind the counter was a thin, gray-haired man wearing one of those red-and-black plaid shirts that always made Amanda think of lumberjacks.

"Hi," he said. "You must be Amanda Price."

Her jaw dropped. She couldn't help it. She'd come here to hide out. How did this man know her name?

"Don't look so surprised," he said. "Everybody knows everything in small towns." He smiled, and he, too, had teeth that were just too perfect. Amanda wondered whether everyone here consumed huge quantities of candy. Or maybe it was something in the water.

"John Heikkinen was in earlier," he said. "Told me all about the pretty woman from Boston who'd moved into the Miller cabin with her daughter. Said you were a TV star back there on the East Coast."

For the first time in many years Amanda felt herself

blushing. "I think 'star' might be overstating it," she said. "Uh, this is my daughter, Ashley." She wanted to change the subject.

"Clarence Carlson," the man said.

"Hi," Ashley said a little bashfully. Apparently spotting something that interested her, the girl wandered off.

Amanda bought a stamp and slipped the letter to her bank into the brass-rimmed slot in the counter marked OUT OF TOWN. When she turned around, Ashley had been joined by a boy with brownish-blond hair. He was about thirteen and in the same gangly stage she was, his body growing this way and that, the various parts trying to keep up with each other. The arms of his blue-checked shirt were about an inch too short. He and Ashley seemed to be getting along pretty well, which surprised Amanda. The girl had always maintained that the boys in her junior high school were so disgusting, she could barely bring herself to speak to any of them. Maybe it was just finding someone her own age. Or maybe her attitude toward boys was changing.

"That's my grandson, Eric," Carlson said. "Helps me out on the weekends sometimes."

Amanda hadn't known it was the weekend. She'd lost all track of time.

"Take a look around," Carlson said. "You'll need some things for that house."

"I'm afraid I'm not going to be a very good customer until my money comes in from Boston. That's what that letter's about."

"Don't let that worry you. Get whatever you want and I'll just put it on account."

"Oh, I couldn't do that."

"Why not? You'll be the only one around here who doesn't." He gave her a fatherly look. "I know you'll need some things for that house. It was only used during the summer, so there's no snow shovel. We have a lot of power failures around here because of the winter storms. The wind'll take 'em down. And it's getting on toward the time of year when we have ice storms. So much ice can collect on the lines that they break under the weight. Anyway, you'll need some candles or an oil lamp. Got any matches to start a fire?"

Feeling like an ignorant city person, Amanda said she didn't think so.

"How about winter clothing?" Carlson asked.

"It gets pretty cold in Boston."

"True, but there's a difference between what you'd wear to go from your apartment to a cab and what you need when you're living in the woods."

Amanda nodded. He was right again. Ashley was wearing a well-insulated water-resistant ski jacket, but the Minnesota cold passed right through Amanda's more fashionable—not to mention more expensive—long coat. And neither she nor Ashley had the right kind of shoes for running around in deep snow.

"Will you help me pick out what we need?" Amanda asked.

"Be glad to."

Amanda and Ashley left Carlson's General Store two hundred and fifty dollars in debt, most if it going for clothing and shoes. As they drove down the street to the grocery store, Amanda said, "What were you and that boy talking about?"

"Eric?"

"Only boy I saw."

"Oh, just stuff."

"Was he nice?"

"Yeah, seemed to be."

It was unusual for the girl to be this uncommunicative. On the other hand, she was almost a teenager, and teenagers never communicated with their parents. They had an unwritten code of honor that strictly forbade it.

The grocery store was bigger than a 7-Eleven but not much. It had four aisles with the meat counter in the rear and three checkout counters in front, only one of which was in operation. Everything was a few pennies more than the same items would cost in Boston, but then Eckstrom's Super Valu was a long way from any major food-distribution points. And it had a monopoly.

Moving along the narrow aisles, Amanda put spaghetti, chicken breasts, ground beef, frozen vegetables, bread, eggs, pancake mix, coffee, milk, flour, sugar, hot chocolate, and orange juice into her cart. She was beginning to realize that this was going to be an enormous grocery bill, because she was stocking a house from scratch. There were no staples in the place. No spices, no catsup, no crackers, not even a box of salt.

"Don't they have any breakfast cereals here?" Ashley asked.

"I'm sure they do," Amanda replied. "We just haven't come to them yet."

She was reaching for a jar of peanut butter when someone said, "You must be Amanda Price."

Turning, she found herself looking at a policeman in a tan uniform. He was in his mid-thirties, tall and broad-shouldered, with thick brown hair and a face that combined boyish innocence with a masculine ruggedness. He smiled, revealing teeth that were only *almost* perfect. But then he was too young to have fallen victim to an insatiable sweet tooth or the water or whatever was putting dentures into the mouths of the community's elders.

She said, "Don't tell me, let me guess. You've been talking to John Heikkinen."

He laughed. "John likes to keep everybody posted on things. I'm Ted Anderson, by the way." He offered his hand and Amanda shook it.

"You the town constable or whatever the correct term would be?" she asked.

"Fiddlehead's too small to have a police force. I'm the sheriff's deputy who's responsible for this area. Work out of a substation down the street."

Getting into the conversation, Ashley said, "I bet there's not much crime around here."

"Most of the trouble seems to come during hunting season. People trespassing on posted land, hunters mistaking each other for deer, shooting at dairy cows." He shrugged. "The rest of the year's pretty peaceful."

"They should let the deer shoot back," Ashley muttered. The girl was fond of animals, and she'd always considered anyone who would shoot them for sport as being on about the same level as muggers or kidnappers.

Amanda gave the girl's shoulder a squeeze, subtly warning her not to be too free with her opinions. She hoped the deputy wasn't a hunter.

"Not many people move into this area in February," he said. "Are, uh, you just here temporarily, or are you going to be with us for a while?"

"I don't know," Amanda said truthfully. It occurred to her that telling the deputy about her situation might be a good idea. At least he'd know to be on the lookout for the man with the strange eyes in the event he somehow located her. She didn't think that was really likely, but she should probably talk to the deputy just to be on the safe side. The grocery store, however, wasn't the place to go into it. She said, "Uh, do you ever make it out Lakeshore Road?"

"From time to time. I patrol the whole area."

"The next time you're out that way, would you mind stopping by? There's something I'd like to talk to you about."

"All right," he said. "Is it anything needs immediate attention?"

"No, no," she said. "Just whenever you get around to it. It's not urgent."

The deputy smiled and said he'd be by within the next couple of days. When Amanda finished picking out the groceries she needed, the top part of the cart was filled to overflowing, and she'd begun putting stuff on the bottom rack, which you usually reserved for big items like cases of soda or twenty-pound bags of charcoal. Her bill was $145.78. The store did not offer to let her put it on account.

As they were driving back to the house Ashley said, "Eric's got a shortwave radio."

"Oh?"

"He says he can get all kinds of stuff. Like from Russia and England and just about everywhere."   .

"Sounds interesting." Amanda wondered where this was leading. Ashley's interest in radio had always been limited to finding the rock music station featuring the screechiest electric guitars.

"He said he'd like to show it to me if I want to come over sometime."

"I see."

"Would that be okay?"

"Sure."

Apparently having said all she intended to on the subject, Ashley turned her attention to the snowbank at the edge of the road. Was this the beginning of her daughter's first crush? Had she finally met a boy she didn't find thoroughly revolting? As she drove, Amanda considered the ramifications of this. Sooner or later, she realized, Ashley and she would need to have the Talk. The one about sex. The one Amanda's mother had never quite worked up the nerve to have with her.

Long ago Amanda had resolved not to make the same mistake with Ashley. She started considering just how she'd go about it—and found herself wishing kids were born knowing everything they needed to so parents wouldn't have to go through the Talk.

"Ashley?"

"Huh?" the girl replied, still watching the snowbank.

"Oh, never mind." The Talk could wait for a few days.

The television station was a sprawling complex on the outskirts of the city. At one end of the building was a small, snow-covered field from which satellite dishes sprouted like enormous upside-down mushrooms. Dexter Buchanan wondered whether someone had to clean the snow out of them after a storm so they'd work right.

It was about three A.M. as he slipped across the station's largely deserted asphalt parking area. Only a handful of people would be at work inside the building, just enough to keep the old movies and commercials running. The place wasn't fenced. This was a low-crime area.

When Buchanan reached one of the building's three rear entrances, he slipped a small carrying case from his back pocket, from which he removed the tools he'd need to pick the lock. Guy in New York had showed him how to do it. It wasn't too hard once you got the hang of it, using two picks at once, getting the tumblers into just the right position. Buchanan checked the door, looking for any indication of an alarm. Spotting nothing suspicious, he went to work on the lock. He knew this was the door he wanted to open, because he'd watched the station this afternoon to see which entrance the news crews used. It took him about a minute and a half to pick the lock, not bad considering that it was a fairly expensive one.

Opening the door a crack, Buchanan peeked inside, seeing a dimly lit, deserted stretch of beige-carpeted hallway. He slipped inside, making sure the door closed silently behind him. Moving cautiously along the carpeted corridor, he noted that the people running the station had made it easy for him. The doors had signs on them. The first one he came to read TAPE EDITING. The next one read NEWSROOM. The door was open, the lights on.

No news people were supposed to be here now. So why were the lights on? Buchanan listened, hearing nothing. He peeked into the room. It was empty. He quickly moved through the doorway.

The room had the same beige carpeting as the hallway. It contained maybe twenty desks, and toward the back were three offices, the signs on their doors indicating they were for the news director, assistant news director, and sports director. On one wall was a large board on which the day's assignments had been written in large blue letters. He noted that Grace had gone to the mayor's news conference at ten A.M. Mike had done a feature on street gangs in Roxbury. To the left of the board, three Teletype machines hummed softly as they printed out the news in dot-matrix letters.

Buchanan moved from desk to desk, opening the drawers and checking the papers inside. He found the desk belonging to Grace O'Brien, whom he assumed to be the Grace who'd covered the mayor's news conference. Another was used by Tom, another by Ralph, another by Lisa. Finally he found one containing a letter addressed to Amanda J. Price—and a framed photograph of the little girl who'd escaped him by ducking into someone's house.

He went through the desk methodically, taking everything out of each drawer, checking it over, putting it back. He found notes concerning New Shipton, but nothing pertaining to the identity of the traitor or the whereabouts of Amanda Price. He had just finished the last drawer when he heard a man's voice come from the hallway. Buchanan ducked behind the desk.

A guy strolled into the newsroom. He was in his mid-twenties, tall, and fairly heavy, mainly flab. He was wearing a tight-fitting sweater that emphasized his protruding belly and his underdeveloped chest. He walked directly to the Teletype machines and tore off the long sheets of paper they'd been slowly spewing out. Using the edge of a desk as a straightedge, he tore off the portions he wanted, threw away the rest, and left.

Now Buchanan knew why the newsroom lights were on. The station probably ran news updates, along with the movies and commercials. And bulletins if anything big happened. The chubby guy had to be an announcer.

Buchanan moved to the news director's office. It was locked, but the lock didn't amount to much. He used a credit card to loid it. The news director had both a desk and a file cabinet. Buchanan started with the file cabinet, finding nothing that would help him, and moved on to the desk. He'd gone through the drawers on the right side when he saw movement from the corner of his eye.

"Don't move a muscle, ace."

Buchanan found himself looking at a security guard in a brown uniform. He was an old guy, about sixty, with a beer gut hanging over his gun belt. The gun itself was in his hand, a .38, and he was pointing it at Buchanan.

Buchanan grinned. "Hey, it's okay. Bob asked me to pick some stuff up for him."

"Yeah, sure," the guard said. "I ask you Bob who, and you say Bob Miller. Let's just skip all the bullshit." The man was looking at Buchanan with steady blue eyes that said he knew how to handle the situation. Ex-cop, Buchanan thought.

"Come out of there nice and slow," the guard said.

Buchanan complied, thinking about the 9-mm Browning automatic under his left arm, the butt not more than two feet from his right hand. But the old guy knew what he was doing. He kept his distance, kept his eyes on Buchanan's hands, held the .38 as steady as if it were in a vise.

"Up against the wall, ace. You know how to do it. I bet you've had lots of practice."

Actually Buchanan had only been busted once, and that had been in New York—the New Shipton cops all worked for the same guy he did. The charges had been dropped, so he'd never served any time in jail. Even now, with a good lawyer, he probably wouldn't see prison if he let this guy cuff him and call the cops. No prior convictions, no clear intent to steal anything. He was illegally carrying an unregistered handgun, but the jails were full, and guys who'd done a lot worse than that were out walking the streets because there was nowhere to put them. But then that wasn't the way Buchanan wanted to play it. He had no intention of letting this paunchy ex-cop take him.

"Move," the guard said.

"And if I don't."

"I'll put a nice little hole in your leg and cuff you while

you're lying on the floor writhing and crying. I know right where to put it so it will hurt the most."

Buchanan believed him. Maybe he was one of those cops who'd gotten kicked off the force for brutality. Too bad they had to meet like this. They were kindred spirits.

Buchanan put his hands on the wall, and the guard said, "Feet back and spread 'em."

Buchanan said, "I can't do it. I have a bad knee, and it'll go out."

The guard sighed. "Why you wasting your time breaking and entering when you could have been a professional bullshitter?"

"It's true," Buchanan said, looking over his shoulder at the guy. "I can't do it."

"Try," the guard said, his blue eyes fixed on Buchanan, letting him know he meant business.

"If I've got to have another operation, I'll sue the station, probably make millions."

The guard said nothing, and Buchanan spread his legs, moved his feet back.

"Feet farther back," the guard said. "Let's quit fucking around and get this shit over with, what do you say?"

Buchanan did as instructed, instantly letting out a cry of pain and collapsing on the floor, clutching his knee. "Oh, Jesus! I'm going to be a cripple, you son of a bitch. Look what you did to me!"

The guard grinned, enjoying the performance. "Okay, asshole, we'll do it your way. Roll over on your stomach and put your hands behind your back."

Moaning as if each movement were sheer agony, Buchanan complied.

The guard came toward him, saying, "All the scumbags running around loose in this town and I had to get a fucking actor."

The guard was moving in from behind him, out of his sight. Buchanan listened to every sound. He heard the handcuffs click together as the guard slipped them from his belt. Then the man was there, putting his knee in the middle of Buchanan's back, touching the back of his neck with the barrel of the gun, just as a warning.

"Don't even think about moving, Mr. Actor."

Then came the moment Buchanan had been waiting for. The gun was withdrawn and there was the soft, familiar sound of gunmetal meeting leather as the guy holstered his weapon, freeing both hands for the task of applying the handcuffs. Buchanan was lean and muscular, deceptively strong. Instantly he flipped his body over, bringing his arm out from behind him and taking a swing at the guy, all in one motion. The guard was quick for a guy his age, pulling his head back in time to avoid the punch. But Buchanan was younger and quicker. Swinging his leg up, he caught the guy in the side of the head, knocking him to the side. Buchanan pulled his Browning as the guard scrambled to his feet, trying to get out his own weapon.

"Who's the asshole now?" Buchanan said, and shot him twice in the chest.

Knowing there were people in the building who would have heard the gunshots, Buchanan was on his feet and heading for the door as the guard hit the floor. Then he was outside, running across the parking lot, the cold night air numbing his cheeks. The Honda he was driving was parked by some other cars at one end of the lot. As he was driving away the door through which he'd left opened, and a man's head peered out. No matter. The guy couldn't make him from there, and even if he got the license-plate number, which was unlikely, the car was stolen.

Buchanan turned left onto a deserted four-lane street and sped away from the television station.

Eight

THE day after the trip into town Amanda and
Ashley spent the morning bringing in firewood and exploring the area around the house. The deep snow made looking
around tough, because its crust would support them for two
or three steps, then suddenly give way, letting them sink in
up to their hips. Despite this difficulty, they kept going.
There was something invigorating about cold, crisp air, the
layer of white, the landscape of bare tree trunks, its bleak
uniformity broken every now and then by the green fullness
of a pine or spruce.

They found the lake, a flat stretch of white with no trees.
A snow-covered lump turned out to be a small dock, its
wood pilings sticking down into ice that looked permanent,
as if it had been here when the glaciers came by, and would
still be here when they came again. It seemed impossible
that the lake could thaw, that the white landscape could turn
green. Amanda had been to other cold places—Bangor in
January, for instance—but she had never before seen a spot
where winter's grip was this absolute.

On the way back to the house she fashioned as good a
snowball as she could from the dry snow and threw it at
Ashley, who was leading the way. It hit the girl in the back,
disintegrating into a white spot on her coat. Ashley turned
around, looking astonished.

"Was that a snowball?" She couldn't believe it.

"I do know how to make one."

"But moms don't do things like that."

"This one does." Amanda began making another snowball.

So did Ashley, who clearly had had more recent practice at this, because hers hit Amanda's shoulder before Amanda had packed together anything she could throw. The snowball fight lasted about thirty seconds before Amanda surrendered.

"If you really feel like acting like a kid, I'll race you to the house," Ashley said.

"No thanks. I don't want to get beat twice in one day."

As they resumed walking—if you could call breaking through the crust into hip-deep snow walking—Amanda again thought of how nice Bob Miller had been to do all the things he had done. Not many people could claim a boss like that, especially in a business where people politicked and backstabbed and changed jobs as much as they did in TV news. She'd called him after supper on the day they arrived, promising to pay him back any money he'd had to spend and pay him rent on the place. Miller had said he was just happy to know they'd arrived safely.

"I insist," Amanda had said. "I won't let you spend any money on us."

"I'm not spending any," Miller had replied. "All the bills are being sent to you."

"You sure?"

"You'll find out when you go to the mailbox. It's the third one from the left in the cluster."

"I'll take care of them. Now let's agree on a reasonable rent."

"I don't want any rent. I'm just glad somebody's finally getting some use out of the place."

"I really should give you something."

"Tell you what. Rent's two hundred a month, which is exactly the amount I was planning to pay you for housesitting for me. Deal?"

Amanda had said it was a deal.

When they got back to the house, they found a police cruiser parked out front. It had a gold star on its door along with the word SHERIFF. Ted Anderson, the deputy Amanda had spoken to in the grocery store, was at the front door.

"Hi," he said, spotting them. "I was wondering where you were. Your car's here, but nobody was answering the door."

"We've been out exploring," Amanda said.

"Find anything interesting?"

"Lot of snow and a frozen lake."

"If you're going to do any serious looking around, you need snowshoes. I've got a couple of pairs if you want to borrow them."

Amanda declined, saying city people like them would probably just get lost in the woods and put everybody to the trouble of rescuing them. She invited the deputy inside and offered him a cup of tea, which he accepted. When the three of them were sitting at the kitchen table with steaming cups of tea in front of them, Anderson said, "What is it you wanted to talk to me about?"

"I'm here because I'm hiding from somebody," Amanda said.

The deputy nodded.

"You don't seem surprised."

"I'm not. Woman and a girl show up all of a sudden in February, not knowing how long they're going to stay. Woman's a TV reporter in Boston, but she's obviously not here covering a story for a Boston TV station. She's not on vacation. People take vacations in February, they go to Florida or Hawaii, somewhere warm. And people with children don't *take* February vacations because their kids are in school."

"Looking at it that way, I guess it was sort of obvious," Amanda said.

"Who are you hiding from?"

"It's a long story." Amanda took a sip of her tea, collecting her thoughts.

"Abusive husband who's threatening to hurt you or the child?"

Amanda shook her head. "I'm not married. Ashley's father and I were divorced a long time ago, went our separate ways. This is something else. I wouldn't even bother you with it except that I think the man who's after me is a professional killer."

She told him the whole story, explaining how the man had tried to grab her at the mall, how the same man had come after Ashley, and how he'd followed them when they left Boston, catching up with them in the middle of a snowstorm. She told him about the break-in at their apartment, the series she'd done exposing the rampant corruption in New Shipton, and about the phone call from her informant, warning her that she was in danger.

"Oh, boy," the deputy said when she'd finished. "I can understand why you were frightened enough to run."

"The man's a professional," Amanda said. "I'm sure of it."

"That was a pretty slick maneuver you pulled in Pennsylvania after he forced you to stop."

"Sheer desperation," Amanda said. "And a lot of luck."

He smiled. "Well, you handled it pretty well."

"That man scares me," Ashley said. "You should see his eyes. They're like . . . like those people in *Night of the Living Dead*."

Amanda nodded. "Every time I think of him, I can feel my stomach tighten up."

"You sure you lost him in Pennsylvania?" Anderson asked.

"I'm sure. A state policeman followed me to make sure. Besides, I think he would have showed up by now if he knew where we were."

"Is there any way he can find out you're here?"

"Only Bob Miller knows. No one else."

"You didn't tell a friend or neighbor or anyone like that?"

"No."

"Did you?" he asked, looking at Ashley.

"No," the girl said.

"You didn't even tell your best friend?"

Ashley shook her head.

"Did you have your mail forwarded?" the deputy asked Amanda.

"No," she said. "I just asked them to hold it until further notice."

"Good, because anybody can go to the post office and get your new address."

"I didn't know that," Amanda said, finding the information a little unnerving. What else didn't she know? "I wrote a letter to my bank in Boston, asking for some money from my account. He can't get the bank to tell him where I am, can he?"

The deputy considered that. "Banks are pretty tight with information. They'll give out some stuff for credit-card reports, that kind of thing, and they have to cooperate with the IRS, but that's about it. I don't think they give away information about their depositors to anyone who comes walking in off the street."

Although his words had relieved her concern to some extent, Amanda wished he hadn't begun the sentence by saying he didn't *think* banks gave out that sort of information.

Apparently sensing that she was still troubled, he said, "Listen, you lost the guy in Pennsylvania, nobody knows you're here except your boss, and you didn't leave a forwarding address with the post office. How's he going to find you?"

"You're right," Amanda said, putting enthusiasm into the words she didn't feel. She didn't want to appear afraid around Ashley, because the girl would worry too. Glancing at her daughter, Amanda smiled confidently, and Ashley smiled back. Maybe they were both acting brave for the sake of the other.

Anderson took out a small notebook. "Let's go over the guy's description one more time. I'll keep an eye out for him and put out a bulletin asking the state police to do the same."

Amanda described him as thoroughly as she could; then Ashley reviewed her impressions of him. Less than an hour ago they'd been having a snowball fight, acting as if they didn't have a care in the world. Now Amanda felt an icy lump of fear circling around inside her. Out of sight, beneath the heavy material of her long-sleeved shirt, Amanda's arms broke out in gooseflesh. She didn't want to talk about the man with the zombielike eyes anymore. She didn't want to think about him.

Putting away his notebook, the deputy emptied his teacup. "That was good. Thank you."

"Another cup?"

The policeman hesitated, glancing at his watch. "Sure," he said. "I've got time for another cup if I don't take too long drinking it."

Amanda had used a saucepan to heat the water, a teakettle not being among the house's limited supply of cooking equipment. As she poured more hot water into Ted Anderson's cup she realized she was glad he wasn't leaving yet. Unquestionably she'd feel safer with a police officer on the premises, but that wasn't it—not all of it, anyway. Amanda had the feeling that Ted Anderson was someone she might like to know better.

"So," he said, taking a sip of his fresh tea, "how do you like winter in the frozen north woods?"

"Better than I thought I would," she replied. "There's something vaguely . . ." She searched for the right word. "Something pristine and crisp and invigorating about it."

"The people are real nice," Ashley said.

"Like the Heikkinens," Amanda said. "John came over with his tractor and plowed out the driveway, then got everything in the house running. Then Barbara came over with our dinner. All we had to do was heat it and eat it." She snapped her fingers. "Which reminds me. I have to return her containers."

"Most people around here are like that," Anderson said. "You familiar with Garrison Keillor, the way he describes Minnesotans?"

Amanda said she'd heard him a time or two on the radio before his show went off the air.

"Well, that's what we're like. My ex-wife—she was from Chicago—thought the people here were too boring, but I guess boring has its good side too."

"You mean, like people helping each other, living quietly."

"Yeah," he said. "Like that."

For a few moments they were quiet, sipping their tea, then Anderson said, "We're both divorced."

"Yes." Amanda didn't know what else to say about it, although she hadn't been surprised to learn he wasn't married. Something, maybe her reporter's instincts, had told her he was single. Or maybe it was just plain old woman's intuition. Amanda promptly dismissed that notion. She didn't believe in woman's intuition.

"Stephanie came up from Chicago, thinking she wanted to get away from the big city, commune with nature. I guess she thought living out here with me would be just the ticket. But it wasn't really what she wanted. She was just fooling herself."

He drank some more tea, then continued. "After a couple of months she got bored. Then she started complaining, was constantly antsy. After a while she started a campaign to get me to move back to Chicago with her. Anyway, it fell apart." He looked at her sheepishly. "And I don't know why I'm telling you all this."

"Any children?" Amanda asked.

"No. Stephanie said she didn't want to raise kids where the schools weren't any good."

"Are the schools here that bad?"

"No local student who wanted to go ever failed to get into college. On the other hand, for a lot of the kids there's a long ride on a school bus, and you won't find classes on subjects like appreciation of impressionist art."

"Who'd *want* to take a class like that?" Ashley asked.

Amanda laughed. "I don't think her future lies in the art world."

Although Amanda wasn't sure exactly how it got started, they found themselves talking about their backgrounds, how they came to be where they were. Both of them were Midwesterners, but while Amanda had moved away from her home state, Anderson was originally from Duluth and had never lived anywhere but Minnesota. He'd graduated from the University of Minnesota in the Twin Cities with a degree in sociology, which proved to be about as useful as a clubfoot when it came to getting a job. Amanda graduated from the University of Nebraska in Lincoln with a degree in journalism. Although the school's big things were agriculture and football, not journalism, she managed to get a job with a TV station in her hometown of Omaha.

She told Anderson how she'd met her husband at the TV station, falling into a marriage that never should have been—except then she wouldn't have Ashley, so it was really a good thing, at least in part. He explained how he'd become a police officer: simply by putting applications in for every opening he heard about anywhere in northern Minnesota. The sheriff's office was the first place to make him an offer. Although he hadn't always been assigned to Fiddlehead, he'd always been in outlying areas. Stephanie had come up one summer with some other Chicago girls, all of them looking for the "pure life" or whatever, wanting to be one with nature. All of them had left promptly after their first face-to-face meeting with a bear except Stephanie, who'd been a more committed idealist than the others. She'd latched on to him as her ticket to the peace and serenity of the north woods, and they'd just sort of fallen into marriage, a marriage that had started disintegrating almost immediately. Amanda had been divorced for seven years, Ted Anderson for five.

All the while they were talking, with Ashley just sitting there listening, not really part of the conversation, Amanda sensed something vaguely tingly hanging in the air between them. What's happening here? she asked herself. Although she'd been to bed with a few men since her divorce—when Ashley was visiting her father—the attraction had been strictly physical. The prickly sensation she was feeling now was more than that, and she didn't understand why it was happening.

She and Ashley had fled, terrified, barely escaping a professional hoodlum on a snowy Pennsylvania highway, ending up here to sit out the winter in one of the coldest spots in the country. And then, the second time she meets him, she starts getting attracted to a cop. Everything was upside down and confused. Maybe all this wasn't really happening. Maybe she was in the hospital having an operation, her mind making up bizarre fantasies while she floated along on the drugs dripping in her veins through an IV tube.

She looked at Ashley. She looked at Ted Anderson. It was no fantasy.

Glancing at his watch again, the deputy quickly downed the rest of his tea. "I've stayed a lot longer than I should have," he said, rising. "I'd rather spend all afternoon here, to tell you the truth, but that's not what the county pays me to do."

Amanda walked the deputy to the front door, and as he was leaving, she said, "Come back sometime when you can stay longer."

Anderson smiled, said he would.

As she closed the door Amanda suddenly felt awkward. Why had she said that? It sounded as if she were coming on to him, inviting him back to see where things might lead. Well, wasn't that what she was doing? The answer was yes and no.

"He's nice," Ashley said as Amanda returned to her

place at the kitchen table. Ashley seemed to be liking everybody lately.

"Yes, he seems to be," Amanda said.

Sipping her tea, she tried to sort out her thoughts. It occurred to her that they still hadn't had the Talk. Maybe now was the time, with the two of them sitting there finishing their tea.

"Kiddo," Amanda said, "there's something we need to talk about." She paused, trying to figure out the best way to get into it.

"About what's been happening?"

"No. About . . . well, about life."

"Oh. This must be where you tell me about sex."

Times had certainly changed. Amanda wouldn't have dared to so much as speak the word around her mother. She sighed. "Yeah, about that."

But before she could say any more, the phone rang. It was an old black desk model that sat on an end table by the couch. Amanda sat down as she answered it.

"Amanda, Bob Miller. You all settled in out there?"

Just from the sound of his voice, Amanda knew something was wrong. Her grip on the receiver tightened; it felt hot in her hand. "We're getting along just fine," she said. "Everyone here seems so nice, so helpful."

"Yeah, you're sure right about that." He paused. Amanda waited. Finally he said, "Amanda, something's happened here I think you should know about. Someone broke into the newsroom last night and killed the security guard, shot him twice in the chest."

"Oh, my God, that's terrible. Which guard was it?"

"Porterfield, the ex-cop."

Amanda had seen him around, but she really didn't know him. A guy with a potbelly and hard eyes. "What happened?" she asked.

"The way the police figure it, someone was in my office, going through my desk and files, and Porterfield surprised him."

"Do you think there's some connection with . . ." She let her words drift off. Ashley could hear everything she said, and Amanda didn't want to alarm her daughter unnecessarily.

"I'm afraid there might be. This afternoon we found out the intruder went through your desk. The interns from B.U. have been using your desk since you've been gone. When Peggy Tyler came in a little while ago, she noticed that everything in your drawers had been rearranged."

"Could the police have done it?" Amanda asked, knowing it hadn't been the cops but trying to make herself believe it was possible just the same.

"None of the other desks got a thorough going through the way yours did." He hesitated. "Amanda, there was nothing in my office that could lead him to you. I'm positive. What about your desk? When you came in to pick up the keys to the cabin, did you stop at your desk, make any notes about where you were going?"

"No, I never went anywhere near my desk."

"Okay," Miller said, sounding relieved. "There's no way he could have learned where you are."

"It's so . . ." Amanda was about to say "scary," but then she saw Ashley standing in the doorway to the kitchen, watching her closely, her eyes full of questions. "I'm sure you're right," she said, putting all the confidence into her voice she could muster.

"Don't worry about this, Amanda. There's no way he could know where you are, no way at all."

When the conversation ended, Amanda sat there, staring at the phone. It had been made by Stromberg-Carlson. She'd never heard of a Stromberg-Carlson telephone.

She had no doubt that the burglar who'd murdered the security guard was the man with the peculiar eyes. Although she'd referred to him as a professional killer, the words had been used with a sort of literary license, for emphasis, to make it clear how vile, how frightening, this man was. She'd had no knowledge that the man had ever murdered anyone. But not anymore.

The man had slain Porterfield, the paunchy but mean-looking ex-cop. The guard would have been no pushover. That the man had prevailed was a further demonstration of his skills. A part of Amanda's mind tried to argue that the intruder could have been anyone; there was no proof it was the man who was after her and her daughter. She rejected the notion that it could have been anyone else. It was *him*.

Next that same portion of her brain tried to convince her that killing an armed guard who was about to apprehend him wasn't the same thing as murdering a woman and a child who were no direct threat to him. But Amanda recalled how he'd tried to pull her into the white car, how he'd aimed a gun at her and Ashley on the snowy Pennsylvania highway, and she had no doubt that he would kill both of them without a moment's hesitation.

He can't know where we are, Amanda told herself. *No way can he know.* And yet she felt as if a huge, invisible hand were squeezing her lungs, making it impossible for her to breathe. The man was determined. He wouldn't give up until he found them. The news from Boston left little doubt about that.

"Who was that, Mom?" Ashley asked worriedly. The girl was still standing in the doorway, watching her.

Amanda forced herself to speak, hoping her voice wouldn't waver. "Bob Miller. He was checking on us, making sure everything was okay."

The girl gave her a look, making it clear she knew there was more to it than that. "Is anything wrong, Mom?"

"Someone at the station died last night. A security guard. I don't think you knew him."

"Oh," Ashley said, seeming to accept the explanation. "Did he die right there at the station?"

"Yes, I'm afraid so."

"Wow. What was wrong with him?"

"His heart stopped."

The girl nodded and dropped the matter.

Tom Price, Amanda's former husband, was sitting in his recliner watching TV that night. His wife Jo-Ann was sitting on the couch, half watching the sitcom and half reading the latest issue of *Vogue*. She was a tall woman whose extremely white skin and blond hair proclaimed her Scandinavian heritage. She had a habit of using her hand to flip her hair back when she was talking to someone, the way Diane Sawyer did.

When a commercial came on, Price let his eyes wander around the room. The Newport Beach condo was nice. They'd lived here two years, and they'd recently replaced their old early American furniture with more contemporary things that seemed to fit the California life-style better. Though too far from the Pacific to have an ocean view, the building was close enough to get the sea breezes at night. During the summer it was nice to step out on the balcony, smell the salt air, get away from the artificial cool of the air conditioner.

He no longer felt like a failure.

He'd felt that way when he was married to Amanda. She'd been making it in TV, while he'd been on a steady downhill slide, getting fired, getting drunk, spending all his time feeling sorry for himself. Maybe working at a shoe store didn't seem like much, but he'd kept the job, quit drinking, stopped blaming the world for things it was up to him to change. Now he was the manager of the chain's outlet in an enormous shopping mall. His was one of the firm's five most profitable stores in southern California, and there was talk about him being the next regional manager.

He harbored no ill will toward Amanda. The marriage was not meant to be; it was as simple as that. She seemed happier without him, and he was happier with Jo-Ann, who made pretty good money selling wholesale cosmetics but who saw him as their main provider. He liked that.

The cordless phone rang. It was on the table beside his chair. He extended the antenna as he answered.

"Mr. Price?" a man said. It sounded like long distance.

"Yes?"

"This is Sam Feldon in Boston. I'm Ashley's English teacher. Before she left, she gave me this number. Could I speak to her, please?"

"Speak to Ashley?" Tom Price said, confused.

"Yes, isn't she there? I promised to call her to tell her what work she'd need to do to keep up with her studies. I've got the assignment from Mr. Bahr too, her social studies teacher."

"What was your name again?"

"Feldon. Sam Feldon."

"Mr. Feldon, I've got no idea what you're talking about."

"You're Ashley Price's father, aren't you?"

"Yes, but—"

"Her mother talked to me before she and Ashley left. She said the girl would be staying with you for a little while, and she wanted me to mail her school assignments so Ashley could keep up. I decided it would be easier to call so I could talk to her and explain everything."

"All I can do is repeat what I said before. I have absolutely no idea what you're talking about."

"Ashley's not there?"

"She certainly isn't."

"Well, is . . . is she expected?"

"Not that I know of."

"Oh, dear. I wonder where Ashley could be. I hope nothing's happened to her."

"Yeah," Price said. "You and me both. When did she talk to you?"

"About a week ago."

"Hmm. Well, if I do hear from her, I'll have her get in touch."

"Yes. Please do that. I wouldn't want her to get behind in school."

Price hung up the phone, frowning.

"What was that all about?" Jo-Ann asked.

He related the strange conversation.

"Why don't you call Amanda?" Jo-Ann asked, flipping her hair, doing her Diane Sawyer thing.

"Good idea." He checked his watch. "Seven-thirty here, ten-thirty there. She'd probably still be up."

"I'll get the number," Jo-Ann said, getting up. She returned a moment later, handing him the blue book in which they kept addresses and phone numbers.

Price looked up Amanda's number and pushed the appropriate button on the cordless phone. The couple of silent seconds passed, and then the phone was ringing in Boston. He let it ring fifteen times.

"No answer," he said, then dialed Boston information for the number of Amanda's TV station. He was mildly surprised to find the switchboard manned and that the operator put him through to the newsroom without hesitation.

"News," a harried male voice said.

"Is Amanda Price there?"

"No, sir. She's on a leave of absence."

"Do you know where she's gone? This is her ex-husband. I need to get in touch with her."

"No, sir. I'm sorry. I don't think she told anyone."

"Do you know when she'll be back?"

"No, I'm sorry."

Price thanked the man and broke the connection. What was going on? Where was Amanda? Where was his daughter?

The next morning he located Ashley's last letter, in which she'd mentioned the name of her junior high school. He phoned the school and was told that Ashley's mother had taken the girl out of school last week. Amanda Price had not left an address or phone number where she could be reached. Nor had she said when her daughter would be returning to school.

"A teacher from your school called me last night," Price told the woman to whom he'd been speaking. "Sam Feldon, her English teacher."

There was a moment's silence before the woman said, "Sir, there's no teacher here by that name."

"Are you sure?" he asked, feeling more concerned for his daughter's safety by the moment.

"Of course I'm sure," the woman said, clearly miffed that he'd challenge her knowledge of the school's personnel.

Price talked it over with Jo-Ann, then called the Boston police.

NINE

DEXTER Buchanan stood in line at the branch post office serving the part of Boston in which Amanda Price lived. Though fairly short, the line wasn't moving. Only one postal clerk was manning the counter, and he had his hands full dealing with a gray-haired woman who was trying to do something that involved two packages and a lot of forms. The clerk looked harried. The woman was explaining something, waving her arms. Having no interest in her problems, Buchanan tuned her out, let his thoughts wander.

The man standing behind him in line let out a loud sigh, letting his impatience be known. Buchanan smelled the booze on the guy's breath. He didn't turn around to look, didn't want to know what the guy looked like. The boozy breath reminded him of his father, a brutal, disgusting drunk who had battered both his wife and son.

Buchanan remembered those days in Baltimore well. The run-down apartment in a sleazy neighborhood. Junked cars on the street. Liquor bottles in the gutter, some of them most likely dropped by his father. They lived like that because his father only worked when he was sober, and he was hardly ever sober. He was a longshoreman, had a good union, made good wages, although the worthless son of a bitch was hardly ever on the job to draw those wages.

He was a big man with greasy dark hair that was receding at the temples, and his body usually reeked of sweat as badly as his breath stank of booze. He sat around the house with a drink in his hand, wearing pants and an undershirt, watching TV, usually sports. Any sports. Wrestling, roller derby, football, hockey—it was all the same to him.

Life around Edwin Buchanan was tense. Look at him wrong, say the wrong thing, and there'd be a foot or a fist coming your way. And it usually wasn't just a single blow. Dexter Buchanan's father liked to make sure his point got driven home. Buchanan took his beatings almost impassively, almost never crying out, rarely flinching. But inside he seethed.

His mother, on the other hand, lived in fear. She screamed and pleaded with him, always to no avail, for the beating came, anyway. Buchanan despised her for her weakness, for giving the son of a bitch the satisfaction of knowing he could have her blubbering and begging for mercy simply by raising his fist.

When his mother killed herself by downing a bottle of sleeping pills, Buchanan's contempt for her only increased. The act showed she was not only weak but stupid. She could have left, simply disappeared. She could have shot the man while he slept—he was usually so drunk, you could have dragged him up to the roof and pushed him off. But not her. She'd escaped by killing herself instead of killing him. Suicide, to Buchanan's way of thinking, had to be the ultimate act of stupidity.

Buchanan had simply bided his time, waited until he was big enough to fight back. When that day finally came, he beat his father so severely that the man was hospitalized for three weeks. He'd had to force himself to stop short of beating him to death. There was no lesson in that. And Buchanan wanted his father to live with the pain, remember the lesson. He'd left before his father came home from the hospital, headed north in a nine-year-old Plymouth.

He hadn't known where he was going when he headed out, but as he was passing through Trenton, New Jersey, he'd decided to stop in New York City, take a look at the skyline, see what came his way. As if drawn to them by some irresistible pull, he found himself in the company of

hustlers and ex-cons and mobsters. A muscular kid, good
with his fists—as his father had discovered—Buchanan
became a collector for a small-time loan shark. When
someone put a bullet hole in the loan shark's forehead,
Buchanan was employed by a bigger loan shark, one with
mob connections.

Although his main job was being muscle for the loan
shark, he did a little moonlighting for the Mafia, usually as
a hit man. He offed three guys. Usually it was some minor
accountant who'd been dipping into the proceeds, someone
not important enough for a big-league hitter but someone
who'd been bad enough to be worth using as an example.
Cheat on us, you see what happens. The advantage of using
him instead of having their own guys do the job was that
Buchanan couldn't be tied to the mob if anything went
wrong.

He was only arrested once the whole five years he was in
New York. One of the loan shark's delinquent accounts had
filed assault charges against him. By the time it was ready
to go to trial, word had got to the guy about what would
happen to his son in California and his daughter in Oregon
if he testified, and all of a sudden he stopped cooperating
with the authorities. The charges against Buchanan were
dropped.

He left New York after his third hit for the Mafia. He got
the word that the cops had gotten a line on him, considered
him their prime suspect in the hit, and that he should
disappear. The people he worked with phrased it as a
suggestion. But it was not the sort of suggestion you could
consider ignoring. In his business there was no such thing as
casual advice from your superiors.

He was told there was work in Boston if he wanted it.
Going to Boston wasn't a "suggestion." The work was there
if he wanted it; he didn't have to take it. But New England
was as good a place as any, so he took the job, becoming a
general-purpose soldier in an organization affiliated with the
New York family he'd done his moonlighting for. It seemed

that he'd found his niche in life. He liked brutalizing people. And he liked killing them.

He would have stayed in Boston—one place was pretty much the same as the next to him—if his boss hadn't been convicted of income-tax evasion. When the guy at the top was taken out of action, there was a scramble to fill the void. And the person who won out had to reorganize things, solidify his power, make sure the people running things for him were *his* people, loyal to him and not some dude whiling away the years in a federal pen. The new power structure wasn't sure of Buchanan's loyalties, so it was "suggested" that he move on. He'd heard there was some action in New Shipton, so he went to check it out. New Shipton was everything he'd hoped it would be.

When Buchanan finally made it to the counter, he handed a slip of paper to the postal clerk. "I need to find out if this person left a forwarding address," he said.

"Cost you a buck to have me check," the clerk replied.

Buchanan gave him a dollar, and the man disappeared through an open doorway behind the counter.

Returning a few moments later, the clerk said, "We're holding her mail until further notice. No change of address."

"Thanks," Buchanan said, turning away from the counter. That was the answer he'd expected, but he had to make sure. Pretty soon he would use up all the options Casperson wanted him to try first. Then he could do the job the way he liked to do it. As he left the post office he held the door open for a woman coming in with a package, smiling warmly at her, wondering whether she thought he was a nice man, a good citizen, the sort of polite fellow she'd like her daughter to marry. He chuckled softly to himself as he walked away from the building.

He used the pay phone outside a convenience store three blocks from the post office to call New Shipton.

"She didn't leave a change of address with the post

office," he said. "I phoned her ex in California last night, and he didn't even know she was gone."

"She would have told him not to let anyone know."

"He was genuinely surprised," Buchanan said flatly. "He wasn't faking it."

"You want to go out there, make sure?"

Buchanan would enjoy that, but it was unnecessary. "Wouldn't be worth the trip," he said.

Casperson was silent for a moment, then he said, "The New Shipton Credit Bureau got the report from her bank. There's nothing in it that will help us."

"She have a good credit rating?"

"Yeah, A-plus. There's a cop on the force here who's got a buddy in the Boston department. The guy in Boston's keeping his ears open, but so far there's nothing."

Absently Buchanan wondered whether that made any sense, to keep your ears open. How could you close them? "How about the killing of a security guard at a Boston TV station? What does the cop hear about that?"

"Cops have no leads. They can't figure it."

"Did I tell you there're no news people on duty at night?"

"Yeah, what does that have to do with anything?"

"Don't you see it? A guy was killed right in the newsroom, and the station's got no pictures of it for the news. Ought to be embarrassing."

Casperson sighed, clearly not giving a damn about pictures the station had for the news. "What's your next move?"

"I'm gonna check with the neighbors, see if anyone knows where she went."

"We're running out of time here," Casperson said. "If this guy's willing to talk to a reporter, he's willing to talk to the grand jury. A lot of people will go down if that happens." The threat was obvious.

"Let me do it my way."

"Your way's very messy. I wouldn't mind if it was out in California, the ex-husband—it's a long way off, so who cares, right? But the local stuff's going to attract attention. At first it might have looked like a psycho grabbed the woman, and maybe a child molester was after the kid. Now, with the woman and kid on the run and with a guard being killed at the TV station, the cops might start putting things together. They might start looking at us. And I don't want that to happen."

"You're the one who just reminded me about the grand jury."

Casperson said nothing, the silence stretching out. Finally he spoke. "Check with the neighbors," he said. "Then do it your way."

Bob Miller was reading the last of the résumés he'd received in the mail that day. It was from a twenty-four-year-old guy in Cheyenne, Wyoming, who thought he was ready to move up to a major market. College degree and two years' experience in the boonies. Miller got four or five résumés a day just like it, from Rapid City, South Dakota; Abilene, Texas; Flagstaff, Arizona; Tallahassee, Florida. People who'd work for a hundred a week or for free or maybe even *pay* him for a chance to work at a network affiliate in a big East Coast city, from which you might be able to move up to New York or L.A. or one of the networks if you were good enough. The vast majority of them would never advance beyond a medium-sized market like Albuquerque or Des Moines, and they'd be out of the business by the time they were in their mid-thirties, having tired of the politicking and backstabbing that made their stomachs twist up at night—not to mention the constant threat of being fired.

Miller, himself, had been fired lots of times, once after only four months on the job, but then news directors and anchors were always the first to go when management started getting antsy about the ratings. The only good thing about it was that having been sacked usually wasn't held against you when you looked for another job. In fact, if you hadn't been canned a few times, you were probably an intolerable brownnose.

Looking at the résumé in his hand, Miller shook his head. As examples of the big stories he'd covered, the guy had listed the crash of a single-engine Cessna in which two people had been injured and a rodeo. A rodeo, for chrissake. The applicant had touched on his background, noting that he'd been an Eagle Scout and a member of the Civil Air Patrol. *Stay in Wyoming,* Miller thought. *Get a job selling high-centered pickup trucks with roll bars and lots of extra lights on top so guys can night-shoot deer and blind the hell out of drivers who don't dim their lights. You'll be happier, trust me.*

Miller was getting ready to toss the résumé in the wastebasket when Sergeant Frederick Ryan stepped into the office. The detective was in charge of the investigation into the murder of the security guard. The cop was a big guy whose round face created the impression of flabbiness, although Miller suspected that assuming Ryan was soft could be a gigantic mistake.

"You find out who killed Porterfield?" Miller asked as the detective sat down.

"No. And unless somebody turns up who got a good look at the guy, or we get a good tip, we're probably not going to." Ryan ran his hand across the crown of his bald head, as if he were smoothing his hair.

Miller said nothing, waited for the detective to explain why he was here.

"You have a reporter here, Amanda J. Price, is that right?"

"Yes."

Miller hadn't told the policeman that Amanda's desk had been searched by the intruder. He'd come close, picking up the phone and starting to punch out the detective's number, but he'd stopped himself. If he'd mentioned Amanda, the police would have wanted to know where she was, and Miller wasn't so sure that telling them was a very good idea.

The New Shipton police had to have contacts within the Boston Department. If the Boston cops knew where Amanda was, then the New Shipton cops could probably find out. And the police chief was one of the New Shipton officials being investigated by the grand jury.

But the police had come up with Amanda's name on their own. What did he do now?

"Where is she?" the cop asked.

"Leave of absence."

"For how long?"

Miller hesitated. "That's sort of up in the air right now." And the next question would be: "Know where she can be reached?" Miller needed more time before he'd know whether to answer that question truthfully, so he said, "The guy who killed Porterfield might have looked through her desk."

Ryan studied him, his expression neutral. "Why didn't you tell me that before now?"

"We didn't know about it. Some of the B.U. interns are using Amanda's desk while she's gone, and nobody knew anything in it had been disturbed until one of them discovered it." Miller hoped the policeman wouldn't ask him exactly when the discovery had been made.

"Was anything removed from the desk?"

"Not that we know of. The intern said that as far as she could tell, everything was there; it had just been rearranged."

"Anything else you haven't told me yet?"

"Yes," Miller said. He told the detective about the attempt to grab Amanda at the mall, the break-in at her apartment, Ashley's close call coming home from school, and how Amanda thought these things were connected with the series she did on New Shipton. "She was terrified," the news director said. "That's why she asked for a leave of absence, so she could get away from this man."

"Why didn't you tell me this before now?"

"Until I discovered that Amanda's desk had been searched, I didn't know there was any connection."

"Why didn't Amanda get in touch with us? It's our job to handle things like that."

"That's what I told her. She didn't want to do it that way. She didn't think you could protect her, especially if there was a strike."

"These other incidents, were they reported?"

"Yes. Boston handled the complaint about the guy trying to grab Ashley, but the other incident, the one at the mall, would have been handled by one of the suburban forces."

"I'll get copies of the reports," Ryan said. "Is there anything else you haven't told me?"

"No," Miller said. "That's everything." Now would come the big question, and Miller was still uncertain how he was going to answer it.

"How do I get in touch with Amanda Price?"

"I don't know." And that was that. He'd made his choice; now he had to live with it.

"She didn't say where she was going?"

"She didn't tell anyone. That's how frightened she was."

Ryan studied him in silence, the cop letting just a little doubt show in his eyes, so Miller would know he wasn't home free if he was lying. But did Ryan actually know he was being lied to, or was he just playing it cool, not taking anything for granted? He knows, Miller decided, but there was nothing he could do about it.

"And you say she thought this might be connected to the story she did on New Shipton?"

"She suspected it, but there wasn't any proof. I mean, the man wasn't wearing a button that read 'I'm from New Shipton' or anything like that."

"I saw those reports she did," Ryan said. "It was a good job. I'd like to see them again."

"I'll arrange it," Miller said.

The detective nodded. "The reason I asked you about Amanda Price is that we got a call from her ex-husband last night. It seems somebody called him, saying he was one of his daughter's teachers and asking if he could speak to the girl. Said his name was Sam Feldon and that he had her English assignments. The ex-husband—who lives in California—doesn't know what the guy was talking about. The girl isn't there, hasn't been there in months, isn't expected. So he starts thinking something's wrong. He calls Amanda. No answer. He calls the TV station, and they tell him she's on a leave of absence, nobody knows where. Then he calls the school here in Boston, and you know what they tell him?"

"There's no such teacher."

"You got it."

Ryan was looking at him again, his eyes asking whether Miller might have suddenly recalled something else he should tell the police. The news director was a little shaken by what the detective had just told him. It meant that someone was looking for Amanda, trying everything he could think of to find her. Miller almost told him where she was, but as he was opening his mouth to say the words he stopped himself, knowing that if he told the Boston police he'd be telling the New Shipton police as well. And how the hell were the Boston police going to protect Amanda out in the north woods of Minnesota? Even the Minnesota authorities couldn't protect her. A lone deputy was responsible for the entire area.

So Bob Miller closed his mouth and said nothing.

TEN

"VERY good," Amanda said after trying the mushroom omelet Ashley had made them for breakfast. "Maybe you'll grow up to become a world renown chef, another Paul Prudhomme."

Sitting across from her at the table, Ashley considered that. "Actually, I think I'd rather be an accountant."

"An accountant? I thought kids always aspired to be astronauts or the president or something like that. Why do you want to be an accountant?"

"I like numbers, you know that."

Amanda put on an exaggerated look of dismay. "My God, I've raised a nerd."

The girl rolled her eyes. "You haven't thought this thing through, Mom. That chef you mentioned, Paul What's-his-name, spends all day busting his butt in a hot kitchen. Nerds, on the other hand, work in nice comfortable offices and make lots of money."

Amanda raised her hands in a sign of surrender. She knew when she'd been beaten. "Want to go to town today?"

"Sure."

"Let's take those containers back to the Heikkinens, then head for the booming metropolis of Fiddlehead Lake."

Ashley didn't reply. She seemed to be thinking about something.

"That sound okay to you?" Amanda asked.

"Mom . . ."

"Yes?"

"Why don't we wait until this afternoon to go into town?"

"Why?"

"Well . . ."

"Well?"

"I told Eric Carlson that I'd stop by to see his shortwave radio the next time I'm in town, and if we go early, he'll still be in school."

I don't believe this, Amanda thought. "I thought you considered boys inhuman, slimy creatures unfit to inhabit the earth."

"Most of them are." Ashley took a big bite of her omelet, apparently trying to get out of the conversation by having her mouth too full to talk.

Amanda waited until she swallowed, then said, "But not Eric."

"He seems nicer than the boys back in Boston."

"Why is he nicer?"

"I don't know," she said uncomfortably. "He just is."

"I guess that's as good a reason as any. We'll run over to the Heikkinens this morning, then hold off on going to town until afternoon."

Ashley nodded in acknowledgment.

Amanda's principal reason for wanting to go into town was to buy more books. Because the house had no TV set, Amanda had picked out some paperbacks at the grocery store and let Ashley do the same. Her original plan had been for them to trade reading material, but their tastes proved too different for that. Ashley had selected a fantasy paperback and *16* magazine. Amanda had chosen two paperback mysteries, classic whodunits. When they traded, Amanda quickly found she had little interest in elves and fairy creatures and none whatsoever in a magazine devoted to fifteen-year-old sitcom actors. Ashley, on the other hand, thought the classic mysteries boring because they were all dialogue and no action. So they were out of things to read.

And Amanda definitely did not want to be out of reading material. For without it there was nothing to do at night but listen to the wind moan in the eaves and think. What she thought about was the man with the lifeless eyes.

Bob Miller had called again last night, to let her know that someone had called Tom, pretending to be one of Ashley's teachers. Clearly the people who wanted to find her were determined. They'd keep trying things until something worked.

Amanda saw herself being pulled into the man's car. And as she did every time she thought of him, she recalled his eyes, twin orbs with all the human warmth of circles that had been cut out of cloth and sewn on the face of an old rag doll. And yet they weren't blank, those eyes, for in them Amanda had seen a coldness as great as the Arctic, as if she were peering into the soul of death itself. She shivered.

"You okay, Mom?"

"Just a little chill. I guess the house hasn't warmed up yet this morning."

Amanda hadn't told her daughter about the phone call to Tom. It was the parent's job to shoulder the worrying. Ashley had already been exposed to considerably more terror than any twelve-year-old should have to endure.

As Amanda watched this miniature version of herself eat breakfast, guilt surged through her, hot and tingling like an electric shock. Ashley was in danger because of her. Because she had done the New Shipton story. And her motives for doing it had been entirely selfish. She had hardly been a crusading journalist, out to rid the world of evildoers. She hadn't done the story because, by exposing its corruption, she could make New Shipton a better place to live. She'd been advancing her career. A heavy-duty piece of investigative work like New Shipton might impress the networks.

A part of Amanda was trying to remind her that pursuing career goals was hardly an evil thing to do, that in fact many people would say it was a very good thing to do. Work hard and succeed. Earn more money to better support yourself and your family. The American way. And yet the guilt persisted, for in her zeal Amanda had endangered her daughter, the most precious thing in her life. And no goals, no matter how well lauded by society, could justify that.

She wished she'd never done the New Shipton story. Didn't she have enough sense to realize that people who thought nothing of murdering other human beings to accomplish their ends wouldn't like having their activities exposed? Hadn't it occurred to her that they might try to get even with her—or that they might want to find out who her sources were, how she had learned as much as she had?

Abruptly Amanda saw a man in a ski mask, a man who insisted that even his covered face had to be electronically distorted. That was what this was all about. The people in New Shipton were trying to find out who had ratted on them. There were only two people who knew his identity: Amanda and the man himself.

Again she chastised herself for not having the minimal foresight required to see this ahead of time. Of course they'd want to know who informed on them. Of course they'd come after her.

"Hey, Mom. Yoo hoo, you in there somewhere?"

"What? Oh, sorry. My mind was just wandering, I guess."

"You're letting your omelet get cold. If it's not eaten while it's hot, the subtle delicacies of its flavor and aroma will be lost."

"You mean it will become ordinary, like scrambled eggs, cease to be a gourmet delight?"

"Exactly."

The girl gave her such a deadpan look that Amanda broke up. She couldn't help herself. She hurriedly polished off the omelet while it still had some warmth left in it.

Amanda concluded that what was done was done. She might be guilty of being naïve, but she had not intentionally endangered Ashley or anyone else when she'd set out to do the New Shipton story. Her task now was to figure out how to deal with the situation, not beat herself over the head with it.

Amanda finished her coffee, then they did the dishes; Ashley washing, Amanda drying. As she put the cups and saucers away, Amanda said, "You ready to return those things to the Heikkinens?"

"Sure. I'll put them in a bag."

Amanda had seen a number of A-frames in the area. The Heikkinens' place was the first one she'd been inside of. Barbara gave Ashley and her a tour. It had three levels. In the basement were things like John's workshop, the washer and dryer, and a spare bedroom. The ground floor, which was taken up by the living room and a huge kitchen, was entirely open, without partitioning walls. The top level was a bedroom loft. One of the structure's sloping walls faced south, and it was all windows, to let in as much solar heat as possible.

"The glass is specially treated," Barbara Heikkinen said. "It lets the sun's heat in but retains the warmth that's already in the house." She and her guests were sitting at the big wooden kitchen table, having coffee and doughnuts. Amanda feared she would gain five pounds and have coffee nerves by the time the day was over.

"Your house is really cool," Ashley said.

"She means she likes it," Amanda said. "She's not commenting on the temperature."

"Oh, Mom, she knows that."

"Thank you," Mrs. Heikkinen said diplomatically. "I'm glad you like it."

Through the kitchen window Amanda could see the big barn in which John kept his treasured snow-removing tractor. He was out there working on it now.

Noting the direction of Amanda's gaze, Barbara said, "He goes out to get some wood, decides to stop and make some minor adjustment to his tractor, and I don't see him again for the rest of the day." She shook her head, but she was smiling warmly, clearly pleased that her husband had something he liked to tinker with, even if she did poke a little fun at him behind his back.

Amanda envied the Heikkinens. Their uncomplicated existence out here in the woods seemed so happy and full of affection. And no professional killers were stalking them. Amanda quickly pushed that last thought back into her subconscious. The man with the lifeless eyes couldn't find them here. She had to stop tormenting herself.

"You need anything from town?" Amanda asked. "We have to run in later today to get some more things to read."

"There's no TV," Ashley said, as if reading were so bizarre that it needed explanation.

"I can help you on both counts," Mrs. Heikkinen said. "John and I both love books, so we've got a pretty good selection. Everything from Dostoyevsky to Elmore Leonard. Feel free to borrow what you like. And there's a portable black-and-white TV set in the spare bedroom."

"Thank you," Amanda said, "but we really couldn't—"

"Sure you could. Nobody ever uses that old set. If you had it, it would not only be doing some good, but I wouldn't have to dust it. Same with the books. They're just sitting there in the bookcase. They need to be read every now and then so they don't feel forgotten."

"I don't think the house even has an antenna," Amanda said.

"Yes, it does. John checked, in case you brought a TV set with you. He said it seems to be in pretty good condition. The wire running to it's probably in the living room somewhere."

"You've already done so much for us," Amanda said. "I don't want to put you out any more."

"So who's being put out? You'll do us a favor sometime. That's the way it works."

Amanda and Ashley selected two volumes apiece from the big bookcases in the living room. Amanda picked a paperback edition of one of Robert Parker's Spenser novels and a hard-bound edition of *The Mayor of Casterbridge* by Thomas Hardy. She chose the Parker novel because Spenser always manhandled the thugs, and she found the idea of thugs getting manhandled appealing right now. Ashley took hard-bound copies of Twain's *Huckleberry Finn* and *The Long Winter* by Laura Ingalls Wilder. That choice, too, seemed appropriate.

Mrs. Heikkinen came up from the basement, carrying a twelve-inch J.C. Penny black-and-white TV set. Noting the girl's selections, she said, "I love the Laura Ingalls Wilder books. I read them I don't know how many times with my children."

"Maybe she shouldn't take anything that's special to you," Amanda said.

"Of course she should take it. Things that are special should be shared." She gave Amanda a look that said there was to be no more arguing. "You know how to hook up a TV set?"

Amanda said she did.

"Okay. Hook the antenna wire to the UHF terminal. That's because all the TV here comes in on translator. You can get the four stations from Duluth but not on the same channels they'd be on if you were in Duluth. Here they come in on channel fifty-four, fifty-eight, sixty-three, and seventy-two. You may have to fiddle with it a little bit, but the set should get them all."

John came in from the garage in time to put the TV set into the car for them. "If you have any trouble," he said, "give me a call and I'll come over and check out the antenna for you. It looked okay, but sometimes the lead-in wire will deteriorate, and you can't tell it from the ground."

As they drove away from the Heikkinens' A-frame Amanda said, "I feel guilty for letting them do so much for us."

"Maybe we should bake them a cake, write thank you on it or something."

"Good idea. We'll pick up the stuff we need to decorate the cake at the store this afternoon."

Behind them, someone honked. Her eyes jumping to the rearview mirror, Amanda saw a green car behind her, right on her bumper. Although the sun was reflecting off the windshield, she could tell there was only one person in the car. The driver honked again—rapid, urgent beeps. No, Amanda thought, don't even *think* it's him. But the sense of déjà vu washed over her just the same. Another deserted two-lane country road, the car coming up behind her. Of course, the situation wasn't exactly the same—the sun was shining this time, the snowbanks were higher, and the area wasn't totally unfamiliar—and yet the similarities overwhelmed her.

Ashley was staring ashen-faced out the back window. The road turned so that the sun was winking on and off through the trees like a strobe light.

"It's him!" Ashley shrieked. "I just saw his face."

Amanda stepped on the gas and pulled away from the green car. The distance between them kept widening. Why was he letting her get away? And then she knew the answer. He had brought help this time. And the help was waiting for her somewhere up ahead. How had he found her so quickly? What had she overlooked?

The green car was coming up behind them again, honking. Amanda drove faster. The road was clear, with relatively few icy spots. It had a couple of sharp curves, though. Amanda tried to remember where they were. The green car was on her bumper again, still honking. Ahead was a curve. Amanda headed into it as fast as she dared. The green car fell back.

"Is there a turnoff anywhere?" Amanda asked. She was sure the green car was herding her into a trap.

"I don't know," Ashley said. "I can't remember."

Amanda came out of the curve, the car shuddering and leaning dangerously to the left. She sped up again, still looking for a turnoff. The green car was dropping back again. Amanda came into another curve. She straightened out as best she could within the narrow confines of the snowbanks, but she'd forgotten that this particular bend was a spiral curve, one that twisted ever more tightly as it continued. She hit the brakes, but it was too late, and the car's rear end broke loose. Amanda saw the trees, a snowbank, the road, more snowbanks, more trees. When the car stopped, she was sideways in the road. The engine was dead. She sat there, her heart pounding, glad she hadn't slid off the road and wrapped the Ford around a tree.

"Mom!"

The urgency in Ashley's voice made Amanda instantly look in the direction of the girl's gaze. The green car was pulling to a stop, its bumper only ten feet from Amanda's door. Her car would have to be jockeyed back and forth between the snowbanks to straighten it, something she clearly didn't have time to do. After the incident in Pennsylvania, Amanda had put the car's tire iron under the front seat. It was still there. She slipped it out. Ashley was watching her, wide-eyed. The girl seemed frozen, unable to move. From the corner of her eye Amanda saw a figure emerge from the green car.

"When he reaches my door, get out and run," Amanda said. She looked straight ahead, not at the approaching man.

"Mom . . ."

"Just do it." She was holding the tire iron, concealing it against her leg. "We're almost to the house. Make sure no one's there, then go in and call for help."

Ashley nodded, but she still seemed rigid and immobile, as if she were a lifeless Ashley doll and not a real girl at all. The man reached Amanda's side of the car. Suddenly Ashley opened her door and leapt out, scrambling up the snowbank.

"Hey," the man said.

Amanda gripped the tire iron, readied herself.

The man tapped the window. "What's the matter with you? You always drive like that?"

Amanda couldn't see his face, just a blue coat. But then he bent down. His face was bony, his eyes blue, his flesh Nordic pale. She had never seen him before in her life. Trembling with relief, Amanda rolled down the window.

"You got some kind of problem, lady?" he asked.

"I . . . I'm sorry. I thought you were someone else. Why were you honking at me?"

The man shook his head, as if to say he'd met some pretty weird people in his time but this took the cake. "I'm looking for the Petersons' place. I thought you might be able to tell me where it is."

The passenger-side door opened, and Ashley got back into the car. "I saw that it wasn't him," she said. She was out of breath.

"Do you know where they live, the Petersons?" the man asked.

"I'm sorry," Amanda said. "I've never heard of them."

The man stood there a moment, looking at her the way a biologist might study a mutant insect, then he turned and walked back to his car. Amanda reached for the ignition switch. Her hand was shaking so badly, she was afraid to drive. The man was sitting in his car now, waiting for her to move.

Amanda let him wait while she took a few moments to calm herself. Then she turned the key, fully expecting the car to refuse to start, but the engine roared to life. It took her a few moments to get the Mustang straightened out, and then she was on her way. The green car followed, staying well back, the driver no doubt thinking she was some kind of a lunatic and best stayed well clear of. Amanda's earlier fear was changing to embarrassment.

Apparently Ashley was feeling the same way, because she said, "I thought it was him. I really did. When I saw him through the windshield of his car, it looked just like the guy."

"It's okay," Amanda said. "I'm just glad you were mistaken."

When they got home, Amanda found the wire leading to the antenna and hooked up the TV set. There was a tiny bit of snow on the NBC channel, but all the others came in flawlessly.

"Which channel's MTV?" Ashley asked.

"None of them. You only get that if you're on cable."

"There's no cable here?"

"I doubt it," Amanda said, thinking that the lack of MTV could be a definite advantage of country living. "You'll have to learn to live without it."

"We don't even have a radio," Ashley said.

"If we're still here then, maybe you'll get one for your birthday." As soon as she said it, she regretted it. Ashley would fill the house with the nerve-jangling din of rock and roll. Amanda wondered whether it was too late to instill in the child an appreciation of Beethoven and Chopin and Vivaldi.

As promised, Amanda took her daughter into town that afternoon, even though they no longer needed books. Amanda wanted to pick up a few things at the store, and she also wanted to stop by the sheriff's substation and talk to Ted Anderson if he was there. She told herself she simply wanted to let him know about the call her ex-husband had received from someone pretending to be one of Ashley's teachers. That was part of it, of course, but somewhere down in the far reaches of her consciousness churned the desire to see Ted Anderson the man, as well as Ted Anderson the police officer. She tried not to think about that; it made her feel silly, like a teenager with a crush. After all, she was an adult woman, divorced, with a child and a career. She was too mature to go around having instant attractions.

Although she knew that thought was flawed, she clung to it. And drove toward the sheriff's substation.

The first indication that there was a town ahead was the community's lone billboard, which read:

ED'S BAIT AND TACKLE
NIGHT CRAWLERS, LURES,
ALL YOUR FISHING NEEDS

"Mom . . ." Ashley was looking worried.

"Yes."

"How am I going to do this?"

"Eric said for you just to stop over, didn't he?"

"Yeah, but I'd feel funny just walking up to his house and knocking on the door. What if his mom opens it? What will I tell her?"

"That you're Ashley Price and that Eric invited you over."

"I don't know."

"Okay, how about this. I'll let you off at the store. You can go in and look around. Eric may be there. If he's not, he might show up as soon as he learns you're in the store. If he doesn't, you could ask Mr. Carlson if Eric's around."

"Just casually, like I'm asking to be polite or something."

"Exactly."

Ashley said that sounded like a good idea, and Amanda dropped her at the store.

The sheriff's substation was one of those manufactured buildings that looked like an enormous house trailer with no wheels. Amanda stomped the snow off her shoes and stepped inside.

"Hi," Ted Anderson said, looking up. He was sitting at one of the two desks in the place. The other was occupied by a heavyset young woman with reddish-brown hair. A counter separated Amanda from the deputy and the woman. Along one wall were three big cages—temporary holding cells, apparently, since they had no plumbing fixtures. All of them were empty.

"You got a moment?" Amanda asked.

"Sure," the deputy replied, getting up. He opened the gate in the counter for her, then led her to a chair beside his desk. When they were both seated, he said, "This is Melinda Stojevich, my dispatcher." Looking at Melinda, he said, "This is the newcomer I was telling you about, Amanda Price."

Amanda and Melinda said hi.

"What can I do for you?" the deputy asked.

She told him about the phone call to her ex-husband. "I just wanted you to know they're still looking for me," she said. "They're not going to give up."

"They're still looking, but they're not learning anything. It seems to me you've covered your tracks pretty well."

Amanda nodded. Then she surprised herself by blurting out the details of what had happened that morning on her way back from the Heikkinens' house. "I was scared to death. I kept expecting to hear shots ring out as Ashley climbed over that snowbank."

"I'm glad it was all a mistake," he said. "I'm glad you and Ashley didn't get hurt when you lost control of the car too." The concern on his face was genuine.

"When it was all over with, I was just sort of embarrassed. I'm not even sure why I'm telling you about it."

"There's nothing to be embarrassed about. Considering what's been happening to you, you've got every right to be on edge. This guy who's after you doesn't sound like anybody to be taken lightly."

She was glad to hear him say that. She wanted to think she was handling things as best she could, not like some panic-stricken movie heroine whose only abilities were screaming and looking terrified.

"Can I get you some coffee? It's pretty fresh. Melinda just made it last month."

"Month before last," Melinda said. "But it's still good."

"Melinda makes bohunk coffee," Anderson said teasingly. "Twenty-four spoons of coffee for each cup. Tastes the same fresh as it does two months later."

"Took him a while to get used to it," Melinda said. "Up till then he'd spent his whole life drinking coffee like a sissy."

Amanda said, "Do you have any tea?"

Everyone laughed. Melinda said, "I've got to run some letters over to Carlson's before it closes. You think you can make tea by yourself, Ted?"

"I can handle it."

Melinda left, slipping into a heavy coat as she went out the door. Ted made two steaming cups of tea and brought them to his desk. "Where's Ashley?" he asked as he sat down.

"Over at Carlson's. I think she has a crush on Eric."

"He's a nice kid. Too bad crushes are here today and gone tomorrow at their age. A few years down the line they'd make a great couple."

"Don't marry her off yet," Amanda said. "I haven't even learned to deal with the fact that she's going to be a teenager in a few weeks." Which reminded her that she and Ashley still had not had the Talk.

They drank their tea in silence for a few moments, then Ted said, "How's everything out at the cabin? You all settled in?"

"As well as we can be, I guess, considering the circumstances. How long will it take before cabin fever begins to set in?"

"Hard to say. About all I can tell you is that around February a sizable portion of the population of Minnesota starts calling the airlines and asking about fares to Hawaii. You figure in that we're used to staying inside and amusing ourselves for several months each year, and that might give you an idea."

Amanda nodded, did some counting on her fingers. "For a city person like me, that works out to March fourteenth."

"Umm. Very low boredom tolerance."

"At twelve-oh-three A.M."

"It'll happen in your sleep?"

"I'll be too bored to feel like staying up and celebrating."

He was looking at her, grinning as if carrying on this silly conversation was the most pleasant experience he'd had all week. He said, "I make it a point to pass by your place whenever I'm on patrol."

"You should stop in, have some coffee. I should warn you that it's sissy coffee, made with only a few spoonsful per pot."

"I will," he said. "I can't do it very often, though, because I'm all the law enforcement this area's got, and I'm not supposed to spend too much time socializing."

He was still smiling at her. She smiled back, and his changed into an almost bashful, boyish grin. He dropped his eyes to his cup. Amanda felt tingly all over, told herself that this couldn't be happening.

"I guess I'd better go over to the grocery store, then pick up Ashley," she said. "Thanks for the tea."

His eyes met hers, and although she wasn't sure, Amanda thought they were telling her not to go. Rising, he escorted her to the gate in the counter.

"Thanks again for the tea," she said.

"Anytime," he replied.

Then she was out the door, walking down the steps and around to the side of the building, where her car was parked. She was slipping the key into the ignition when someone tapped on her window. It was Ted Anderson. She rolled down the window.

"Have you tried the Lake Café yet?" he asked.

"No."

He was bending down, looking in the window at her, the bashful grin back on his face. "It's not much, but then it's the only restaurant in town. Anyway, uh, if you and Ashley would like to meet me there in a while, I'd be happy to buy you dinner."

Amanda started to think about it, then decided to heck with thinking about it and said yes, they'd love to.

The Lake Café was a small wooden building that looked like a 1950s diner inside. It had a faded turquoise Formica counter and stools with round swiveling tops, their chrome stems bolted to the floor. Booths lined one wall; there were no tables. The only thing missing from the anachronistic scene was a garish jukebox with remote-play terminals along the counter and at each booth.

Thank goodness for that, Amanda thought. Had there been a jukebox, Ashley would have played something by the "Eardrum Splitters" or the "Nerve Janglers."

The three of them were sitting in a booth, Amanda and Ashley on one side of the table, Ted Anderson on the other. Amanda noted that deer heads had been mounted on the end walls, staring at each other above the customers, who were eating things like meat loaf or pressed turkey or pork chops.

"Eric's radio is really neat," Ashley said. "While I was there he tuned in Radio Moscow and the BBC."

"Were the programs interesting?" Amanda asked.

"The programs? Not too, I guess. They just talked about the world situation and stuff."

"Nothing important."

"I mean, it's not what they're saying that's interesting," the girl explained, "but that Eric can get all that stuff."

"I see. Why is it I don't think radio's what you're interested in?"

Ashley reddened, giving her mother a dirty look. Clearly saying such things—especially in front of the deputy—was a no-no.

The girl had been doing most of the talking since they'd entered the restaurant. Amanda and Ted Anderson had been silent, letting their eyes meet, hold for a moment or two, then drift away to look at something else. Amanda felt vaguely silly doing this, and yet she seemed unable to stop.

She was also beginning to wish Ashley was dining with Eric and his parents tonight.

"Eric's got another radio that gets the police calls too," Ashley said. There was a hint of defiance in her voice, as if warning her mother not to say anything else that might embarrass her. "He hears you talking to your dispatcher," she said, looking at the deputy. "This morning, before he went to school, he heard you going to rescue a woman."

"To rescue a woman?" the deputy said. "I don't remember rescuing any women this morning."

"Eric said her name was Stromquist."

He laughed. "Oh, that rescue. Mrs. Stromquist is about eighty. Her husband just died recently, and she's been a little panicky since then. Not that I blame her, finding herself alone after all these years. In any case, she called about dawn, saying there was someone breaking into her house. It turned out to be a squirrel. She's got a bird feeder on the rear of her house by the back door, and somehow a squirrel got into it and was having a field day."

Amanda said, "Is it safe for an eighty-year-old woman to live out here all by herself?"

"I go by and check on her every day," Ted Anderson said. "She hires a guy to plow out her driveway after a snowstorm. Too bad she doesn't live closer to John Heikkinen. He'd do it for free."

"But what if the phone or the power was out and the roads were blocked?"

"She keeps a good supply of wood."

"But she could have a heart attack or something, and there'd be no way to get help."

"That's true," the deputy said, "but the same thing could happen right in the middle of Minneapolis. City people die in their homes and no one finds them for days. Besides, out here people help each other; they keep an eye out. Lots of people go by to check on her. It's not just me. And there're no thugs to knock her down and snatch her purse.

"Most important of all," he continued, "this is where

Anna wants to be. She's spent most of her adult life in the north woods, and right here's where she wants to spend what's left of it."

"How about you?" Amanda asked. "This where you want to spend the rest of your life?"

"If I can," he said.

"Don't you miss stores that sell clothes other than jeans and parkas, good restaurants, bookstores?"

"And record stores and cable TV," Ashley added.

Anderson smiled. "I'm not going to give you a commercial for living in the woods. It suits me, but it doesn't suit everybody. As for shopping, most of us make an annual trek into Duluth or the Cities—that's what we call the Twin Cities, just the Cities. We buy whatever we need, eat out if we want, and by the end of the day we're usually glad to be heading home.

"I guess you get so you're not used to big towns. The air in the Cities always smells like exhaust fumes, sort of like a bus just passed you, except the smell never entirely goes away. They had to build sound barriers along the freeways so the people living next to them wouldn't go crazy." He paused, then said, "I think I just broke my promise. I'm giving you a commercial for living in the woods."

"You ready to order yet?" the waitress asked. She was about fifty, blond, big-boned but not chubby. Amanda realized she had yet to look at her menu. She'd been too busy looking at Ted Anderson.

"Cheeseburger," Ashley said without hesitation. "And a Coke."

"I'll have the special," the deputy said.

"I'll have the same," Amanda said, although she didn't recall what the special was. She didn't want to fumble with the menu, make a fool out of herself while everyone waited for her to make up her mind.

The special turned out to be hot roast-beef sandwiches with instant mashed potatoes and overcooked green beans.

Amanda suppressed the desire to ask for a wine list, just to
see what would happen.

"Best thing they serve here," Anderson said, "is the fried
smelt. But you can only get it in the spring, when they're
running."

"What are smelt?" Ashley asked.

"Little fish."

"Like sardines?"

"Little bigger than that. They swim upstream from Lake
Superior to spawn. People from all over the state will go for
the smelt run, line up along the streams with nets. For
people on the North Shore, it's not officially spring until the
smelt start running."

"You had smelt in Milwaukee," Amanda told her daughter. "Don't you remember?"

"I was just a little kid then," the girl said. "How could I
remember?"

Ashley sounded miffed, and Amanda wondered whether
it was because of what she'd said about the girl and Eric
Carlson. Or could Ashley sense what seemed to be happening between her mother and Ted Anderson? Was she
jealous, afraid of losing her mother's affections? Amanda
gave the girl's leg a loving squeeze. Ashley smiled; everything seemed to be okay. Maybe Amanda was just imagin-
ing things.

When they'd finished their meal, the deputy said, "I can
wholeheartedly recommend the pie. David and Jeanette
Lindström own the place, and Jeanette makes all the pies
herself."

He and Amanda had cherry pie, while Ashley had apple
with a slice of cheese on it. Anderson was right; the pie was
delicious.

As they were leaving the restaurant, getting into their
separate cars, Amanda said, "Thanks again for dinner,
Ted." It was the first time she'd used his given name, and
he grinned at her across the roof of his police cruiser.

"I'll stop by in a day or two. To check on you."

The sun had set while they were eating. As Amanda drove into the cold Minnesota night she found herself watching for headlights in the rearview mirror, but none appeared. The man with the strange eyes wasn't following her. And Amanda realized suddenly that this was the first time she'd thought of him in a while. He hadn't come up in the conversation over dinner, hadn't even popped into her thoughts all the time she had been in the restaurant.

But then it wasn't the restaurant that had made her cozy and warm and unafraid. It was Ted.

ELEVEN

DICK Kilmer rolled over. The young blond woman next to him stirred in her sleep, mumbled something incomprehensible. She'd drifted off after their lovemaking, while Kilmer lay awake, letting his thoughts wander.

He wondered whether he'd ever be able to settle down, get married—or even live with someone. At this point in his life he was unable to imagine it. Giving up the chase, the satisfaction of constantly having someone new and different to make love with was . . . well, it was unthinkable.

Kilmer had the knack. He didn't have any well-honed lines or approaches, because it was nothing he'd learned. Rather it had come to him naturally; he'd been born with it. At thirteen he had been seduced by a fourteen-year-old girl who lived down the street, and from that point on, he'd had girls. In a bed when his parents or hers were out of the house. In the backseats of cars. On a blanket in a culvert after slipping away from the church picnic. Now that he was grown-up and had a place of his own, hardly a day went by that Dick Kilmer didn't find a girl who was new and interesting and horny.

The blond was named Bernadette Cole. He'd met her at the Laundromat. Having run out of clean clothes, he'd been forced to do his laundry. Saturday morning was the best time for finding women at the Laundromat, but he hadn't been able to wait until then, so he'd gone, fully expecting to find the place deserted—except maybe for a couple of thugs who wanted to break into the change machine. But the thugs hadn't been there. And Bernadette had.

It was the same old never-fail magic. He'd smiled, she'd

smiled, and the next thing you knew, they were talking. Kilmer really didn't know what it was about him that attracted women. He was fairly good-looking, he supposed, but he'd seen much better-looking guys who didn't have nearly his success with women. And uglier guys who seemed to score nearly as often as he did. So it wasn't looks.

The closest Kilmer could come to explaining it was to say it was his easygoing manner. Women relaxed around him, talked to him naturally, nothing forced. When you made people feel at ease around you, they liked you, and when women liked you, they wanted to go to bed with you. At least that was how it worked in Kilmer's experience.

Because of AIDS, condoms were in these days. Kilmer always insisted on using one, and a lot of the women he met insisted as well. His father had always said that using a rubber was like taking a shower with a raincoat on, but Kilmer didn't find prophylactics objectionable. The sex act was nice, but it was the finale, the conclusion of the fun. What you did getting there—the part that didn't involve protection—was just as important as the act itself, if not more so. Kilmer was a good lover. He tried to make sure his partner experienced every last bit of pleasure she was capable of having.

As he lay there, sleep still eluding him, Kilmer found himself thinking about Amanda Price. Although she was nearly ten years older than he was, Amanda Price had the looks to get the attention of any man who wasn't attracted to other men. Though nice, her legs and figure weren't what did it. It was something about her face, the way her dark hair set off her big green eyes, her warm smile, her small, upturned nose. She was one of the few women at the TV station who had successfully resisted Kilmer's charms. Not that he'd really tried. He'd never really tried. He was just a nice friendly guy who put people at ease. He'd done most of Amanda's field camera work for the last year. Amanda had been at ease. But nothing had happened. It worked that way sometimes.

He wondered where Amanda was. Nobody seemed to know. He wasn't even sure whether Bob Miller knew. A guy had tried to grab her, and a few days later he'd tried to grab her daughter. Amanda had panicked and run. It seemed to him she might have overreacted, but then it wasn't his decision to make. You come right down to it, it wasn't really any of his business. As Dick Kilmer came to that conclusion he sank slowly into sleep.

He was dreaming that somebody was poking him with a pipe. He was shooting the mayor's weekly news conference, and somebody was standing behind him, poking him with a length of pipe. Leaving the tripod-mounted camera to take care of itself, Kilmer angrily turned around, prepared to yank the pipe away from whoever was pestering him with it. Muttering an obscenity, Kilmer flopped over onto his back and found himself wide awake.

The lights came on.

Blinking, still half asleep, Kilmer tried to find the details of the room in the glare. Beside him, Bernadette groaned, buried her face in the pillow. Kilmer sat up, squinting, his eyes adjusting to the light, his surroundings coming into focus. A man stood by the light switch.

He had a gun.

And Kilmer had seen enough movies and TV cop shows to recognize the fat cylinder fitted to the automatic's barrel. It was a silencer. Kilmer's grogginess vanished, the way a close call can sober a drunk. His heart was pounding madly, the sound reverberating in his head, the blood rushing by his eardrums like white-water rapids.

"Get up," the man said.

He was tall and thin with a lean face that remained expressionless, almost as if he were bored. There was something odd about his eyes, as if they weren't flesh and blood but something painted by an artist who lacked the talent to put life into his work.

"Get up," the man said again, his tone making it clear that he was definitely serious.

Kilmer slid his legs over the edge of the bed and stood, the covers falling away from his naked body. "What do you want?" he asked.

Bernadette sat up, rubbing her eyes, the covers slipping off her small breasts. "Dick, what the hell's going on?"

Then she saw the man and quickly pulled the covers up over her breasts, her eyes widening. She looked at Kilmer questioningly.

"Stay in bed and keep quiet," the man told her. Bernadette stared at him with terror-filled eyes and said nothing.

To Kilmer he said, "Get dressed."

Kilmer obeyed, feeling strangely distant from his actions. Hands pulled on his briefs, his T-shirt, his slacks. He was uncertain whose hands they were, although they didn't seem to be his. Finally he stood there, fully dressed.

"Good," the man said. He swung the pistol toward Bernadette, and it coughed twice, holes appearing in the covers she was holding across her chest. A look of total disbelief appeared on her face. Her mouth hanging open, she stared at the man who'd just shot her, and then her eyes seemed to lose their focus, and she toppled sideways onto the bed, the covers slipping down, exposing the side of one breast.

Stunned, Kilmer stared at her, his brain refusing to accept what it had just seen. The man stepped over to him, jabbing the gun into the small of Kilmer's back.

"Move," he said.

But Kilmer was unable to move. His body seemed rigid, as if it had petrified into a Dick Kilmer of stone that would forever stand there and stare at the bed in which Bernadette Cole had just been murdered, a statue erected to mark the spot where a young woman had died. He recalled the way her eyes had dimmed as life had left her. It was the same way the man's eyes looked. Out of the confusion of swirling thoughts in Dick Kilmer's brain emerged an insane but powerful notion.

I've just met Death, he thought.

Although Death appeared to be a man, it was unable to hide its true identity. To see through its facade you had only to look in its eyes.

"Move," Death said, more forcefully this time.

"Why?" Kilmer heard himself ask. "Why did you do it?"

"I couldn't leave her there to call for help, now could I?"

Kilmer made no attempt to answer.

"If you don't move," the killer said, "I'll do the same to you. What'll it be?"

Kilmer allowed himself to be guided out of the bedroom. "Where are we going?" he asked, his voice far away.

"We're going to the country, you and me. So we can have a little talk."

Though dazed, Kilmer knew the man was probably going to kill him. He tried to force his brain to work. He couldn't just go passively to his death.

As if aware of what Kilmer was thinking, the man said, "Don't do anything stupid, okay, Dick? Once we've had our little talk, you can go about your business."

Kilmer's apartment was on the second floor. They took the elevator down. The man guided him to a red car parked around the corner. A few blocks away, a cab went through an intersection; otherwise the city seemed deserted. Kilmer wished with all his might for a police car to come down the street, but none appeared.

Opening the rear door of the red car, the man said, "Get in."

Realizing that this was probably going to be his only chance to make a stand, Kilmer leaned forward, as if meekly complying then pushed away from the car, whirling around as he did so and launching a wild swing at his adversary. The man might shoot him, he knew that, but it was simply a chance he had to take.

The man, apparently anticipating such a move, stepped nimbly out of the way of Kilmer's desperate roundhouse punch. Then a fist rammed into Kilmer's gut, doubling him over. Bile rose in his throat, and his lungs were struggling to suck in air that didn't seem to be there, as if he'd been shoved into a vacuum. He tried to straighten himself, to continue the fight, but no amount of willpower could force his body to act. Quickly moving behind him, the man slipped a cloth over Kilmer's face, and when he was finally able to take in a desperately needed breath, it smelled of a strong chemical.

A moment later he was falling.

Tumbling into bottomless blackness.

Opening his eyes, Kilmer saw daylight. He was in the backseat of a car. There wasn't room for him to stretch his legs out; he felt sore and stiff. The rear door of the car opened, cold air rushing in, and he was pulled into a sitting position. He felt nauseous. His head felt as heavy as an oversize cannonball.

Death was looking at him.

Blinking his surroundings into focus, he saw that he was somewhere in the woods. Snow, leafless trees, isolation. And Death, he thought groggily. Can't forget about Death.

"You ready for our little chat?" the man asked.

Kilmer made no attempt to answer. If he opened his mouth, he might throw up.

"Where is she?" the man asked.

"Who?"

"Amanda Price."

"Amanda?"

"Yes. Where is she?"

"I don't know."

"Tell me what you do know."

"She's on a leave of absence. Nobody knows where she went." The contents of Kilmer's stomach rose, then settled back down. This, he realized, had to be the man who'd tried to grab Amanda and her daughter.

"Surely she told you, her number-one cameraman."

"She didn't tell anybody. I swear it."

"No one?"

"The only one who might know is Bob Miller, the news director, and I'm not even sure he knows."

"Who was the man whose face and voice were electronically distorted?"

It took his drugged brain a moment to figure out what man he was talking about. "You mean the guy in Amanda's New Shipton series?"

"Yes. You shot the tape for that, so you saw his face. You know who he is."

"I don't know who he is."

"Don't make me angry, Dick. That would be a mistake."

"I don't know. I swear I don't."

"What'd he look like, then?"

"I don't know."

"You saw him, didn't you? I'm running out of patience here, Dick."

"Yeah, I saw him, but he was wearing a ski mask. He said he'd be doubly protected. He'd wear the ski mask *and* be electronically distorted. It's the truth. It's what he wanted."

"Who besides Amanda knows who he is?"

"Nobody. Just her."

The man yanked Kilmer out of the car. The contents of Kilmer's stomach rose unstoppably and spewed from his mouth. The man let go of him, and Kilmer leaned against the car, vomiting into the snow, icy perspiration beading on his forehead. Finally he had a few dry heaves and then his stomach settled. The man led him to a picnic table, guided him onto a snow-covered bench. Kilmer was barely aware of the cold seeping in through the seat of his pants.

Sitting down across the table from him, the man said,

"Now we're going to find out if you've been telling the truth."

Kilmer just stared at him.

Brushing the snow off the table, the man placed an object on it. It looked like a cigar cutter.

"These used to be popular once upon a time," the man said. "As you can see, it's a miniature guillotine with a razor-sharp blade. Actually it's a trick guillotine. You're supposed to be able to put your finger into it, slam the blade down, and nothing happens. Looks like magic. But this one's been fixed so the trick feature won't work."

For the first time Kilmer saw something come into the man's strange eyes, the hint of a gleam. The sight made Dick Kilmer start to tremble uncontrollably.

"Put your finger into the guillotine," the man said. He was pointing the gun at Kilmer's head.

Buchanan used a pay phone in the heated entrance of a suburban discount store to call New Shipton. Because people were going in and out, he was cautious about the words he used.

"The gentleman I spoke to was unable to answer my questions," he said.

"You mean it was a different cameraman?"

"No. He was the one."

"Then why couldn't he tell you?"

"The, uh, person he was dealing with was dressed for skiing."

"He was wearing a ski mask during the interview?"

"Seems he was a little paranoid."

"Crap."

"This means more messy business, I'm afraid."

"What do you mean, 'you're afraid'? You *like* messy work."

Buchanan said nothing.

"Do what you gotta do," the voice from New Shipton said.

• • •

Amanda sat in the recliner, reading another book she'd borrowed from the Heikkinens. This one was the book-club edition of *Watchers* by Dean R. Koontz. Barbara Heikkinen belonged to three book clubs. She'd joined them, she explained, because it was the only way to get the current books without driving forty-five miles to the closest bookstore.

It was Saturday, and Ashley was off snowshoeing with Eric Carlson. Since meeting Eric, Amanda's daughter had certainly discovered a wealth of new interests. Shortwave radio, snowshoeing, and she'd even mentioned the possibility of attempting cross-country skiing—with Eric, of course. This from a girl who'd once referred to boys as slimy scuzballs.

They'd finally had the Talk, which turned out to be a lot more traumatic for Amanda than for her daughter. Amanda had stumbled and fumbled her way through the things she thought the girl should know about sex, only to find out that Ashley already knew all of it, wasn't the least bit embarrassed by any of it, and understood that doing it could get you pregnant—even the first time.

Ashley had asked a couple of questions about birth control, which Amanda answered, and they both agreed that if, a few years hence, Ashley felt she needed birth control, her mother would arrange it. Amanda had put great stress on the part about a few years hence. To Amanda that meant about eight years hence, and she hoped Ashley didn't interpret it to mean three or four.

In any case, her daughter had reached the age at which she started to find boys interesting, armed with all the information her mother could give her—even if the girl had already known most of it.

Ted Anderson was stopping by every other day or so, ostensibly to check on her, make sure the man with the weird eyes hadn't located her. They both knew this was just something they were telling themselves, because that was less complicated than dealing with all the complexities admitting to a relationship would involve. Amanda's concern that Ashley might resent Ted's intrusion into their lives had been unfounded. The girl genuinely seemed to like Ted. He'd stopped by one evening carrying a Monopoly game, set up the board on the living-room floor, and asked who wanted to play. Ashley had been delighted. When the game ended, the board had been awash in little red plastic hotels, nearly all of them Ashley's. Amanda and Ted had been soundly trounced.

Amanda's finances had reached the state at which she'd started wishing all that Monopoly money was real. Instead of sending Amanda's money, her Boston bank had mailed her some forms to be filled out and notarized. She was becoming frustrated at how difficult it was for her to get her own money. Having little choice, she'd driven into town and located the only notary, a man named Toivo Kuusisto, who was also the local real-estate agent, insurance salesman, income-tax preparer, and accountant. Fiddlehead Lake apparently wasn't big enough to support much in the way of specialists.

She'd stopped by the store to let the Carlsons know her money hadn't arrived yet but that she'd pay her bill just as soon as it did. Clarence Carlson had said he was sure she was an honest person, that she could pay up when she was able, not to worry. In the meantime, anything she needed could go on the tab.

Several days had passed since she'd heard anything from Boston, which she assumed meant Bob Miller had nothing to report. Perhaps the man with the peculiar eyes had given up. Unbidden, the image of what had happened that day at the shopping mall popped into her head. She felt the man grab her, hold her with his incredible strength. She looked into his eyes.

Amanda shivered as fear gripped her insides with icy fingers. She shouldn't remember that day, shouldn't think about the man at all. Ashley and she were safe here. There was no way he could find them. And yet fear's icy fingers refused to relax their grip.

Deep down inside, did she really believe they were safe? Or was she just hoping, trying to convince herself? Putting down the book, Amanda closed her eyes, tilted the chair back, forced herself to think about something else. Clearly her stay here was going to be a long one. Maybe she should enroll Ashley in school. Amanda thought of Ashley on the school bus, taking the fifteen-mile ride to the nearest junior high school. The girl would be gone the whole day, in a place where Amanda wouldn't know what was happening to her, couldn't help her. Abruptly a new image popped into Amanda's head: the man following the school bus, waiting for his chance to grab her daughter.

Stop it, Amanda told herself. She was making monsters where there didn't need to be any. Only Bob Miller knew where she was, and he understood the need for absolute secrecy. She was safe. Ashley was safe. Everything was all right. Ashley was off somewhere snowshoeing, and Amanda had been worried that she might wander into the woods and get lost, her body and Eric's not being found until spring, their remains half eaten by wild animals. She'd heard there were timber wolves around, and bears. It was a mother's job to worry about such things, and Amanda had let these concerns trigger her other fears as well.

"Well, it's time to stop this nonsense," she said aloud to the empty room.

Suddenly uncertain about what she expected to accomplish, Amanda picked up the phone and called Mrs. O'Donnell, the old woman who lived across the hall from her in Boston.

"Hi," she said when the phone was answered. "It's me, Amanda."

"Amanda! How are you? Are you back?"

Mrs. O'Donnell was a good friend, so Amanda had told her why she was leaving. Not being able to tell her where she was going, Amanda had—rather limply, looking back on it—told her she didn't know precisely where she was headed. Now the old woman would want to known where she was, and Amanda would have to find some way to avoid telling her.

She said, "No, I'm not back. I'm still out of town. I just called to see whether everything was all right."

"Where are you calling from? Are you and Ashley okay?"

"We're fine."

"Well, where are you?"

"I'm just checking to make sure everything's okay," Amanda said, ignoring the question. "Anything happen I should know about?"

"No problems at all. I've been watering your plants, following your instructions to the letter."

"Thank you. I appreciate that, I really do."

"Amanda, is there some reason why you don't want to tell me where you are?"

Amanda hesitated, drawing in a slow breath. She said, "I'm sorry, but . . . well, I just can't tell anyone where I am. I guess all I can do is ask you to understand. I'm fine and Ashley's fine. We're perfectly safe."

"Amanda, I don't mind telling you all this is a little scary. Are you sure everything's all right?"

"We're fine. Honest."

Mrs. O'Donnell was silent for a moment, then she said, "When will you be back?"

"I don't know. Probably not for a while. I hope I'm not imposing by asking you to keep on watering the plants for me."

"Oh, no. It's no bother at all."

"Well, thank you again. I'm sorry I have to be so mysterious about everything, but I wanted to keep in touch even so."

"I'm glad you called. I was wondering about you. I'm glad to know you're all right."

"I guess I'd better go now."

"Oh, I just remembered. Your uncle was looking for you."

"My uncle?"

"He said he was from out of town somewhere. Detroit. Or was it Denver?"

The icy fingers were back, squeezing with all their might. Amanda could feel her arms crawling with gooseflesh. Her only uncle lived in Iowa. "What . . . what else did he say?"

"Just that he was dropping in unexpectedly, hoping to surprise you, and nobody was home. He wondered if I knew where you were. I told him you were away and that I didn't know for how long or where you'd gone."

"When was this?"

"Oh, dear, let me see. It was several days ago. I don't recall the exact day. Too bad you missed him after he went to all the trouble of stopping by."

"What did he look like?"

"Let me think a moment. Oh, I'd say he was over six feet tall. Thin, real thin, but strong-looking, if you know what I mean. Probably one of those joggers, someone who takes care of himself."

"What about his eyes?"

"His eyes?"

"Was there anything unusual about them?"

"Well, yes, now that you mention it. I know a woman whose husband collects toy soldiers—antique ones. And, well, if you don't mind my saying so, your uncle's eyes reminded me of the eyes on those toy soldiers, sort of painted on. Does that make any sense?"

To Amanda it made a great deal of sense. The gooseflesh had spread to her thighs, and a chill was working its way up her spine.

"Do you know which uncle he was?" Mrs. O'Donnell asked.

"I know who it was," Amanda said.

TWELVE

"But he didn't learn anything," Ted said. "You knew he'd try."

They were sitting on Amanda's couch. The deputy had shown up about an hour after her telephone call to Mrs. O'Donnell. Looking out the window and seeing his car in the drive, Amanda had been filled with relief, barely able to resist the temptation to throw herself into his arms. And now, as she sat here on the couch with him, Amanda wondered why she'd held back. Explanations circled in her head like debris sucked into a whirlwind, but she was uncertain whether any of them made sense.

Because the threat hanging over her made this a bad time to get too deeply involved with anyone.

Because she was afraid to have a serious relationship with any man, ever.

Because she wasn't certain what Ted's reaction would be.

But these were just speculations, confused random thoughts. Her feelings about Ted were all mixed up, too jumbled to unravel. There was a part of her, she knew, that wished she hadn't held back, that wanted him to hug her and comfort her and tell her everything was all right.

"It's just that he's trying so hard," Amanda said. "He'll never give up."

"It's not how hard he tries," Ted said, "but whether he has any luck."

Amanda shuddered. "How do I know he isn't having any luck?"

"Did he find anything at the TV station? Did your neighbor in Boston know anything that would help him?"

169

"No, but I don't know what else he's tried. Maybe something worked."

"What could he try?"

"I don't know."

"Listen, I don't blame you for being scared. That man's clearly no one to fool around with. But you're making a nervous wreck out of yourself. It seems pretty unlikely that he can find you." While Ted had been talking, he'd taken her hand. He was looking into her eyes. "And if he did locate you, you'd need to have your wits about you. Have you thought about what you'd do?"

Amanda shook her head.

"Make a plan, just in case. Consider what weapons you have available, what exits you could use to get out of the house in a hurry, what you could do to make the place more secure. Think of it like preparing for a fire. You don't ever expect to have one, but it's a good idea to be prepared, regardless."

"Yes," she said. Ted was right. Instead of just worrying all the time she should think about fighting back, trying to survive, just in case.

"What about Ashley? She's off with Eric, snowshoeing. She wants to go cross-country skiing with him. A thirteen-year-old boy who can't protect her."

"No, he can't. But you can't keep her locked up in the cabin, either. A girl her age needs to get out, needs contact with other kids. All you can do is tell her to be cautious but without scaring the daylights out of her. Make sure she understands the need for caution but don't terrorize her."

"It could be a fine line," Amanda said unhappily.

"Not really. She already knows what's going on. All you have to do is tell her to keep her eyes open. Tell her what I just told you, that it's like a fire. It's pretty unlikely you'll have one, but it pays to be careful, to take a few precautions. That's not too scary. Besides, Ashley's a good kid, with a level head on her shoulders. Look at how well she handled the attempt to grab her after school and the incident in Pennsylvania. The way she's coped with all that should make you proud of her."

"It does," Amanda said.

"Well, she's had a good mother, someone who cared, raised her right." He was still holding her hand, still looking into her eyes. He smiled.

For a moment they just sat there like that, looking into each other's eyes. And then Ted was leaning toward her, his lips approaching hers, his arm slipping around her. Automatically Amanda's arm slid around him, her lips parting to accept his. The kiss was gentle, more tender than passionate, and when it ended, Ted pulled back a little, studying her face, apparently waiting for permission to continue.

Amanda stared at him, dazed. And then, barely even aware that she was doing it, she pulled him to her again. This time the kiss was longer, more passionate. Little prickles erupted throughout her body, long dormant desires suddenly awakened. When the kiss ended, Amanda realized that Ted's breathing was abnormally rapid. It took her a moment to realize that hers was too.

"Should . . . should we be doing this?" she asked, surprised at the husky breathiness of her voice.

"What do you think?" Ted said. He gently caressed her cheek with a finger, sending a whole new wave of tingles surging through her.

"I don't know what I think," she said. "But I don't want to stop."

They kissed again, with still more fervor, his tongue exploring her mouth, then withdrawing so hers could explore his. He hugged her tightly, breathing gently in her ear, nibbling its lobe. They kissed again, his hand finding her thigh, softly stroking it through the material of her jeans. Desire erupted like a blaze, her legs parting, inviting him to touch its source. She was already moist, wanting him, needing him.

Their clothes began to come off, each of them undressing the other. He unhooked her bra with one hand, slid it off.

He cupped her breasts, admiring them, and then his tongue was on her nipple, circling it, teasing it, sending waves of pleasure swirling through her.

"Oh, God," she heard herself moan.

Then they were heading toward the bedroom, each one leading the other. Already naked, they slipped under the covers, pulling themselves tightly together. His fingers found her clitoris, gently stroked it, while her hands found his erection. He groaned. Just as Amanda thought she was about to explode, he gently guided her astride him and entered her.

When it was over, they lay in bed, just holding each other. Amanda felt drained. "I wasn't expecting that to happen," she said.

"Neither was I," Ted replied. "But I'm glad it did."

"It never happened three times before," she said. With Tom, orgasms had been few and far between.

"You've never been in the hands of a master before."

She leaned on one elbow. "Not only is he a great lover but he's humble too."

"And good-looking."

"Umm, if you like the macho-cop type."

"Am I the macho-cop type?" He seemed worried about it.

Amanda pretended to think it over. "I guess not. But you are a great lover."

He grinned at her. "It takes two to make great love."

"Why, Ted," she said in a mock Southern accent, "I do believe that was a compliment."

"You're a perceptive devil."

She snuggled tightly against him. "I wouldn't mind doing that once a day."

"Only once?"

"You haven't proved you're up to more than just once yet."

"That a challenge?"

"Me, a respected journalist from Boston, going around hurling sexual innuendos at rural policemen?"

"In these particular circumstances your words did seem to hint at things sexual, yes."

"Who the hell was hinting?" she asked, and nibbled on his earlobe. "That was a double-dog dare, an out-and-out challenge. Let's see what you can do, mister."

"Oh, my God," he said, putting his hand on his forehead. "I'm going to become a sex slave, held captive so my body can be ravished mercilessly."

"You only wish," she said, and they both laughed.

They made love again, and it was nearly as good as the first time. Afterward they lay in the afterglow, lazily drifting toward sleep. Ted broke the silence.

"I realize this wasn't supposed to happen," he said, "but I think I'm falling in love with you."

Amanda didn't know what to say. She wasn't even sure how she felt about him. Attracted by him, yes, in all sorts of different ways, but he seemed to be suggesting a commitment she wasn't sure she could make.

"You're supposed to say you're falling in love with me too," Ted said.

"Ted, I . . . well, maybe I am. But if we let this thing happen, where will it take us?"

"The only way to find out is to try it and see."

"But we barely know each other."

"That's easily taken care of."

"I don't know how long I'm going to be here. Eventually I'm going back to Boston, resume my career. What happens to us then?"

"Why worry about that now?"

"Well, because we have to."

"No we don't. I think we've got a nice thing here, don't you?"

"It's nice, yes."

"Let's see where it takes us for however long it can last. What's wrong with that?"

"It's so . . ." She searched for the right word.

"Risky?"

"Yes, risky."

"I'm willing to chance it if you are."

She was silent for a moment, then said, "So am I." And she realized a part of her had known all along that's what she would say.

"Let's see if we can find some way to seal the bargain." He began kissing her neck.

"Again? You're kidding."

He wasn't kidding.

Bob Miller's BMW hit a bump in the road, causing something in the back to rattle. Miller frowned. Cars this expensive weren't supposed to rattle. He'd just finished playing racquetball with Rex Danielson, the TV station's general manager. Although Miller wasn't particularly fond of racquetball, the boss was, and joining him on the court from time to time was good politics. Which, he supposed, was a euphemism for sucking ass. But what the hell, a little ass sucking now and then—along with good ratings—kept him in the expensive house in the Boston suburbs and enabled him to afford the German-made status symbol he was driving.

Stopping at a red light, he picked up the car's telephone and punched out his home number. Miller was on a minor two-lane thoroughfare lined with leafless trees that would turn the street into a tunnel of shade come summer. Never having liked expressways, he stuck to the smaller roads whenever he could. His wife answered the phone.

"Hello." There seemed to be something odd about her voice.

"Anything wrong, Mary?"

There was a brief silence, then she said, "Uh, no. I . . . I just had a frog in my throat."

"Gee, Mary, you'll eat anything."

He expected her to laugh, but she didn't. She didn't say anything.

"I just called to let you know that I'm on my way. Be there in about fifteen."

"Okay," she said lightly. "See you then." She broke the connection.

Frowning, Miller hung up the phone. Why had she sounded so . . . so tight? Had one of the kids done something horrible, so atrocious that she wasn't going to tell him about it? She did that sometimes, to spare them the good scolding—and occasionally the good paddling—they'd get from him. Mary spoiled them hopelessly. Her idea of discipline was that if the kids were about to blow up the house, she might step in and politely ask them not to because it would make such a mess. He decided that's probably what it was, something he'd learn about a month or two from now, most likely at breakfast. True confessions over Count Chocula and Suger Frosted Flakes.

His phone rang. It was Julia, one of the weekend reporters. "Sorry to bother you, Mr. Miller," she said. "But there's a police officer here to see you, a Sergeant Ryan."

Miller said he'd be there in about twenty minutes, then he called his wife to tell her he'd be delayed. Again her voice seemed strained, but Miller dismissed it from his thoughts. Whatever the problem was, he'd learn about it eventually. Mary worried too much about things. She didn't know how to relax, go with the flow.

He wondered whether he should tell the policeman about Dick Kilmer. The cameraman had failed to show up for work the last few days. Miller's secretary had phoned him, getting no answer, but the guys Kilmer's age did things like that sometimes. After a few days of shacking up with some woman or an unauthorized trip to Florida they'd show up with some lame excuse and expect everything to be all right. They always seemed so surprised when Miller would tell them it wasn't all right and fire them. He shook his head. Young people today had no sense of responsibility. To them life was a big party, do whatever you want. And then they looked so wounded when it was time to reap the consequences.

Kilmer was one of his best cameramen, and he hoped the young man would come back with proof that he'd been suffering from amnesia or something like that, which was about the only way he'd be able to keep his job. The news director sighed. He supposed he should get the photo director to start looking for a replacement.

As it turned out, Miller didn't have to mention Kilmer to the policeman, because as soon as the two men were seated in the news director's office, Sergeant Ryan said, "You have a guy named Dick Kilmer working for you?"

"Yes," Miller said, bracing himself for what he was sure would be bad news.

"When did you last see him?"

"A few days ago. Why?"

"He's dead."

"Dead? What happened?"

"Found his body out by Quabbin Reservoir. Some guys snowmobiling discovered it. You got any idea why he'd be out there?"

"No, none. How did he die?"

"Somebody shot him."

The news director was stunned. "Shot him?"

"In the head. At close range."

"Jesus Christ," Miller said, stunned. "What the hell was he into?"

"That's what we'd like to know," the cop said.

"I . . . I don't know anything that will help you. He was good at his job, one of the best I've got—or had, I guess I should say. I don't know anything about his private life. I heard he was a real ladies' man, making it with a different woman every night. But . . . well, that's just what I heard."

"There was a woman in his apartment when we checked

it out," the cop said. "She was dead, shot with the same gun."

Miller stared at the detective, dumbstruck. Finally he found his voice. "Guys like Kilmer, guys who have a lot of women, sometimes they get into trouble with husbands, jealous boyfriends. You think that's what happened?"

"At first I thought it might be. The dead woman was in Kilmer's bed, naked. Her name was Bernadette Cole. Mean anything to you?"

Miller shook his head, waited to hear the rest.

"The first thing that made me have my doubts about it being a jealous husband or boyfriend was the other thing that had been done to Kilmer. All the fingers of his left hand had been cut off. A rejected lover usually doesn't go that far. One could, of course, but they don't usually."

"My God," Miller said. He felt as if an icicle had just formed in his gut.

"In the meantime we've learned that the girl wasn't married and hadn't been real deeply involved with anyone for quite some time. The jealous-lover theory was getting pretty weak, but it still seemed possible until this morning, when we had ballistics compare the bullets from Kilmer and the girl with another bullet we have—one we dug out of a stud in the wall over there." He inclined his head toward the spot where the security guard had been killed.

"You mean, Kilmer was shot by the same guy who killed Porterfield?" The chunk of ice in Miller's midsection was growing as the implications of what he'd just learned began to dawn on him.

"Kilmer, Bernadette Cole, and Porterfield, all killed with the same weapon," the cop said. He was studying Miller's face, looking for his reaction.

"What does it mean?" the news director asked.

The detective was still studying him, his eyes asking if maybe there wasn't something Miller would like to tell him, something he'd been holding back. Miller forced himself to meet the policeman's gaze, hoping he didn't have the sheepish look of a little kid who'd just told a big lie, knowing there wasn't a chance he'd be believed.

Kilmer had been Amanda's cameraman on the New Shipton series. Someone killed the woman Kilmer was with, took him out into the boonies, and tortured him. The same guy who'd killed a security guard here at the station after looking through Amanda's desk. Poor Kilmer, the news director thought. The cameraman didn't know what the killer wanted to learn. How much agony had he endured, with no way to end it by telling the man what he wanted to know? Miller tried to tell himself he had no proof that it had worked that way, that he was just making assumptions.

I'm the only one who has the information the killer wants, Miller thought. His internal organs seemed to have stopped working, as if they had just frozen solid.

"Something wrong, Mr. Miller?"

"No," he said. "I . . . I was just thinking about Kilmer, what was done to him. Was he mutilated after . . ." He let his words trail off.

"No. He was alive."

Miller had known that would be the cop's answer, but he'd had to ask, just in case he'd figured it out wrong. The detective was still looking at him, waiting for him to say something. The news director had absolutely no idea what to do.

If there was any chance at all that he was in danger, he should tell the detective where Amanda was. And yet he was still certain that whatever he told the Boston police would promptly be learned by the New Shipton police, who were controlled by the corrupt officials running the town. Cops had all sorts of back channels of information. Could he put Amanda in jeopardy like that?

Then something Amanda had said came back to him. One of the reasons she was so insistent on leaving was that there was no way the cops could protect her. They were talking strike, and in any case, they didn't have the manpower to give her twenty-four-hour security. Well, nothing had changed. A police strike was still possible, and the cops couldn't protect him and his family twenty-four hours a day, either. Hell, in his case they probably wouldn't even consider it. No one had attacked him.

Whenever anyone asked, he said he didn't know where Amanda was. That word could have filtered back to the man who was after her. Still, if there was even the remote possibility that he'd put himself and his family in danger, he owed it to them to let them know. When he got home, he'd tell his wife. Inwardly he groaned. Mary would be worried sick. She fretted over the possibility that a car payment would get lost in the mail and their credit rating would be ruined, so what would she do with the notion that a hired killer could be after them?

Miller decided he should tell Amanda what had happened, then talk it over with his wife. If Mary wanted him to tell the police about Amanda, he'd let Amanda know what he was going to do, give her a chance to get out of the cabin, just in case the New Shipton cops decided to have her picked up by the Minnesota authorities on some phony charge, then he'd get in touch with Sergeant Ryan, tell him everything.

"You look like you're wrestling with something," the detective said.

"Wrestling with something? Like what?"

The detective shrugged. "You tell me."

"I can't get all this out of my mind," the news director said. "We see death and suffering all the time in the news business, but it's different when it's somebody you know. Those people in the stories, they're always strangers. I can't stop thinking about Kilmer, what it must have been like."

For a long moment the cop just sat there, his eyes fixed on Miller's. Finally he said, "I'll need to talk to the people who knew Kilmer."

"You already have the names and addresses of everyone

in the department. They all knew him, of course, but I can tell you who he was most friendly with."

"Please," the detective said.

After the police officer had gone, Miller called Amanda, telling her what had happened and that he hadn't mentioned her to Sergeant Ryan because of his fear that the New Shipton cops would learn her whereabouts. He didn't inform her that he was going to reevaluate that decision after talking things over with his wife. There was no point in worrying her about it yet. Amanda had started crying when she heard what was done to Kilmer; she was already upset enough.

THIRTEEN

A peculiar numbness spread throughout her body as Amanda hung up the phone. She sat on the couch, staring at a spot on the wall. The room seemed abnormally quiet, the silence almost a presence in the house. She could hear the beating of her heart, the shallow inhaling and exhaling of her breath.

Although she tried not to think about Dick Kilmer's ordeal, about the unspeakable agony and terror he'd endured, her mind kept seeing his fingers come off one by one, feeling his pain, as if she had been inside him at the time. Realistically she didn't know how it happened, what implements had been used for the amputating, but the images seemed no less real, no less terrifying.

Amanda held up her hands, made sure all her fingers were there.

It was her fault. The pain Dick Kilmer had endured, the death of the woman he'd been with. All of it, all her fault. Dick had been tortured to force him to reveal where she and Ashley had gone. And he hadn't known. He'd had no way to end his torment. The images of horror refused to leave her mind. She knew who had done this to the cameraman. She saw his dull, expressionless eyes staring at her, devoid of human feelings. Then he snipped off one of Kilmer's fingers, and the eyes began to glow.

Amanda heard a sound that made her jump. It took her a moment to realize that she had made the noise herself. A short, high-pitched yelp of pure terror.

Someone she'd worked with and liked was dead because of her—along with the security guard and the young woman whose body had been found in Kilmer's apartment. How many people would die? Were she and Ashley truly safe here, or was it only a matter of time until the man found them?

Suddenly panic seized her, and Amanda rushed into the bedroom, got her suitcase from the closet, opened it on the bed. She'd pack her things, then Ashley's, and as soon as the girl got back from snowshoeing, they'd leave. Hurrying to the dresser, Amanda scooped up the contents of the top drawer, carried them to the suitcase, and dumped them into it, dropping a bra as she went. She picked up the bra, flung it at the bag, missing it, and hurried back to the dresser, yanking open the second drawer down. Then she stopped, suddenly uncertain whether she was doing the right thing. She had no money to run with—to buy gas and lodging on the way, to get a place to stay once she got there. There? Where was there? She had nowhere to go.

And she had an unpaid bill at the general store, where her honesty had been accepted. She had Ted, and despite her confused feelings about the relationship, she didn't want to leave him. And if she did have to leave him, she couldn't just gather up Ashley and run away, disappear without a word.

Hopelessly confused, Amanda stared at the open dresser drawer. What should she do? Would she and her daughter be safer staying here or going elsewhere? Having almost no money, she might be forced to use her credit cards, which would leave a trail. The corrupt New Shipton officials had access to the FBI, the credit bureau, whatever they needed. How could you hide from people like that? Maybe this was the safest place she and Ashley could be. Amanda simply stood there, unable to sort out her thoughts, unable to reach a decision.

Suddenly she rushed back into the living room and picked up the phone, dialed the sheriff's substation.

"Sheriff's Department," a woman answered. It wasn't

Melinda but someone else, someone whose voice she didn't recognize.

"Ted Anderson, please."

"He's not in. Can I take a message?"

"Uh, this is Amanda Price out on Lakeshore Road. Could you tell him to stop by here as soon as he gets a chance?"

"Sure. Do you need him right away? Is it urgent?"

Amanda started to say it was but stopped herself. As far as she knew, the killer was still in Boston, still unaware of her hiding place. It was urgent to her because she was panicking, but to the authorities in Fiddlehead Lake, Minnesota, her circumstances weren't nearly so dire. She said, "Just sometime today. If he could. It's fairly important."

The woman said she'd pass the message along, and Amanda sank onto the couch. Now she had nothing to do but wait. Wait for Ted to come. Wait for the Carlsons to bring Ashley home. Amanda wished her daughter were there now, so she could see the girl, know she was safe. On the other hand, maybe it was just as well that Ashley wasn't able to see her mother this upset, this helpless and confused and terrified.

Amanda resisted the urge to look at her watch. No more than a few seconds had passed since she had put down the phone. Ted might not have even received her message yet. It could be hours before he got there. If he had calls to which he had to respond, he might not make it until tomorrow. Suddenly Amanda felt alone, a desert's worth of alone, a polar ice cap's worth of alone. She heard noises outside and hurried to the window, her heart pounding. A squirrel leapt from a spruce tree to the power line and scampered away like the nimblest of high-wire performers.

Amanda sat down again, and the loneliness washed over her like the granddaddy wave surfers dreamed of. Her body began to shake, and then tears were streaming down her cheeks.

• • •

Ted showed up about forty-five minutes after she'd called. Amanda had a good cry on his shoulder, then told him why she was so upset.

"It's my fault," she said. They were sitting together on the couch. Ted was holding her hand.

"For exposing a bunch of assholes?"

"I could have left it alone and no one would have been hurt."

"Except the people who got in their way."

"But *I* wouldn't have caused that."

"Look at it this way. Maybe people got hurt because of your actions, but other people might have been hurt through your inaction."

"I can't take the blame for those who got hurt because I *didn't* do a story."

"You can't take the blame for the ones who got hurt because of the story, either. You were doing a good thing, shedding some light on something that needed exposing badly. You were sort of like an X-ray machine exposing a cancer. What X-ray machines do is good. You don't blame them if the cancer is too nasty to be cured and the person dies. I wish more reporters did stories like the one you did. Instead we get traffic accidents and pointless banter."

"I don't feel like an X-ray machine. Or a crusading reporter, either. I feel like a naïve woman who stirred up something that should have been left alone."

Ted shook his head. "The scum in New Shipton are to blame. They were killers before you stirred them up. You're the good guy. They're the bad guys."

"Some knight in shining armor I am. I rode into battle without bothering to find out the rules of the contest, knowing in my heart that good would triumph—and that it would look great on my résumé."

"Hey," he said, taking her face in his hands, "stop being so hard on someone I'm quite fond of. She's a pretty special person to me, and I get offended when people say bad things about her."

"Gonna beat me up for badmouthing myself?" Amanda tried to manage a small smile, but it just wasn't in her. "What am I going to do?" she asked.

"Stay here and let the local law protect you. I hear that deputy they got over there has got an enormous crush on you."

"The local deputy's sweet," she said. "But he has other duties, other people to protect."

"True, but he doesn't have a crush on any of them."

Amanda sighed. "You're going to make me feel better no matter how desperately I want to be miserable, aren't you?"

"Being miserable doesn't help."

"No." She sighed. "But sometimes you can't help it. And I still don't know what I'm going to do."

"Stay put. I'd miss you too much if you left."

"What am I going to do to make sure Ashley and I don't end up like . . ." She let her words trail off.

"As I said, stay put. You have people here who care about you. If you run, you'll be all alone. You're short on money and you have nowhere to go."

"But . . . what if he finds me here?"

"Amanda, he could find you anywhere."

"Bob Miller knows where I am."

"So do the Heikkinens and the Carlsons and Melinda and some other people. Someone will always know where you are."

"But Bob Miller's in Boston."

"And so far we have no reason to believe the killer knows that Bob Miller knows. What did he tell the other people at the station?"

"That I'm on an extended leave of absence and that he doesn't know where I've gone."

"Maybe that situation's not perfect, but it beats heading off into the unknown with what little money you have left."

Amanda nodded. "You're right."

"Whew! For a minute there I thought you were going to get up and start packing."

"I already have."

"Will you unpack now?"

"Yes. I . . . well, I was just so scared when I heard what happened to Dick."

"I can understand that. I want you to keep on being scared, so you'll keep your guard up. But don't panic, okay? If something else happens, call me. Maybe I can figure something out. Maybe I could find another house to put you in, let everyone know that your whereabouts are to be kept secret."

"Like your place?" She did her best to give him an impish smile.

"I wish. My place happens to be a bunk bed at the substation. Not only is it barely big enough for one, but the bedsprings squeak." He eyed her lecherously.

Amanda laughed. A few minutes ago she would have believed herself incapable of it. "There's always my place," she said.

He looked wistfully at her. "In a community like this, everyone would know. Besides, what would Ashley say?"

"I know," she said. "I was just wishing it could be, that's all."

"You won't get any arguments from me."

They made small talk for another few minutes; then Ted said the good citizens of Fiddlehead needed protecting, and he had to go. As she watched him pull away, the loneliness settled over her again, but this time Amanda tried to fight it off. She watched TV until Ashley came home. The girl was exuberant. Snowshoeing was great. The Carlsons were fantastic. And Eric was . . . well, Eric was what she talked about for the rest of the day.

Amanda didn't mention the news from Boston.

Pulling into the driveway of his white two-story house, Bob Miller pushed the button on the remote control, and the left-side door of the attached two-car garage began going up. He drove through the opening, parking his BMW beside his wife's Pontiac station wagon.

At the door that led to the kitchen he pressed a button on the wall and the garage door began closing by itself. When he'd called Mary from the office to let her know he was once more on his way home, she'd acted strangely again. Because Mary was a worrywart, he was still pretty sure it was some minor thing that was troubling her. He dreaded telling her about Dick Kilmer. She might disintegrate, leaving behind nothing but a pile of shattered nerves.

On the other hand, people like Mary could fool you sometimes. Although they fell apart over little things, they could be rocks when it came to major disasters. Bob Miller had never been able to understand people like that.

"I'm back," he said, stepping into the kitchen.

No one answered, which probably meant everyone was in the den, which was at the other end of the house. Miller hung his jacket in the small coat closet by the door, then walked across the ceramic-tile floor to the side-by-side refrigerator-freezer. Looking into the refrigerator side, he spotted a Moosehead beer in its green bottle. He used an opener to remove the top without even checking to see whether it would twist off—those things were murder on your hand—and poured some of the frothy liquid into a beer glass. Miller leaned against the counter and took a swallow.

The kitchen was spacious, with oak cabinets, countertops made out of a synthetic material that looked like marble, and was practically indestructible, an island into which had been built one of those electric ranges with a continuous smooth surface, no visible cooking coils. The kitchen was one of the things that had sold them on the house. They'd moved three times in Minnesota, never once having a place with a truly nice kitchen.

Taking another gulp of beer, he ran his fingers through his blond hair. Mary was blond, too, and so were their two sons, Pete and Ryan, ages seven and nine respectively. In

Minnesota, where damn near everybody was blond, the Millers had fit right in, even though neither he nor Mary was Scandinavian. Miller, himself, was English-Irish; Mary was Polish and German.

He swallowed some more beer. He was just postponing his talk with Mary, he knew that. Ultimately he would have to march back to the den, explain the situation to her, see what happened. Drinking a beer and thinking about how to phrase it was just delaying the inevitable.

He drank some more beer, made no effort to move.

Miller didn't like being the only one who knew where Amanda was. Someone was looking for her, looking hard. Someone who was willing to kill people, to do terrible things to them. And yet he had no reason to believe that the man looking for Amanda would try to get the information from him. The word he'd put out had been that she hadn't told him where she was going. Why should she? A leave of absence was no different than a vacation in most respects, and employees going on vacation rarely left itineraries. In fact, if he hadn't offered Amanda his Minnesota cabin, he truly wouldn't have known where she was going.

Again he thought about what it must have been like for Dick Kilmer. A homicidal lunatic demanding to know where Amanda was. And Kilmer unable to tell him. The killer demanding the identity of the man whose face and voice had been distorted. Kilmer not knowing that, either, because the man had worn a ski mask during the interview. And because of what he didn't know, Kilmer had suffered.

Should have told Sergeant Ryan back at the station, Miller decided. Should have told him everything.

But that would have been the same thing as telling the people in New Shipton where to find Amanda and her daughter. He had to give Amanda some notice, so she'd have time to get away if that's what she wanted to do. And he had to talk to Mary about this, because he could have endangered her and the kids as well as himself.

Being a news director wasn't supposed to be like this.

You were supposed to worry about the ratings, your job security, the infighting between members of your staff. Those were the things that were supposed to turn your stomach so sour you were unable to sleep at night, not murderous madmen with zombie eyes. Miller had the feeling that he'd stepped into a script from *Friday the 13th* or *A Nightmare on Elm Street,* which was where crazed killers with zombie eyes belonged. They did *not* belong in real life. Especially in *his* life.

As he polished off the beer Miller wondered whether he'd ever assign another hard-hitting investigative piece. Suddenly stories like the kid's mammoth tree house or the dog that rescued its master seemed a lot safer, nice human-interest stuff that didn't piss anyone off. Miller shook his head. He'd run news departments like that, happy news and happy talk as dictated by the consultant. He'd done it because that's what he'd been hired to do, but he never liked it.

Getting another beer from the fridge, he headed for the den. Might as well get it over with, he decided. After all, what was the worst thing that could happen? His constantly anxious wife would have a nervous breakdown and go away to a hospital where everybody wore white pajamas, leaving him to take care of the kids. Hell, it wasn't as if anything *serious* could happen.

The house had four bedrooms, one for himself and Mary, one for each kid, and one for company. This was the first home of its size Miller had owned, and in a way he wished he didn't have that empty, available bedroom. Relatives, both his and Mary's, were always stopping by on their way to Maine or Canada, or sometimes just to see New England or just plain visit. And relatives were a pain in the ass. Miller stepped into the den. Mary and the boys were sitting on the couch, staring at him.

"Why are you looking at me like . . ." He let his words trail off because he'd just realized that the three of them were holding their hands behind their backs. As if they were tied. And their eyes were filled with terror.

Miller spun around.

And found himself looking at a man with a gun.

For a moment Miller just stared at the gun in the man's hand. He'd heard that robbery victims often couldn't remember anything *except* the gun, and now he knew why. The gray metal weapon was an evil-looking thing—instant pain, instant damage to your vital parts, instant death. He forced his gaze from the pistol to the man's face, and he immediately knew that this was the same man who'd attacked Amanda and her daughter. It was the eyes. The lifeless eyes of a corpse.

A part of Miller's mind was telling him, *Hey, you made it, man. Here you are in your own private* Nightmare on Elm Street. *An actual zombie has you and your family right where he wants you. And you know what? You're ankle-deep in shit, that's what.*

Miller stared at the man, speechless, his brain trying to tell him this isn't real, *couldn't* be real, and at the same time he was terrified because he knew it *was* real, because he knew this man was a flesh-and-blood killer, because he and his family were in terrible danger.

"Who are you?" Miller asked, his voice tremulous.

"Lie down on the floor," the man said.

Miller just stared at him.

"Lie down or I'll put a bullet in your leg. Your choice."

Miller complied, and the man tied the news director's hands behind him with a length of thin rope, which he pulled painfully tight.

Backing away from Miller, the man said, "Okay. Everybody up. We're going upstairs."

Miller stood, meeting the bewildered, terrified gazes of his wife and children. What would this man do to them? Would he hurt the children? Surely not, he told himself. No one would harm children.

The man waved the gun toward the doorway. "Go," he said.

Mary's eyes met his, trying desperately to communicate something, but Miller had no idea what. At least she seemed to be coping. She was afraid but not hysterical. They moved down the hallway in single file, Miller in front, then the two boys and Mary, all of them with their hands tied, the gunman following them. When they reached the stairway, Miller stopped, waited for further instructions.

"Up the stairs," the man said.

Miller led the way, his mind desperately searching for something he could do—anything. But with his hands tied, he was helpless. And even if he did have some way of resisting the man, he had no way of protecting the kids or Mary while he did so. Could he throw himself at the man, knock him down, yell for Mary and the boys to run? He didn't know. He didn't even know whether they *would* run. It was possible they'd just stare at him, too confused and afraid to do anything.

He also knew the man would kill him if he tried anything. *He'll kill you, anyway,* a part of Miller's mind said. But he didn't want to believe that. There had to be hope that they'd get out of this. There just had to be.

"In there," the man said as they reached the top of the stairs.

They moved into the master bedroom. It had always been a familiar, friendly place with its queen-size brass bed, Mary's big mirrored dressing table, the portable TV on which they watched late movies and Johnny Carson in bed at night. Mary had decorated the room, choosing wallpaper and carpet and curtains in varying but compatible shades of blue. But the room wasn't a cozy place anymore. The man with the gun had violated it. And the blues seemed icy, merciless.

Blocking the doorway, the man said, "You and you, sit down there with your back against the bed."

He'd indicated Mary and Ryan, but no one moved. All

four members of the Miller family were just standing there, as if too confused to make sense of even the simplest command.

"P-please," Mary said, her voice a high-pitched whisper. Her eyes met Miller's again, and they seemed to be pleading with him to do something. But Miller had no idea what to do.

The man aimed the gun at her legs. "Get on the floor or I'll put you there my way."

A shiver traveled through Mary's body, working its way from her head to her legs. Then she slowly sank to the floor.

"Put your back against the bed," the man said, and Mary scooted the three feet to the brass frame at its foot.

"Now the boy."

Ryan hesitated, eyeing the man defiantly, but his boldness was a momentary thing, and he lowered his gaze and complied with the man's order.

Looking at Miller, the man said, "Take the other boy into the corner and stay there."

Miller took Pete to the indicated corner. The man pulled a piece of cord from his pocket and tied Mary's already bound hands to the bed. Producing another piece of cord, he did the same to Ryan. Mary made a noise that was part gasp, part squeak.

"You and the boy," the man said to Miller. "Let's go."

He guided them down the hallway and into the main bathroom. Again he blocked the doorway. Looking at Pete, he said, "Get into the tub."

The seven-year-old looked at his father for direction, his blue eyes darting from his dad to the man with the gun.

"Why do you want him in the tub?" Miller asked.

"You'll see."

"Leave him alone. He's just a little boy. He's never done any harm."

The man aimed his gun at Pete's midsection. The boy stared at him, his face white, his eyes wide. He seemed incapable of moving. A tear trickled down his cheek.

"Either he gets in the tub or I'll shoot him in the belly. I don't care which."

"Pete," Miller said, "get in the tub. Go ahead. Get in."

Slowly the boy's gaze shifted from the gun to his father. He looked befuddled, as if his father's words hadn't made any sense.

"Pete, get into the tub. Please."

Hesitantly the boy stepped into the tub. When he was standing in it, the man said, "Sit down."

Pete obeyed slowly, as if every second he delayed might be a moment longer he could live. And Miller knew that might be the case. They could all have just moments left to live. He tried frantically to free his hands, but the cord held them tightly. His fingertips were numb.

The man pushed the lever that closed the drain, then turned on the water in the tub. The water reached the boy's shoes, then the cuffs of his pants.

"What are you doing?" Miller demanded. "Tell me what you're doing."

The man swung the gun from the boy to Miller. "Watch. You'll see."

"Please," Miller said. "Stop this."

Without answering, the man shifted his attention back to the tub. Pete, his hands still tied behind him, was sitting in water two inches deep now, staring at the two men in the room with eyes that seemed enormous. He was shaking.

The sound of the water flowing into the tub seemed unnaturally loud. It filled the room with noise, pounded the insides of Miller's skull. The water covered Pete's legs now, and it was still getting deeper. At least there was no steam rising from it. If the man had turned it on full hot, Pete would be getting scalded. Suddenly the man grabbed the boy, pulling him forward, pushing his head under the water, which bubbled around Pete's ears. The boy thrashed violently with his legs.

"No!" Miller screamed. "What do you want? Goddammit, tell me what you want!" He fought with his bonds with every bit of strength he owned, but the effort was useless.

Pete's struggle was getting weaker, and still the man held his head under the water. The water covered the boy's ears entirely now. A gurgling moan bubbled to the surface. That his hands were bound and that he'd be no match for this man even if they weren't suddenly didn't matter. Nor did the likelihood that he'd die. He couldn't just stand here and do nothing while his son drowned. Miller hurled himself at the man.

But his adversary had been expecting him to do just that. A blow landed in Miller's midsection, doubling him over. Then another blow landed on the back of his head, propelling him forward. His face hit the doorknob, the door itself slamming back into the wall so forcefully that the wood cracked and the doorstop popped loose and sailed across the room. Miller landed on the floor. Dazed, he sat up. He could feel the blood trickling from his nose. It took a moment or two for his vision to clear. Pete was sitting up in the tub, coughing, taking ragged breaths. At least Miller's charge had forced the man to release his drowning son.

The man was looking at him. "If I put the boy under water again, I won't let him up until he's dead. You want that?"

Miller seemed unable to find his voice. He shook his head.

"All right," the man said. "Who was the guy in Amanda Price's documentary?"

"I . . . I don't know," Miller said. "I swear it. Amanda never told me. She's the only one who knows."

"Where's Amanda Price?"

Miller hesitated, then said, "Florida. The Starlite Motel in Orlando."

"That's a lie," the man said.

He reached for Pete, and the boy tried to scramble out of the tub, but the man was too quick for him. Grabbing Pete by his shirt, he yanked him back into the water, pushed his head beneath the surface.

"Minnesota!" Miller screamed. "We've got a summer place there. We . . . we never sold it. Fiddlehead Lake. Route 1, Box 227-B."

"Where?" the man said, his eyes boring into Miller's.

"Fiddlehead Lake, Minnesota. Route 1, Box 227-B. Please let my boy up. Please. I've told you where she is."

"Who else knows?"

"No one."

"Not your wife?"

"No."

"No one at the TV station?"

"No. Let Pete up. Please. He's drowning."

The man let go of Pete, who sat up gasping, water running from his nostrils. Miller wanted to grab the boy, pull him from the tub, but he couldn't do it with his hands tied—even if the man would let him.

"Can he get out of the tub now?" Miller asked. "Please." He knew he was begging, but he didn't care. In places like Chile and South Africa, political prisoners had to beg their torturers. Passengers on hijacked planes had to beg their captors. Sometimes begging was all you could do.

"Get out of the tub," the man said, and Pete scrambled out, rushed over to Miller, still coughing and sucking in deep, ragged breaths. Miller wanted desperately to put his arms around the boy, hold him close, but his bonds made it impossible.

"I told you what you wanted to know," Miller said. "There's no reason for you to do anything else to us. I told you the truth. I swear it."

The man nodded. "I believe you," he said. He turned off the water, then opened the tub's drain. The water in which Pete had nearly drowned began flowing out.

What happens now? Miller wondered. There was a thought buried deep in the reaches of his subconscious, a horrible, terrifying thought he'd been trying to ignore. But now it asserted itself, swam doggedly toward the surface of his consciousness. The man couldn't let them live, couldn't let them warn Amanda before he got there, couldn't let them identify him.

Miller tried to think of something to say, find words that would persuade the man to let them live, convince him that neither he nor any of his family would say anything about what happened here today. But there were no words with that much power, no argument that would mean a thing to this uncaring monster, this killing machine with the inhuman eyes.

"Back to the bedroom," the man said. "Let's go."

Mary and Ryan were still tied to the bed. The boy looked at Miller with eyes that were full of confusion and fear, but Mary seemed unaware of his presence, as if she had withdrawn into a place deep within herself, a place that was safe, where horrors such as this did not occur.

Pete was sopping wet and covered with goose bumps. Water dripped onto the bedroom floor from the cuffs of his pants.

Fully aware that the man would be better off with them dead—no witnesses, no one to warn Amanda—Miller opened his mouth to do the only thing he could think of: beg. But before he could speak, Ryan leapt off the floor, dashed past their startled captor and into the hall. The boy's arms were free. Somehow he had untied himself.

Caught by surprise, the man hesitated before whirling around, stepping into the hall, and bringing up the gun. Knowing his son would be dead if he didn't do something, Miller rammed into the man as hard as he could, throwing off his aim. The gun fired, the bullet coming nowhere near Ryan, who had reached the stairs and started down them. Although Miller had fallen, the man had not. Ignoring Miller, the intruder went after the boy. Getting to his feet, Miller ran after the two. His bound hands making it impossible to grab anything for support, Miller tumbled down the last half of the stairs. At the bottom he scrambled to his feet in time to see the intruder rush down the short downstairs hall and into the den. Miller ran after him.

He heard a crash, and when he arrived in the den, the sliding glass door leading to the deck was in pieces, icy winter air rushing into the room. No more shots had been fired, so Ryan, unable to stop, must have run right through it. The man was standing in the doorway, looking to his left. Ryan must have made it. He *did* make it, Miller told himself. He did, he did.

Suddenly Miller realized he shouldn't just be standing there. There was something he could do now. Ryan had given him the chance. He rushed back down the hall. Mary, still deep within herself somewhere, was coming down the stairs with Pete. They both still had their hands tied behind their backs. After freeing himself apparently Ryan had untied the cord holding his mother to the bed, then run out of time before he could unbind her hands.

"Hurry," Miller said in an urgent whisper. "Let's get out of here." He backed up to the front door, turned the knob with his bound hands.

Although Pete was urging her on, Mary was still moving slowly, zombielike, as if unaware of anything around her.

"Goddammit, Mary!" Miller said. "Hurry!"

The door was open now. He left it, hurrying over to his wife, who'd just reached the bottom of the stairs. He used his body to herd her toward the door.

Suddenly, as if someone had switched her on, Mary came to life. For a moment her eyes met Miller's, and they were alert, filled with purpose. "Run!" she shouted at Pete. "Run!"

And then the man was there, looking at them with eyes that contained not the tiniest drop of human warmth. Turning toward the door through which Mary and Pete were fleeing, he raised the gun. Miller hit him with a low body block that knocked the man's legs out from under him. The man hit the floor. Miller threw himself on top of him.

FOURTEEN

DRIVEN by absolute terror, Ryan Miller ran as hard as he could. As he fled down the hall, away from the man with the gun, he kept expecting a bullet to hit him in the back. For a moment the boy thought he *had* been shot when the gun fired. But there was no pain, no warm wetness to indicate he'd been wounded, and he all but threw himself down the stairs, skidding on the living-room carpet, then dashing along the downstairs hall and into the den.

Suddenly the glass door was there, right in front of him. The nine-year-old hit it with bone-rattling impact, fully expecting to bounce off the heavy glass and land dazed on the floor, where the man would find him and do awful things to him. To Ryan's surprise the door shattered, the shards spilling out onto the deck, and then he was outside, trying his best not to slide off into the snow-covered rosebushes.

Managing to maintain his balance, Ryan turned left and ran down the three wooden steps into the backyard; then he rounded the corner of the house, taking himself out of the line of fire from the deck. He didn't know where he was headed; he was just going, getting away before the man hurt him—or killed him.

Suddenly he realized that the man could have reached the corner of the building, could be aiming the gun at him. Ryan veered to the right. The tall wood fence was in front of him, blocking his escape. The boy leapt, grabbing its top and pulling himself up, his feet kicking wildly as they sought purchase. His toe found one of the horizontal boards to which the vertical wood was attached, and he was up and over, scraping his arm as he went. He fell into the snow in the Murphys' yard, instantly scrambling to his feet and running. Dashing onto the front porch, he rang the bell, then pounded on the door with his fists.

No one answered.

Tears started running down his cheeks. The Murphys had to be home. They *had* to be. He kicked the door as hard as he could, then kicked it again. And again. Then he just stood there crying, feeling utterly defeated.

Gathering up all the strength he had left, Ryan forced himself to calm down and think. The man could still be coming after him. Or he could be back in his house, getting ready to hurt his mom and his dad and his brother. Ryan had to get help, had to save his family. He ran to the sidewalk, turned right because it had been kept shoveled in that direction while the other way was snow-packed and slippery-looking. Again he had no idea where he was going. To the extent that he had a plan at all, it was just to keep running until he saw a house where the people were obviously home. Or until a car came by. He hoped a police car would appear, but even at the age of nine he'd had enough experience with fate to know how unlikely that was.

His lungs sucking in air as fast as they were able, Ryan ran, compelling his legs to keep moving him forward. Ahead was the intersection where his street met Regis Drive. He scrambled over the snowbank, dashing into the street, looking in both directions for any signs of someone who could help. The street was deserted. Ryan hurried across it. As he climbed the snowbank on the other side, the boy glanced behind him, seeing no one. As far as he could tell, the man wasn't pursuing him. Maybe he wasn't hurting Ryan's family, either. Maybe he'd left, run away before the police could show up. Maybe if Ryan went home, he'd find out that everything was all right now. He stopped on top of the snowbank, panting, his heart racing. Should he go back, or should he keep on looking for help?

After a moment he concluded that he had to get help, for

the man could still be there, could be doing bad things to his brother again. What had the man done to Pete? Why had he been all wet? Had the man tried to drown him?

Ryan leapt off the snowbank, forced his tired muscles to function. He ran blindly, thinking that he might be doing this wrong, but uncertain exactly what the right course of action was. Should he run up to another house, knock on the door? Abruptly he discovered that he was in an open area, the bareness broken only by the trees sticking out of the snow. Then he saw the swings, the miniature kid-powered merry-go-round, the slide. He was in the little park he and the other neighborhood kids often played in.

And on the other side of the park was the help Ryan had been looking for. A fire station. There were always people at a fire station. Filled with relief, Ryan found a new energy and hurried through the park. Dashing across the street without looking, he ran up to the big doors at the firehouse and began pounding on them with his fists.

"What's the matter, boy?" It was a fireman. He'd stepped out of a small door in the front of the building.

"My . . . my mom and dad and brother," Ryan said. "A bad man, he . . . he tied us up. He . . . he . . ." Ryan fought to catch his breath, struggled to make his mouth speak the necessary words.

"Someone's in your house?"

The boy nodded vigorously. "He . . . he has a gun."

"I'll get the police," the fireman said. "Where do you live?"

Ryan pointed toward the park. "Fifty-two twelve Linwood."

"Come on," the fireman said, moving toward the door, but Ryan was already running again, heading for his house.

When he got there, out of breath and terrified of what he would find, he discovered that the front door was open. The boy approached it cautiously because he knew the gunman could still be inside. As he approached the open door he heard his mother sobbing. The sound drained him of his caution, and he rushed inside. His mother and father and Pete were on the floor. His mom and Pete were on their knees. His dad was just lying there. His mom and brother looked up as he stepped into the room. His dad did not.

"He shot Daddy," Pete said. Tears were running down his cheeks. "Daddy saved us. He fought with the man, so Mommy and I could get away."

Ryan heard sirens. They were getting louder.

"This is delicious," Ted said, taking another bite of one of Amanda's homemade biscuits. "And to think it was cooked by a city woman."

"People in New England do make biscuits," Amanda said, "although this was my mother's recipe."

"Old Nebraska farm recipe?"

"Actually my mother was a secretary at an insurance company. And I think she got the recipe from a Betty Crocker cookbook."

Ted sighed. "I think all the old recipes are gone, the ones that were used by the pioneers, when everything was made from scratch."

"That's because they involved things like milling your own flour by hand or churning your own butter. It can take all day to do things like that. There'd be no time left for stuff like earning a living."

Ted said, "I was figuring that the little woman could mill the flour and churn the butter while I worked to support the family."

"Sexist," Ashley said. She'd put down her fork and was staring at him.

Suppressing a laugh, Amanda said, "Ditto."

Chastened, Ted went back to his meal, eating in silence.

They were sitting at Amanda's kitchen table. She'd invited Ted over for Sunday brunch because it was a time at which he was almost certain to be free. Most of the area's residents would be in the town's only church, which was Lutheran and had services in Swedish the first Sunday of every month, so Ted rarely had to do any police business on Sunday mornings.

Ted's job made having a relationship with him difficult. Because he was on call twenty-four hours a day, you could never count on his being able to show up at the time you'd agreed upon. He might not even be able to warn you that he was going to be late, which made things like cooking elaborate dinners that had to be eaten at once rather risky. About the only way you could get together was for Ted to just stop by whenever he got the chance. It was hard to plan anything with that sort of relationship.

Amanda had made all the things she'd thought Ted would like. Scrambled eggs, hash browns, sausage, biscuits, orange juice, coffee. She usually didn't eat this much for breakfast—or this much cholesterol—but apparently she'd been right about Ted's taste. He was gobbling everything up, as if the meal would have to hold him for a week.

"Do you know when they're going to get the TV signals fixed?" Ashley asked. "All the stations went off the air yesterday, and they still haven't come back on."

"Power's out to the hill where the translators are located," Ted said. "Electric company will probably get someone up there to fix it tomorrow."

"Tomorrow?" Ashley said. "Why is it taking them so long?"

"Things happen slower out here in the country."

"How come?" the girl asked.

Ted shrugged. "They just do."

Amanda groaned. "Does this mean I'm going to have to play endless Monopoly games tonight?"

"You've just got to keep trying, Mom," Ashley said. "You'll win one eventually. You've got to learn which properties to buy and start buying houses sooner. You'll get the hang of it."

Amanda didn't want to get the hang of it. She'd enjoyed the game as a girl, but she was grown-up now. A life of nothing but Monopoly got boring after a while.

She felt a lot better today than she had yesterday after learning that Dick Kilmer and a woman had been murdered. For one thing, Ted was here, and his presence made her feel cozy and safe. And protected, although she had trouble coming to terms with that particular feeling. Amanda liked being independent, self-sufficient, things that were at odds with needing protection. And then there was the whole weak female and macho-male thing. Amanda didn't like feeling that she needed a man to defend her.

Still, she did like Ted. And the problems she was having trying to figure out how to handle their relationship weren't because of anything he'd done. They were within herself, things she'd have to sort out on her own.

Ted's presence wasn't the only reason Amanda felt better today. She'd had a chance to think things over, and although she felt terrible about what had happened to Dick Kilmer, she and Ashley were probably safe. The man with the strange eyes would have to lay low now that he'd killed three people. And he hadn't found her, even after taking such drastic steps.

Although she didn't like thinking about what was done to Dick Kilmer, Amanda made herself consider what the cameraman might have told his killer. As far as Dick had known, no one had any knowledge of her whereabouts. Bob Miller had spread the word that he didn't know, and there was no reason for Dick to doubt him. Also, the cameraman would have revealed that the informant who appeared in Amanda's series of reports was wearing a ski mask, that only Amanda knew who he was. The man with the lifeless eyes would have to admit defeat, give up, leave Amanda and her daughter alone.

Although a part of Amanda knew there were weak points in this logic—if not outright holes—she didn't want to listen to that part of herself, for its message of horror was too much for her to deal with right now. It started her thinking about how Dick Kilmer had been tortured, how a similar fate could await her or Ashley if the killer found them.

She and Ashley were safe for the time being. She had to believe that, for if she couldn't, she'd go crazy.

"I heard on the radio there's a big storm moving in," Ted said.

"How big?" Ashley asked.

"Big. A blizzard. A foot of snow or more."

"When's it supposed to get here? I'm supposed to go cross-country skiing with Eric." She looked panicky, as if missing out on a chance to see Eric could ruin her life forever.

"Not till after dark," Ted said.

"Should she go?" Amanda asked, worried. "I mean, what if she and Eric got lost out there? With a blizzard coming, we'd never find them."

"There's a trail we're supposed to follow," Ashley said quickly. "It circles around and back to town. Takes an hour and a half or so. We'll get back in plenty of time, Mom. Honest."

Amanda said, "Ted, is it really safe? I mean, with a storm coming and everything."

"I was planning to ask you whether you wanted to go snowshoeing."

"Snowshoeing? Me?"

"It's fun, Mom," Ashley said. "You ought to try it."

"I'm not real athletic," Amanda protested.

Besides, the way she had things figured out—at least before learning about the blizzard—was that they'd drop Ashley off at the Carlsons', then come back and spend the afternoon making love.

"Aren't you getting cabin fever yet?" Ted asked.

"Well, yeah, a little." But the fever could be cured *in* the cabin too.

They discussed it for about ten minutes or so, after which it was agreed that Ashley could go cross-country skiing with Eric if she promised to be back by three at the absolute latest and that Amanda would try her hand at snowshoeing. Ashley promised to be back by three.

• • •

Sitting in a window seat, Dexter Buchanan watched the ground fly by as the jetliner thundered down the runway at the Minneapolis-St. Paul International Airport and lifted itself into the air. The plane would stop in Duluth, then continue on to Hibbing. He'd be there before noon.

Things had not gone the way he'd intended at the Miller house. His plan had been to kill all four of them, so no one could warn Amanda Price that he'd learned where she was. Then the boy got loose and messed everything up. Buchanan had been sure he'd tied the kid up quite well, but then knot tying wasn't his specialty. He'd never been a Boy Scout.

Well, no matter. It had all worked out.

Only Miller and the youngest boy had been in the bathroom when Buchanan had learned where Amanda Price was hiding. The kid's ears had been under water at the time. And Miller himself wasn't going to tell anyone. According to the Boston all-news station Buchanan had been listening to before he left town, Miller was in a coma, his condition grave.

Buchanan hadn't asked the wife or boys anything. He'd waited for Miller. So no one even knew why he'd been there. No one who could tell, anyway.

The only disappointment was that he'd missed out on the pleasure of killing them.

As the seat-belt sign winked out, Buchanan tipped his seat back and closed his eyes, emptying his mind. It was a funny notion, an empty mind, since such a thing was actually impossible. You were always thinking about something. What had just happened, what would happen tomorrow, how the material in your pants had been manufactured, what kept the plane in the sky. Your mind was always filled with memories, questions, doubts, all sorts of idle thoughts. True emptiness, a complete shutdown . . . well, there was only one way to obtain that. You had to die.

What people actually meant by emptying their minds was

simply letting their thoughts wander where they pleased, lazy and relaxed, no worry, no urgency. And that's what Dexter Buchanan did now. But after a few moments of thinking about unimportant things he found himself recalling what proved to be the turning point of his life. The showdown with his father.

Buchanan had waited a long time for that day, planning for it, dreaming of it. He'd worked out in the school gym, doing sit-ups and pull-ups, bench-pressing, practicing on the punching bags. He tested his skills by taking on the toughest guys in school. By the time he was a senior, he *was* the toughest guy in school. Some of the boys were bigger, some stronger, some quicker, but none of them fought with the same disregard for their own safety, the same desire to administer punishment no matter what, the same killer instinct that Buchanan had.

The last guy he'd had to beat was named Randy Mohr, a big freckle-faced blond kid whose nose was always peeling. Buchanan was waiting in the parking lot when Mohr and two other boys came by. No one was with Buchanan. He was a loner who found friends more trouble than they were worth.

"Hey," Buchanan said, "it's Randy the Dandy Mohr, dumbest, ugliest fuck in school."

Mohr said, "Hey, look, a talking dildo." He continued on, not interested in fooling with Buchanan.

But Buchanan had no intention of being ignored. Moving in quickly, he punched Mohr in the face, knocking the surprised boy off his feet. Mohr stared up at him, the look of surprise disappearing, turning into rage. His two companions backed away. This was between Buchanan and Mohr.

Buchanan was wiry, which gave him speed and strength. But Mohr was enormous, weighing over two hundred, none of it flab. If this was a contest of brute strength, Buchanan wouldn't have a chance. But then he had no intention of letting it become such a contest. As Mohr got to his feet, his face still reddening with rage, Buchanan stepped in close enough to land a couple of quick punches, nothing that would hurt him but guaranteed to infuriate him even more. Mohr bellowed and came after him. Stepping to the side, Buchanan landed a solid punch in the boy's midsection.

"Your mother gave me a blow job last night, Mohr. If I'd known how bad her breath smelled, I wouldn't have let her do it. Had to wash my dick for twenty minutes afterward."

Mohr had to know what Buchanan was doing, that he was making him furious on purpose, so he'd be wild, ready to explode, too enraged to fight well. But rage was burning inside Mohr now, feeding on itself, well beyond the point at which logic could still extinguish it.

Mohr's eyes were wide, smoldering. Buchanan could almost see the hatred dancing in them, the need to destroy. "Tell your mother to quit following me around," he said softly. "I won't let her suck me off again even if she doubles the hundred she gave me last time."

Mohr lunged, two hundred pounds of fury intent on demolishing this person who said such things about his mother, this piece of shit who was making a fool of him in front of his buddies. Ducking under Mohr's roundhouse swing, Buchanan hit him solidly, throwing his weight into it. The blow stopped Mohr as if he'd run into a hundred-year-old oak. His feet came out from under him, and he hit the ground with the impact of a wrecking ball slamming into a wall. Buchanan kicked him hard, burying the toe of his shoe in the soft flesh just below Mohr's rib cage. The air rushed from the boy's lungs. Buchanan kicked him again. Pulled his foot back, brought it forward another time, brought it back, swung it forward, kicking him mercilessly. As he punished his fallen adversary Buchanan felt none of the rage that had driven Mohr. In fact, he felt nothing at all. Challenging Mohr had been the right thing to do, and now kicking him was the right thing to do. He didn't hate Mohr; he didn't even care about him. Kicking him was just the thing to do, that was all.

A large crowd had gathered. Buchanan hadn't realized it until some of the boys intervened, pulling him away from Mohr. "Jesus," one of them said, "you could have killed him."

Buchanan shook himself free of the boys' grasp, then turned and left. He had done what he came to do.

He was now the toughest kid in school, not that the position won him much admiration. The other kids avoided him, were careful not to meet his eyes, and when he did catch them looking at him, he'd seen a mixture of fear and revulsion in their expressions before they quickly looked away. None of this concerned Buchanan at all. Other people's opinions were unimportant.

About a month after the fight with Mohr, Buchanan was ready to take on his father. When the confrontation came, his father was sitting in the living room, watching the wrestling matches on TV, long hairy arms hanging out of his T-shirt, smelling of sweat and booze. A glass of bourbon sat on the arm of the threadbare chair. When his father picked it up to take a swallow, Buchanan knocked it out of his hand.

"What the fuck you think you're doing?" his father demanded, his cruel eyes narrowing.

"New rules," Buchanan said. "No more booze in the house."

The older man shook his head, as if he weren't sure this was happening. "Who the fuck you think you're talking to?"

"A worthless piece-of-shit drunk."

His father's eyes narrowed to slits. "You think because you're almost grown-up you can run things, do you? I can see I'm going to have to teach you some respect, show you who's in charge."

Moving around behind his father's chair, Buchanan grabbed it and overturned it, spilling the man out on the floor. The lazy drunk started to get up. He never made it. Buchanan kicked him in the face, the blow rolling him over.

Buchanan let him get up then, let him try to make a fight of it. It was no contest. The boy was younger, stronger, and all the working out had developed his muscles superbly. Slowed by alcohol and inactivity, the older man didn't have a chance. Buchanan beat him far worse than he'd beat Mohr, managing to stop himself just seconds before he would have killed him. It was what he'd dreamed of and planned for, worked for with a rare determination, and when it was done, Buchanan felt nothing. Not satisfaction, not relief, not even hatred for the man who'd made his life so miserable. As with Mohr, he had simply done what seemed the right thing for him to do. Now it was over. It no longer mattered. Buchanan never saw his father again.

Now, sitting in the airplane, recalling the event, Buchanan still thought of it as the turning point in his life, for it was after that that he'd left Baltimore and discovered his life's work. But he still didn't feel anything about it. That it was a turning point was an intellectual conclusion, not an emotional one.

It wasn't until later in life, when he was with the New York mob, that Buchanan started to enjoy hurting people. It wasn't that he got a huge amount of pleasure from it. The satisfaction was very brief and not at all intense. But at least it was a tingle of enjoyment, however short-lived. Nothing else in life provided him with even that much satisfaction.

Buchanan turned his thoughts to Hibbing. He would have to rent a car, drive the forty-five miles to Fiddlehead Lake, then find out where the rural-route address was. Buchanan thought about these things, unaware of the blond man who sat four rows behind him.

He hadn't noticed that the man was behind him at the ticket counter at Logan. Nor had he noticed the blond man when he, too, changed flights at O'Hare and again in the Twin Cities, always behind Buchanan in the terminal buildings, always close enough to make sure he could overhear what Buchanan told the ticket agents.

But then Buchanan was accustomed to being a predator. It had never occurred to him that he would ever be stalked.

FIFTEEN

"ARE you sure it's in there?" Amanda asked.

She and Ted were standing at the base of a hillside. He had just pointed out the spot where a bear's den was concealed by snow. All Amanda could see was unbroken white.

Ted said, "She's in there, all right. Mama black bear and two cubs."

"Well," Amanda said, "that's one way to avoid cabin fever. Sleep through the winter."

"Bears aren't true hibernators, you know. They don't sleep as deeply, and their body temperature doesn't drop as much. If the weather warms up a little, they'll come out and look around, see what's happening."

"What would we do if she came out right now?"

"Get the hell out of here."

"Are they dangerous, the bears?"

"They can be. They've got pretty short tempers."

"They cause much trouble?"

"They're responsible for most of the prowler complaints I get during the summer," Ted said. "People up from the city will hear a commotion outside, like somebody's destroying something. Turns out to be a bear raiding the garbage can. They're not real gentle about it, and they can make quite a racket."

"Is there any other wildlife around here I should know about?"

"Raccoons. They like garbage cans almost as much as the bears, but they're smaller, so they don't make quite as much noise. I guess the biggest problem animal is the skunk. If

213

you have a dog, he'll probably get sprayed four or five times during the summer. Fred Hanson's got a German shepherd must have got it fifteen times one year. Dog never did quit stinking."

"Makes quite a slogan," Amanda said. "Fiddlehead Lake, land of garbage-eating bears and ten thousand skunks."

"I don't think the powers-that-be would go for that one. They prefer to stress things like the fishing and hiking and clean air."

"How can the air be clean if it's filled with all that skunk odor?"

"Unless you're so bighearted that you absolutely can't make your dog stay outside until the scent works off, it's really not that big a problem."

Amanda considered that. If she lived in a place like this, Ashley would want a dog, and Amanda could not imagine the girl making her dog spend the night outside, no matter that essence de skunk would permeate everything in the house. But then there was no chance of this becoming a problem. She and Ashley lived in an apartment in Boston to which they would eventually have to return, and her lease prohibited pets.

And yet more and more lately she had been thinking about what it would be like to live here permanently. It was natural, she supposed, when you encountered a life-style different from your own, to mentally try it on, see how you might like it. Even so, Amanda seemed to be doing that a lot lately, more than idle curiosity would call for. She wasn't sure why she was doing it—or maybe she did know why and was just refusing to admit it to herself.

"You ready to head back?" Ted asked.

Amanda said she was, and they started off, moving with the flat-footed sliding motions necessitated by the snow-shoes. They'd been walking in the wooded countryside for about an hour and a half, Ted pointing out frozen streams that flowed into Fiddlehead Lake during the warmer months, summer cabins that were inaccessible by car this time of year because the roads leading to them weren't cleared, a rocky outcrop from which a distraught city girl had tried to leap to her death only to end up in a pine tree, unhurt but embarrassed.

About half an hour after leaving the site of the bear's den, they arrived at the crest of a low hill overlooking Fiddlehead Lake. The sheriff's substation was about a hundred and fifty yards away. They stood side by side, looking down on the town.

"I'm exhausted," Amanda said, leaning against Ted as if she were too pooped to stand unassisted.

"It's good for you," Ted said. "People spend all winter inside, and when they try to get out to do something physical, they have a heart attack."

"Tomorrow I'm going to be sore in places I didn't even know I had muscles."

Ted put his arm around her, just held her while they looked down on Fiddlehead Lake. After a while she looked up at him, met his eyes, and he kissed her, a gentle brushing of the lips that soon grew more intense. When it ended, Amanda said, "There were other forms of exercise we could have indulged in besides walking around, making our muscles sore."

Ted smiled warmly at her. "I like you, Amanda Price."

"Like me? A while back you were falling in love with me."

"I still am, but you can fall in love with someone without really liking them. When you like someone, you really enjoy their company, you want to be friends, to hang around with them. Love, all by itself, is more possessive, more prone to things like jealousy." He grinned sheepishly at her. "Philosophy of life by that renowned expert Ted Anderson."

She returned the smile. "I like you, too, Ted."

They kissed again, so passionately that Amanda actually entertained notions of doing it in the snow, an idea she quickly dropped when it occurred to her that bare flesh, snow, and temperatures in the low twenties were not compatible.

"We should stop this," Amanda said. "The dispatcher could be watching us from the back window of your office."

"She'd need binoculars to see much at this distance, and substation order number twenty-two prohibits looking out the rear window with binoculars." He shook his head in mock seriousness. "Instant dismissal, forfeiture of your pension, and disparaging articles will be written about you in all the law-enforcement magazines."

"A serious offense," Amanda said.

"Definitely."

For a few moments they just looked at each other, reluctant to go back to where there were other people, hesitant to give up this solitude in which the two of them were all that mattered. Finally they started down the hill.

At the substation Amanda returned the snowshoes she'd borrowed from Ted, thanked him for the nice time, and headed for the general store to see whether Ashley had showed up yet.

"Nope," Eleanor Carlson said. "She and Eric haven't come back yet."

She was a short gray-haired woman with flawlessly clear blue eyes. She was Eric's grandmother. With Eric's parents, grandparents, and the boy himself, there were five people who worked in the store, and you never knew who might be on duty when you came in. Amanda supposed Eric and his wife would someday run the place, and maybe his kids and their kids. The image of Eric and Ashley married and working in the store popped into Amanda's head, and she pushed it away. Eric was the girl's first fling. There would be many others before she was old enough to think about marriage.

There was a newspaper rack beside the counter. Amanda got a copy of the Sunday Duluth *News-Tribune*.

"Those just got here," Mrs. Carlson said. "The truck delivers them broke down. Last time that happened, I got the Sunday papers on Monday." She shrugged.

Amanda paid for the paper. "I don't know whether to wait for Ashley or go on home and let her call me. How long do you think they'll be?"

"It's only a quarter of two, so they could be another hour yet. Why don't you just go on, and I'll have Sue run her home for you." Sue was Eric's mother.

"I don't want to put her to any trouble."

"No trouble at all. There's no reason for you to wait around or drive all the way back into town."

Amanda thanked her and headed for home. Ted had suggested that she drive her own car into town, just in case some emergency police business came up and he had to leave her. Also, his only transportation was his sheriff's cruiser, which he wasn't supposed to use for personal business, such as romancing women from Boston.

The sky had been white all day, warning of the impending storm. Amanda switched on the radio. After a few moments the announcer in Hibbing informed her that the Weather Service was still predicting that a major winter storm would hit the area this evening. Snow and blowing snow, with accumulations of a foot or more likely in some areas. Travel this evening was being discouraged. The announcer added that anyone who was already traveling and wouldn't reach his destination before nightfall should start looking for a place to hole up until the storm was over.

Amanda remembered the storm in Pennsylvania. A thought occurred to her, and although it was foolishness, nonsense, the idea was so scary that it made her shudder. The man with the strange eyes had caught up to her during the last snowstorm. Maybe he would do it again during this one.

Ridiculous, Amanda thought. Silliness.

And yet her uneasiness would not go away.

• • •

Eleanor Carlson looked up as the bell over the door tinkled. A stranger stepped in, glanced around, then walked up to the counter. He was tall with a thin face. Although he was wearing the right kind of clothes for the woods—high-top insulated shoes, jeans, thick hooded coat—everything looked brand spanking new, as if it had just been bought.

"Sign out front says this is the post office," he said.

"It is, but I'm not supposed to conduct any post office business on Sunday."

"I just need some directions," he said.

As Eleanor Carlson looked at him, she realized there was something odd about his eyes. They had no sparkle, no shininess the way eyes usually did. They reminded her of the eyes in the stuffed deer head her uncle had on the wall in his den, eyes that stared at her glassily, unseeing.

"Who you trying to find?" she asked.

"It's Route 1, Box 227-B."

"Box 227-B," she said, concentrating. "Sounds familiar. Oh, I know why. That's the Miller cabin, where the Price woman is staying. You a friend of hers?"

"Yes, from Boston. But all I was given was the mailing address. I don't know how to find it."

While the man was talking, another stranger came in, a blond man. Two strangers showing up at the same time on a Sunday afternoon in February was pretty unusual, so Eleanor thought they must be together. However, the man at the counter glanced at the blond man, then looked away, apparently not having recognized him.

Eleanor said, "You follow the highway out of town." She pointed in the appropriate direction. "Go three miles and you'll come to a group of mailboxes on your right. The last one in the group will say J. Heikkinen on it. Turn there and go about two miles on that road. The place you're looking for is white with a blue roof, on the left."

The man thanked her and left. A moment later the blond

man left as well, without buying anything. Eric and Ashley came in, passing him just outside the door.

"Hi, Gramma," Eric said. "Ashley's mom been here?"

"Just left. I told her your mom would drive Ashley home."

"I don't want to be a lot of trouble to anybody," Ashley said.

"No problem," Eleanor Carlson said. "Sue's been figuring on it all along."

"Come on," Eric said. "Let's go over to the house." They hurried out the door before Eleanor Carlson thought to mention the man who'd asked for directions to Route 1, Box 227-B.

Eric was certainly infatuated with Ashley Price, and Eleanor wondered whether discovering girls would mean the end of the boy's fascination with radios. Time moved on, she supposed. Not that long ago Eric had been a pudgy little baby, her first grandchild. Soon he'd be going to high school, getting a driver's license, and before long he'd be married and she'd be a great-grandmother if she was still here.

She stared at the door through which the two kids had left, and she abruptly found herself wondering about the man who'd just been here asking about Amanda Price. Why had he only known the mailing address? If Amanda had told him how to get here, she would have given him directions. Maybe she wasn't expecting him. Maybe he was a former lover and she'd come here to get away from him. Although that might be a little fanciful, Amanda Price's arrival in Fiddlehead was definitely a puzzlement. Eleanor had lived here her entire life, and this was the first time anyone had moved in during the dead of winter. Especially someone who brought a child along and then didn't put that child in school.

She suspected that Ted Anderson knew why Amanda was here, but Ted was keeping it to himself. And then Eleanor thought she had the answer. Amanda Price could be in a witness-protection program of some sort. That would explain why Ted had remained mum on the subject and why Amanda and her daughter had showed up here at this time of year. It even explained the man with the odd eyes. He was a government agent. It was just like the government to send him out here without directions for finding the place.

Pleased with herself, Eleanor Carlson nodded. She was almost certain she'd just figured out what was going on. She could hardly wait to try her theory on her husband, see what he thought. Everyone in town thought Amanda Price's arrival was a bit of a mystery. Perhaps Eleanor Carlson would be the one who solved it.

"He's certainly in a hurry," Sue Carlson said. She was driving Ashley home in her Bronco. Ashley was sitting in the rear seat with Eric. She glanced up to see a blue car speed past them, then let her attention return to Eric.

"You'll get the hang of it," he said. "It just takes a little practice."

"I'm not so sure about that," Ashley said. "Every time I tried to move, I fell down."

"Everybody does at first."

"Did you?"

"Sure," Eric said. "I spent more time on the ground than I did on the skis."

"Every time I fall down, I feel so . . . so stupid—like a klutz."

"You're not a klutz," Eric said quickly. "I think you're graceful."

"Really?" Ashley thought it was the nicest thing anyone had ever said to her.

Blushing, Eric nodded. For some reason, saying nice things embarrassed him. Saying nice things was hard for boys apparently, even for Eric, who was the only truly nice boy she'd ever met. For all Ashley knew, he could be the only truly nice boy in the world, which showed just how special he was.

"Thank you for the compliment, Eric—even if I don't deserve it."

"You do deserve it," he said, his face reddening still more.

Ashley felt warm all over.

They drove in silence for a few moments, then Ashley said, "Mrs. Carlson, do you ski?"

"Eric's dad does. I stay at home so I can have a hot toddy ready when he comes back in." She was a small woman with curly blond hair and a round face. She always gave Ashley cookies when she was visiting Eric. Ashley thought she was very nice.

"Maybe I should be like your mom," Ashley said to Eric. "Stay home and make the hot chocolate." She didn't say "hot toddy" because she thought it was an alcoholic drink and she didn't want to give the wrong impression.

"Don't give up yet," Eric said. "You'll like it if you get the hang of it."

"That's up to Ashley," his mom said. "If she doesn't feel comfortable on skis, then you shouldn't force her."

Quickly Ashley said, "Oh, I don't mind trying again."

"Well, just as long as you want to and feel safe," Mrs. Carlson said. She turned onto Lakeshore Road.

"If you don't want to, I don't mind," Eric said. "I mean, there's lots of other stuff we can do."

"I'd like to try it at least once more," Ashley said. "Before I make up my mind." Ashley enjoyed trying new things, and she didn't like giving up just because they didn't go well at first. Besides, anything she did with Eric was fun—even listening to the not terribly exciting programs on his shortwave radio. She resisted the temptation to regard the broadcasts as dull, since Eric was so fond of tuning them in. Instead she tried to think of them as informative.

Ashley was almost home when Mrs. Carlson suddenly hit the brakes, bringing the Bronco to a stop. The blue car that had passed them earlier was in the middle of the road with its hood up, blocking the way. There was no one around the car. For a moment Sue Carlson simply looked at it, then she said, "Maybe we can roll it out of the way."

Feeling real uneasy about the situation, Ashley said, "I think we should stay in the car."

"We can't just sit here all day, Ashley," Eric's mom said. "That's not a very nice thing to do, to leave the car blocking the road like that. The driver should have gotten it as close to the shoulder as he could."

"Yeah, we gotta try to move it," Eric said. "With all of us pushing, we should be able to do it. I hope it's not locked."

From the corner of her eye Ashley saw movement. Turning to look, she saw a man scrambling over the snowbank toward them. She gasped. It was *the* man.

"It's him!" she shrieked. "Get out of here. Hurry, it's the man."

"What man?" Sue Carlson asked.

But she didn't wait for an answer. Apparently the urgency in Ashley's voice had gotten through to her, for she put the Bronco in reverse and stepped on the gas. The wheels spun, then grabbed, and the Bronco sped backward, away from the man, who had been almost close enough to grab the door handle. He turned around and ran toward the blue car.

Mrs. Carlson was having a hard time driving backward at this speed. The Bronco kept weaving from side to side, scraping the snowbank on one edge of the road, then the other.

"Mom!" Eric shouted. "Turn around so you can go forward."

She spun the wheel, and the Bronco slid sideways, then rolled backward into the snowbank. Sue Carlson shifted into drive and stepped on the gas, but the tires spun. She looked ready to panic, lose control.

"Use four-wheel drive," Eric said.

She put the Bronco into four-wheel drive and tried again. It pulled itself out of the snow. The blue car had already turned around. It was coming. Mrs. Carlson floored the

Bronco, and they were speeding back toward the main highway. Looking behind them, Ashley saw the blue car. It was rapidly closing the gap.

"It's gaining on us, Mom," Eric said anxiously.

Sue Carlson sped up but only a little. Apparently she knew how fast you could drive on this road, and she wasn't going to exceed it. Remembering how her own mom had lost control on a curve on this same road, Ashley thought that was wise. The blue car continued to get closer. As if she had the ability to use mind over matter, Ashley thought, *Wreck! Spin out! Slide off the road!* The blue car was unaffected by her mental commands.

Ashley could see the man's face now, the narrow, bony features. At least she couldn't see his eyes, his horrible zombie eyes. The blue car was still closing the gap. It was nearly on their bumper.

Sue Carlson rounded a curve, then accelerated into a straight stretch of roadway. The blue car stayed with her. Abruptly it swerved to the left, started trying to pass.

"Mom!" Eric yelled. "Drive in the center of the road. Don't let him get beside you."

His mother pulled over, cutting the blue car off, hogging the road. The highway was up ahead. There would be more traffic there. Maybe they'd run into Ted Anderson or a state policeman. Sue Carlson drifted to the left, and the blue car was instantly trying to take advantage of the opening by passing on the right. Sue jerked the wheel, bringing the Bronco back into the center of the road, but she did it just as she entered a right-hand turn. And just as she hit a patch of glare ice that neither the traffic nor highway department salt had been able to remove from the road's surface. Instantly the Bronco was spinning, sliding sideways, then backward, then sideways again, the tires hitting clean asphalt again and screeching in protest.

Sue Carlson made a squeak.

Eric shouted something Ashley was unable to comprehend.

Then there was a thump, snow spraying past the windows, Ashley's seat belt digging into her flesh as her body was hurled first one way, then the other. The Bronco bounced. Ashley felt weightless. Then there was a crash, and she was pitched to the side so violently that she thought her seat belt would surely break. But it didn't.

The Bronco was motionless, the only sound the hissing of steam from the ruptured radiator.

Dazed, Ashley simply sat there, trying to make her brain function, struggling to hang on to consciousness. Finally one thought snapped her out of it. The man. He was still out there. Quickly surveying her surroundings, she determined that the Bronco was upright. In all directions she saw trees and snow, which meant it had plowed through the snowbank and into the woods. Eric was beside her, motionless, blood oozing from a cut on his forehead.

"Eric," she said, clutching his arm. When he didn't respond, she shook him. "Please, Eric. Say something." Tears were running down her cheeks. She thought he was dead.

The boy moaned, and Ashley felt her heart beat faster. Thank goodness, she thought. Oh, thank goodness.

Looking into the front seat, she saw that Mrs. Carlson was leaning forward, her head almost touching the steering wheel, the seat belt keeping her from collapsing on it. The car was tipping slightly forward, Ashley realized. She'd been too confused to be aware of it until now.

"Mrs. Carlson," she said. "Can you hear me?"

No response.

Ashley knew she had no more time to waste here. The best thing she could do was to get out of there, get help. And she had to do it right now, before the man showed up. She pressed the release button on her seat belt. Nothing happened. Putting one thumb on top of the other, she pushed with all her might, and it still refused to release.

The belt was the kind that only caught when there was pressure on it, so she pulled gently on it and found it came out of its holder easily. Once she'd pulled enough slack, Ashley worked herself out of the belt. Pulling the handle, she pushed on the door, which was stuck. She hit it with the weight of her body, and it popped open, causing Ashley to fall out of the car and into the snow. She scrambled to her feet. She had to get help, had to get away before the man found her.

The girl could see the hole in the snowbank where the Bronco left the road. She moved away from it, because that was where the man would be. The crust on the snow kept giving way under her weight, and she wished she had the snowshoes she'd borrowed from Eric the time they went snowshoeing. It had been fun, more fun than cross-country falling down—what she'd done today with Eric could hardly be called skiing.

Thinking of Eric made her struggle harder against the deep snow. She had to get help before he and his mom went into shock, or lost too much blood from internal bleeding, or lost too much body heat. But these were things she knew almost nothing about. She'd heard about them; that was all. She really had no idea how seriously injured her companions might be.

Once she'd gone far enough from the hole in the snowbank, Ashley climbed toward the road. Near the top of the snowbank, she peered over it, seeing no sign of the blue car, no sign of the man. She crested the snowbank, ran onto the road, headed toward the highway as fast as she could go. It was about a mile away, so she had to pace herself, move fast enough to make good time but slowly enough so that she didn't wind herself. At least that's what her PE teacher had said. Ashley hadn't paid much attention at the time. Now she wished she had.

Hearing a noise behind her, she spun around.

The man grabbed her.

SIXTEEN

USING the cheap, yellow-handled broom she'd bought at the general store, Amanda swept the dirt into a small pile in the center of the living room. The job would have been a lot easier with a vacuum cleaner, but her Hoover was back in Boston. She used a plastic dustpan to pick up the dirt.

As she carried the dustpan into the kitchen and emptied it into the trash, Amanda wondered where all the dirt came from. She hadn't seen a patch of exposed earth since she came here. Everything was under a thick layer of snow. And then she remembered that the roads were all full of the sand-salt mixture highway crews applied during the winter to melt the ice and provide traction. The stuff was everywhere. It collected underneath the cars and fell off in the driveway. And both she and Ashley probably collected it on their shoes when they went to town. As mysteries went, that one proved to be pretty short-lived.

Leaving the dustpan and broom in the kitchen broom closet, Amanda returned to the living room. Earlier she'd taken the throw rugs outside for a good shake. They were piled on the couch. Amanda returned them to the floor, putting one in front of the couch, the other in the open space by the front door.

She switched on the TV set, finding nothing but snow. The translators were still off the air. It was a sign that she should do some more housework, Amanda decided, so she went into the kitchen, got out scouring powder and a sponge, and scrubbed the sink. When she was done, it was four o'clock. Where was Ashley?

Amanda considered phoning the Carlsons and rejected the idea. She didn't want to seem the worrying overprotective mother. The girl was probably at the Carlsons', spending as much time as possible with Eric. Ashley hadn't been instructed to phone when she and Eric got back from cross-country skiing. Nor was there any rush for her to get here. Dinner was still two hours away, and they were having leftovers, so Amanda needed no help in preparing anything.

Still, a vague feeling of foreboding had settled over her. She tried to push it away. She'd had such feelings before, and they usually just meant she was tired or depressed about some minor thing. Amanda was unable to recall an occasion when her feelings of foreboding had actually preceded something terrible happening. It was probably just the weather, the white sky graying as the short winter day neared its end. And maybe she was worried, just a little, about being out here in this isolated house during the blizzard that was forecast to hit tonight.

"The thing for you to do," she said to the empty house, "is to keep busy."

Amanda cleaned the bathroom, working for a good five minutes on the brown stain in the toilet without removing even a trace of it. When she was finished with the bathroom, it was almost four-thirty, and Ashley still hadn't come home. Amanda debated with herself for about a minute, then decided to phone the Carlsons. It was getting darker by the moment, there was a storm coming, and Amanda wanted to know where her daughter was. Sitting down on the couch, she lifted the receiver. The phone was dead.

"Damn," she said. "Doesn't anything ever work around here? First the TV and now the phone." She felt silly for talking to the empty room. But then what did it matter? No one was here to see her do it.

Amanda replaced the receiver. The feeling of foreboding was back, stronger now. In the back of her mind she'd known that everything was okay because the Carlsons would have phoned her if anything bad had happened. But now she no longer had that assurance. The phone was out. The Carlsons couldn't call.

Sitting on the couch and staring across the room, Amanda tried to figure out what to do. If she drove into town, she might miss the Carlsons bringing Ashley home. She didn't even know what kind of car they drove. For about ten minutes Amanda just sat there, listening for the sound of a car pulling into the driveway. All she heard was a gust of wind that blew through the leafless trees and pushed against the side of the house, a precursor of the coming storm.

Finally Amanda got up, put on her coat, and walked to the end of the driveway, hoping to spot a pair of headlights approaching on the road. The wind gusted twice more, a few snowflakes fell, and what was left of the daylight disappeared from the blackening sky. The feeling of foreboding grew stronger, like a powerful fist, tightening its grip on her innards, squeezing, twisting.

Amanda shivered. Her feet felt like blocks of ice. It was too cold to stand outside and watch the road. Taking one last look in the direction from which Ashley would come, Amanda reluctantly headed back to the house. As she passed her car she remembered the newspaper she'd bought earlier. She'd forgotten to take it inside; it was still in the car, on the backseat. She got the paper and went back inside the house.

Amanda tried the phone again. Still dead. She decided to make five-thirty her deadline. If Ashley hadn't come home by then, Amanda would drive into town. Going into the kitchen, she laid the newspaper on the table, then put some water on to boil. When it was bubbling, she made herself a cup of tea, sat down at the table, and opened the newspaper. Another gust of wind came up, slapping the side of the house and groaning in the eaves. It was an eerie sound, and it made the dark woods seem full of ghosts.

The banner headline concerned the Middle East. The

Israelis were beating and killing Palestinians in the occupied territories, and the Iranians were still behaving like madmen. Duluthians living on the north shore of Lake Superior were up in arms over plans to extend Interstate 35 northward out of the city, because they felt the freeway would despoil the lakefront. Amanda pulled out the comics, pushed the rest of the paper away from her.

When she'd finished the comics and her tea, it was five-oh-five. Another twenty-five minutes and she would go look for Ashley. All sorts of horrible possibilities circled at the edge of her consciousness, and although she tried her best to ignore them, the terrible images kept popping into her head—Ashley in a car wreck, Ashley lost somewhere in the woods with Eric, Ashley with a broken leg.

Ashley in the hands of the man with the lifeless eyes.

Amanda realized she was trembling. Another gust of wind hit the house, making it shudder and issuing a long, pitiful wail as it sought out cracks in the walls through which it could suck out the structure's warmth.

The man doesn't know where we are, Amanda told herself. He couldn't have Ashley. It was just her mind, dredging up her worst fears. She looked at her watch. Five-fifteen. Almost time to go and look for her. Amanda pulled the Duluth *News-Tribune* back in front of her, opened the second section. An attempted hijacking had been foiled by airport security personnel in Athens. She began flipping through the pages absently, without really seeing any of the words. She stopped on page B-4, when she spotted the word Boston. The headline read: INTRUDER SHOOTS BOSTON NEWSMAN.

She hesitated, reluctant to read more because some unidentifiable instinct was warning her that this was going to be terrible news. The only sounds were the wind, which was blowing lightly but steadily now, and the hammering of her heart. Amanda read the story.

An armed man had forced his way into TV news director Bob Miller's house, tying up his wife and two sons, then waiting for the newsman to arrive home. When Miller showed up, the intruder forced them all to go upstairs, where he tied Mrs. Miller and the older boy to the bed, taking Miller and the other boy into the bathroom. The boy, seven-year-old Pete, said the intruder had filled the bathtub with water and held his head under it.

Miller was shot twice by the intruder during a struggle.

The Miller family said the man was a stranger, and they had no idea why he'd forced his way into their house. Miller, according to police, was in a coma, unable to shed any light on the situation. The hospital listed his condition as critical.

The imaginary hand squeezing Amanda's insides was gone now. She felt as if she had no insides, as if she were hollow, containing nothing but emptiness, as cold and black as the depths of space.

Bob Miller in critical condition.

His wife and children terrorized.

Amanda knew who had done it. The man with eyes as cold and empty as she felt inside right now. A merciless killer who wanted only one thing: to find Amanda Price and her daughter. Thoughts swirled through her consciousness so rapidly Amanda was almost unable to discern any of them.

It was her fault, all her fault.

A gun firing, Bob Miller falling.

The gun firing again.

Blood on the walls . . . on the furniture . . . everywhere.

The man's cold, dull eyes brightening abruptly.

The man's voice, as garbled and demonic as the voice of the possessed child in *The Exorcist* saying, "I want Amanda Price and her daughter."

A terrified Bob Miller pleading for the lives of those he loved.

Then telling the man where to find Amanda.

Amanda checked the story. It had happened yesterday.

By air the man could get here from Boston in a couple of hours. He could be here now. He could already have Ashley. No! Amanda thought, firmly rejecting the notion. No, no, no, no! She couldn't let herself believe that, because if it was true, all was lost. Ashley was late, that was all. Just late, nothing more.

Still, Amanda and the girl had to get out of here quickly. She had to assume the man knew where she was. Her hideaway was no longer safe. Getting up so quickly that she knocked over the chair, Amanda dashed into the bedroom, grabbing the suitcase and throwing it on the bed. She pulled out a dresser drawer, carried it to the bed, and dumped it into the suitcase. Dropping the drawer, she got another, did the same thing with it.

Abruptly she stopped. Tears were streaming down her cheeks, tears for Bob Miller. He was a kind man, the best boss she'd ever had, one of the world's truly nice human beings. And because of her, he was in a coma, in critical condition. Which meant it was touch and go, that Bob Miller was on the edge of death.

She threw herself onto the bed, her body landing on top of the suitcase, and she began to sob. "I'm sorry, Bob," she said through the tears. "I'm so goddamn sorry."

The man who had shot him was a conscienceless monster who pursued his prey with single-minded determination. He was like an automaton that had been programmed to seek out its objective mindlessly, never resting, never giving up.

Amanda forced herself to stop crying. She had to get out of here, find Ashley and get away from this place while there was still time. As she stood up, a number of things occurred to her all at once, conclusions so staggering that she had to sit down on the bed and try to sort out her churning thoughts.

She had no money.

She had nowhere to go.

How could she leave with a major winter storm perhaps only minutes away from striking the area?

Getting up, Amanda went to the window and peered into the darkness. A pair of snowflakes drifted past the glass. If she tried to leave now, she could get stranded. It happened, even here in Minnesota where people were accustomed to severe winter storms. Drivers would get stuck, be forced to try to survive the freezing temperatures in their cars. Some would suffer frostbite and lose hands or feet. A few would die of exposure or from carbon monoxide leaking from the exhaust systems of stationary cars. Others would try to walk out, and their bodies wouldn't be found until spring.

At least if she couldn't get out, the man couldn't get in.

Amanda checked her watch. Five-thirty. It was time to go look for Ashley. Leaving the mess she'd created in the bedroom, Amanda hurried into the living room, grabbed her coat, and headed for the door. As she was reaching for the knob, headlights illuminated the front window and she heard a car outside. Thank God, Amanda thought. She resisted the temptation to rush out to throw her arms around her daughter, hugging her joyfully and scolding her for worrying her mother all at the same time.

Taking off her coat, she waited. She'd discuss things with Ashley reasonably and calmly. It wouldn't do any good to let the girl see what a panic she was in. These thoughts instantly evaporated when someone knocked on the door. Ashley wouldn't knock; she'd use her key. Who was there?

Telling herself it wasn't the man—absolutely, positively wasn't—she moved to the window and peeked out. A strange man was at the door, a young guy, maybe twenty, dark-haired, with a pale complexion. He knocked again, and Amanda opened the door.

"Amanda Price?" he asked.

"Yes."

He handed her an envelope. "Guy gave me fifty bucks to deliver this to you."

"A man? What man?"

He shrugged. "I don't know. Just a guy. We were both at the Standard station on the edge of town, and he gave me that envelope and asked me if I'd deliver it to a place out on Lakeshore Road for fifty bucks. I said sure."

"What did he look like?" Amanda demanded.

"He was just a guy. He had the hood on his coat pulled up. I couldn't really see much of his face."

"What about his eyes? Did you notice his eyes?"

"His eyes?"

"Yes, his eyes. Was there anything . . . anything unusual about them?"

"I don't know, ma'am. I really never noticed."

"Are you sure? Think. Please."

"Look, I don't know what this is all about, but I'm just the delivery boy. Whatever's going on between you and this guy isn't any of my business."

"What kind of car was he driving?"

"A blue one, a Chevy." Before she could ask him anything else, the man turned and hurried back to his pickup, which was parked behind Amanda's Ford.

Amanda closed the door and sat down on the couch, staring at the envelope. It was blank, nothing written on it, not even her name. It was just an ordinary legal-size envelope, and yet it was the most frightening and ominous object she had ever seen. Amanda didn't want to open it. And yet she had to. Her hands shook as she tore it open.

Inside was a single sheet of paper on which the message had been neatly printed with upper- and lowercase letters.

I have your daughter. Drive to the end of Lakeshore Road and stop with your lights off. Come alone. If you're not there in half an hour, the girl dies. If you stop on the way, the girl dies. I'll be watching.

For a few moments Amanda simply sat there, unable to think, unable to move. Slowly a hard, cold reality settled over her. Her worst fears had come true. The man had Ashley. Amanda was unable to call for help because the phone was out. She had no time to drive into town because she had only a half hour to get to the end of the road, and the storm was about to settle in. If she stopped at the Heikkinens' or anywhere else on the way, the man would kill Ashley.

He'd probably kill her anyway.

The thought hung there.

There was nothing Amanda could do except follow the man's instructions. If she didn't, he'd kill Ashley, and it would be her fault. If she complied with his instructions, at least she'd be there to try to save her, although she had no idea how she was going to handle a professional killer whose ruthlessness and physical prowess were beyond anything she'd ever encountered before. And yet she had to try, for only she could save Ashley. Only she could save herself.

Rushing into the kitchen, Amanda got a sharp knife from the drawer. She didn't know exactly how she could use it against her adversary, but at least she had a weapon. Returning to the living room, Amanda put on her coat, slipping both the letter and the knife into one of its large pockets.

The wind whipped her hair and stung her face as she hurried to her car. As she started the engine and switched on the headlights, the snow began to fall heavily.

Dexter Buchanan sat in the driver's seat of the rented blue Chevrolet. In the other bucket seat, bound and gagged, was Ashley Price. He was parked at the end of Lakeshore Road, waiting. He didn't know why the road went this far. There were no houses here, only some mountains of snow that had been piled up by the plows.

He wasn't watching Amanda Price, as he'd indicated he would in the note. Watching her was unnecessary. He was sure she wouldn't take the chance that her daughter would die because she'd violated his instructions. Buchanan had considered going to the house in which the Price woman was staying, but he'd decided on this plan for two reasons. First, someone could always stop by the cabin and interrupt him. Second, and most important, what he had in mind could be better handled in a place like this than at the cabin.

And then there was the psychology of the thing. Making Amanda Price come to him, knowing that she'd be heading toward her own death and coming all the same. She'd be terrified, desperate to save her daughter, which suited Dexter Buchanan just fine. Soon he'd be back in New Shipton with the name of the traitor.

In the darkness of the car's interior the girl was just a shadow. Buchanan switched on the interior light so he could look at her. Green eyes enlarged by fear stared back at him. Her hair was in disarray, from her being locked in the trunk while Buchanan was at the gas station.

The girl looked a lot like her mother. She would be beautiful when she grew up. She was already quite attractive, although her body was in that transitional stage in which she was neither child nor adult. She shrank against the door as Buchanan reached over to pull the gag from her mouth.

"You can speak if you want to," he said.

She stared silently at him with her large green eyes. That was fine with Buchanan. Whether she talked to him was unimportant. Switching off the interior light, he turned on the headlights and watched the snowflakes swirl around in the beams. Already half an inch or so had fallen. After a few moments he switched off the headlights, sat in the darkness, and waited.

The wind had let up, and except for an occasional click from the car's cooling engine, the north woods were absolutely quiet, a stillness that only snowfall seemed capable of producing. Nothing moved outside the car except the snowflakes. Then the wind picked up again, whistling past the windows of the car and breaking the silence.

As it often did when he was forced to wait, Buchanan's mind began plucking random memories from his subconscious. He briefly revisited the beating he'd given his father, his mother's suicide, the day he arrived in New York

City. And then, apparently prompted by the presence of Ashley Price, he found himself remembering another girl, one he'd known when he was sixteen.

Darla Everton had been a little too thin, with lifeless brown hair and a face prone to zits. In short, she was homely, the sort of girl boys usually paid no attention to.

But Darla Everton was one of the most dated girls in school. The reason was simple. She'd spread her legs on the first date for any boy who took her out.

She was the only girl Buchanan had been out with his entire time in high school. And he'd only gone out with her once. He'd stolen a car for the occasion, a restored '57 Chevy convertible that had been sitting in the parking lot of a shopping mall with the keys in the ignition. He and Darla had driven to a wooded spot outside the city known to almost everyone in his high school. Pulling into a clearing filled with beer cans and liquor bottles and used condoms, he switched off the lights.

Not one to waste time, Darla slid across the Chevy's bench seat and slipped her arms around him, kissing his neck, nibbling his ear. Buchanan just sat there uncertain what to do. Darla kissed him, plunging her tongue into his mouth and pulling herself tightly against him. Following her lead, he pushed his own tongue into her mouth, squeezed one of her small breasts.

"Oh, baby," Darla whispered.

Buchanan felt nothing. Still, this was sex, the thing he'd heard so much about, the thing that occupied the minds of just about all the guys in school, so he pressed on, searching for the wonderment boys seemed so obsessed with.

Darla pulled off her blouse and bra. He felt her bare breasts, finding them small and soft and uninteresting. Taking his hand, she guided it to her crotch. He rubbed her there and she moaned.

"I'm ready whenever you are," she said breathlessly.

But Buchanan wasn't ready. His penis lay between his legs, limp and useless. Apparently sensing that he needed some additional encouragement, Darla unzipped his fly, worked his flaccid organ out of his pants, and put it in her mouth. It grew a little, then went soft again.

Darla sighed. "Nothing's going to happen, is it?"

"No," he replied.

"Oh, well, don't worry about it. I've known other guys it's happened to. It's nothing to get embarrassed about."

Buchanan wasn't embarrassed. If women didn't arouse him, it was just a fact, nothing to get upset about. Darla could tell people about this, he supposed, but he really didn't care. No one would tease him about it because no one would dare. He drove her home, then left the stolen convertible at a used-car lot.

As the memory faded away he said to Ashley, "I've got some things to do outside. If you try to get away, I'll hurt you very badly. You understand that?"

Ashley said nothing.

"Hey," he said, "I asked you a question. You understand what I just said?"

"Yes," Ashley said, her voice as dry as last year's fallen leaves.

"Good," Buchanan said.

He got out of the car. The wind began to blow still harder, howling through the leafless trees, snowflakes hitting his face like fistfuls of gravel.

SEVENTEEN

TED Anderson sat at his desk, thinking about Amanda Price, picturing her dark hair and green eyes and slender, shapely body. He was smitten, head-over-heels-can't-live-without-her smitten, and he had absolutely no idea what to do about it. Sooner or later she would go back to Boston and resume her career as a TV reporter, leaving him here to patrol his beloved north woods.

Smitten though he was, Ted Anderson didn't see how they could have a life together. He'd be miserable in Boston; he was sure of that. And although Amanda seemed to be developing an appreciation for the woods, he didn't really see her giving up her career for life in the boonies. Ted didn't want to lose her, but he didn't see how he could keep her.

Which left him in a peculiar mood. A part of him was aglow with his rapidly growing feelings for Amanda, while another part was saddened by the certainty of losing her.

His dispatcher this evening was Rachel Lind, who sat at the other desk. She was a tall woman, at least five-eleven, with long brownish-blond hair. Looking over at Ted, she said, "By the time my shift's over, all the roads'll be closed. You still got that cot?"

"Still got it," Ted replied. "How's Roger gonna feel about you and me spending the night here together?"

She shrugged. "He won't like having to fix the kids' breakfast in the morning, but that's about it. Roger's not exactly what you'd call the jealous type."

"Even when his wife's locked up with a handsome devil like me?"

She laughed. "Not even then. Although I'll tell you who should be jealous. Whoever your Boston friend has back in Massachusetts."

"What do you mean?"

"You two are the talk of the town. Every time you get together you're both acting like a pair of starry-eyed teenagers. You might say you're an item."

"I didn't know it's that obvious."

"It's that obvious."

Ted felt on the verge of doing something he hadn't done in years: blushing. He managed to avoid it—he thought. To change the subject he said, "It's sure been quiet. I don't think the phone's rung in three hours."

"That's typical for a day like this," Rachel said. "When it snows, everybody stays home."

"But there's usually a couple of people wanting to know the road conditions between here and Fargo or something like that."

"Maybe the phone's out." Rachel picked up the receiver, put it to her ear. "It's dead," she said, looking mildly surprised.

"Call the phone company, get them to fix it."

For a second Rachel looked as if she might actually do it, but then she held up her fist, making a face at him over her knuckles. "Nobody likes a smartass, Anderson."

Ted shrugged and gave her an innocent look, as if to say, *A smartass—who, me?*

Rachel switched the radio in front of her to the state police frequency, called the Hibbing dispatcher, and asked her to contact the phone company, let it know that the phone was out at the Fiddlehead Lake police station.

Meanwhile Ted had gone back to thinking about Amanda—not about Amanda herself but about her problem. If a professional hit man was looking for her, there were things he should have done and hadn't. Fiddlehead Lake was a tight-knit community that looked out for its own, and for the time being, Amanda Price was one of its own. He should have alerted the people at places like the restaurant, the general store, and the gas station to let him know if anyone came around asking about Amanda. If anyone did, he'd learn about it at once. Ted stood up and got his jacket from the coatrack.

"You get the sudden urge to make a snowman or something?" Rachel asked.

"I'm going to walk over to see the Carlsons."

"Store's closed."

"I'll go to their house. After that I may go to the Lindstrom and the Hakala places." They owned the restaurant and the gas station, respectively. "I want to let everybody know to keep an eye out for someone asking about Amanda Price."

Although Rachel looked puzzled, she didn't ask for an explanation. "You sure you don't want to wait until morning?"

"I think I'll do it right now."

Rachel gave him a look that suggested if he didn't have enough sense to stay inside where it was warm during a blizzard, for chrissake, then there wasn't anything she could tell him. As if to prove her point, a gust of wind shook the building.

Actually Ted enjoyed getting out in the snow. As the wind-driven flakes stung his cheeks, he sucked in a deep breath of cold air, closed the door behind him, and headed toward the Carlson place. Snowflakes swirled along the street in currents and eddies of white. A drift was forming in front of the grocery store. Ted inhaled more cold air and watched the spectacle. He felt exhilarated.

Because Fiddlehead was so small, you could walk from any point in town to any other in five minutes, even in a blizzard. His cheeks had barely gotten cold when he knocked on the door of the Carlsons' two-story white house.

Larry Carlson, Eric's father, opened the door. He was a tall, broad-shouldered, blond-haired Scandinavian who looked more like a lumberjack than a store owner. "I was just about to come looking for you," he said. "I tried to call you, but the phone's out."

"It's out at the station, too," Ted said. "Must be out all over town." He stepped into the Carlsons' living room. It was spacious, with wall-to-wall carpeting and furniture that was old but solid. "What did you want to see me about?"

"I'm worried about Sue and Eric. They went to take Ashley home a couple of hours ago, and I haven't seen them since."

An uneasy feeling skittered along Ted's backbone. "What were they driving?"

"The Bronco. I would have checked on them myself, except the Bronco's the only four-wheel-drive in the family. And the chains for my dad's car are broken in about six places. I went to get another pair from the store and we're out of that size."

"You should let me do it, anyway," Ted said. "I'm in constant contact with the dispatcher over the radio. If there's any problem, all I have to do is grab the microphone."

"Want me to come with you?"

Ted shook his head. "If you're anxious to know what's going on, you can monitor my transmissions on Eric's scanner radio."

"I'll do that," Larry Carlson said.

"They haven't been out there very long, and Sue's lived here all her life. She knows what to do. I don't think there's much to worry about."

"I just want to find them before they get stranded out there and have to spend the night."

"I'll find them," Ted said, turning to go.

"What was it you came to see me about?" Larry asked. "Anything important?"

"I just wanted to ask a favor of you," Ted said, again facing Carlson. "I'd like you to let me know if anyone shows up at the store asking for Amanda Price. Spread the word, let everyone in the family know."

"Someone was asking about her today," he said.

"Who?" The uneasy feeling skittering along Ted's backbone had just turned to fear and moved to the pit of his stomach, crawling around in there like a many-legged insect.

"A man. It was Mom who saw him. She said she thought he was a government agent and that Amanda Price was probably in some sort of federal witness-protection program."

Ted had no idea what he was talking about, and he didn't hang around to find out. Reminding Larry Carlson to listen to his son's scanner, he hurried out the door. Moving as fast as he could against the wind, his heart thudding like a bass drummer gone berserk, Ted made his way through the blizzard and back to the substation. He'd put chains on his cruiser earlier, as soon as the snow had started falling, and now he was very glad of his foresight. Reaching the substation, he hurried inside to tell Rachel what was happening, but before he could open his mouth, she rushed over to him, holding up a newspaper.

"I think you should see this," she said.

Ted was about to tell her he didn't have time to look at the paper when the headline she was pointing to registered. Grabbing the newspaper, he read the story. When he finished, his hand was shaking. Rachel was staring at him.

"Jesus," he said, his voice barely audible.

Then he realized he had to move, find Amanda, find out what had happened to Sue and Eric Carlson and Ashley Price. He quickly told Rachel what was happening, watching her eyes widen as he did so.

"Call the Hibbing state police dispatcher on the radio and see if he's got any units in this area that can lend me a hand," Ted said.

She turned and hurried to her desk. Ted rushed out the door.

• • •

Amanda held the steering wheel with a death grip. Snowflakes whirled and swirled and danced in the car's headlights. In some places the wind scoured the pavement, keeping it spotlessly clear, while in others it piled the snow into drifts that kept getting deeper and deeper. The car would hit them, slowing, almost floating, and then it would burst through on the other side. If they got much deeper, she might get stuck. The car was equipped with so-called all-season radials, which were good enough for winter in Boston but not for weather like this.

Amanda imagined herself stuck in a snowdrift, unable to get the car out, time running out on the deadline for reaching Ashley. But then what made her think she could do anything to save her daughter in the first place? She was up against an armed adversary for whom she was absolutely no match. What could she do? What chance did she have?

She pushed these thoughts away, concentrated on driving. She was going to try. She *had* to.

Ahead was the biggest snowdrift she'd encountered yet, maybe two feet deep. Knowing she couldn't simply drive through it, Amanda stepped on the gas. The car shot forward, hitting the drift, snow flying in all directions, the car wobbling, slowing, feeling light, and then she was through it, not going more than two or three miles an hour. If the drifts got much deeper, she was going to have trouble.

Her knuckles were beginning to ache, but she didn't relax her grip on the wheel. She needed a plan, some way she might have a chance of saving Ashley and herself. She forced her brain to concentrate on that, but nothing came to her. An icy drop of perspiration trickled down her neck.

She saw light ahead, the Heikkinens' A-frame, and she considered going inside, asking them to call for help. Maybe the man wasn't really watching her. Maybe Ted could come, get some other policemen to help him. She slowed the car, not sure what to do. Inside the A-frame was warmth and help, and it was so tempting, so very, very tempting.

If you stop on the way, the girl dies. I'll be watching.

Although a part of her was all but begging her to pull into the Heikkinens' drive, Amanda stepped on the gas and sped by the A-frame. Maybe the man was watching and maybe he wasn't, but Amanda couldn't take the chance.

She thought she caught a glimpse of someone standing by the Heikkinens' woodpile, but she couldn't be sure. Maybe it was John Heikkinen, getting some wood. Maybe it was just a shadow, a tree silhouetted against a lighted window. Or maybe it was *him* watching her. She shivered.

The rectangles of light that were the Heikkinens' windows disappeared behind her, and there was nothing but blackness and the swirling white flakes. Amanda felt as if she'd left her last chance for warmth and human contact behind her, as if she were driving into a world in which there was nothing but blackness and cold and emptiness.

A cruel and uncaring world in which she and Ashley might die—unless she could find some way of preventing it. And she still had no idea how she might go about it.

The white flakes filled her field of vision.

The wind buffeted the car.

A tear or a drop of cold sweat trickled down Amanda's cheek. She was uncertain which.

The tire chains on Ted's cruiser clattered as he drove across a stretch of Lakeshore Road that had been scoured by the wind. The storm was getting worse. He was beginning to encounter snowdrifts that were difficult to get through, even with tire chains.

"Fiddlehead substation to Unit 129," Rachel said over the radio.

"Go ahead."

"Be advised that the closest SP unit is about ten miles away. He's en route, but with these road conditions it'll take him a while to get here."

"Ten four, Rachel. I'm on Lakeshore now, but I haven't seen anything."

"Ten four. Keep me advised."

Under ordinary circumstances he might be able to call in a State Police helicopter, but there wasn't a chopper built that could fly in weather like this. Suddenly Ted saw something that made him step on the brakes. A hole in the snowbank, where something might have plowed through it and run off the road. He pulled up to the spot and stopped, shining the car's spotlight over the edge of the road. The snowbank blocked his view, and he saw nothing but bare trees and falling snow. Telling Rachel what he'd found, Ted got his flashlight and went for a closer look. He discovered the Carlsons' Bronco about ten feet from the road, against a tree.

Suddenly one of the doors opened, and Eric Carlson got out, waving his arms. "My mom's inside!" he shouted. "Her leg's hurt, but except for that she's okay."

When Ted reached the Bronco, Eric looked as if he'd jump on him and hug him. Sue was stretched out in the backseat, covered with a blanket. Ted leaned over the front seat to get a better look at her.

"I think my leg's broken," she said, "but I don't think I'm hurt inside or anything. Eric wanted to go for help, but I made him stay here. I was afraid he'd get lost in the blizzard. We were both unconscious, and when we woke up, it was already snowing and Ashley was gone."

"I think the guy in the blue car might've gotten her," Eric said.

"What guy?"

Eric told him how a man in a blue car had forced them to stop and how his mother had lost control of the Bronco while trying to get away from him. "He could have Ashley," the boy said. "He could've taken her."

Ted wasn't sure which was worse, Ashley out there lost in a blizzard or Ashley in the hands of a killer. "I'm going to have to go look for her," the deputy said. "Can you and your mom hold out here a little longer?"

The boy nodded. "The Bronco's stuck, but the engine starts, and we can use the heater a little. But it overheats. I think the radiator's leaking."

"Keep the window open a crack when you run the heater, and don't run it too much."

"I know," the boy said. "You'd better find Ashley."

"I'm going now. I'll tell Rachel what I found here, and she'll get someone out here to get you and your mom."

"How long will it take?"

"Not long, I hope."

"Find Ashley," the boy said again.

When he was back in his car, Ted explained the situation to Rachel. "See if you can get Hal Townsend to come out here with his Wagoneer. He's got a CB radio in it, and he can stay in touch with his wife. He shouldn't have too much trouble getting here, but if he does, then you'll have to get Ralph to fire up his Sno Cat."

"Ten four. Larry Carlson's here. He says he'll go over to get Hal."

"Ten four."

Ted went back to the Bronco to let Eric and his mother know that Hal Townsend, who was the paramedic for the volunteer fire department, would be coming for them in his Wagoneer. Eric and his mom said they'd be fine.

Back in his car, Ted headed for Amanda's cabin. He didn't know for sure that Ashley was in the hands of the man in the blue car, and he didn't know where Amanda was. Checking out her cabin was the only thing he could think of to do. Maybe Amanda was there, safe but worried sick about Ashley. Maybe the man was there. With Ashley.

Ted recalled how less than an hour ago he'd been thinking about how smitten he was with Amanda and how he was so certain he'd lose her. He'd been thinking of her eventually going back to Boston. Now he was afraid he'd lose her today, this minute, and in a much more terrible manner than just watching her drive away, heading east.

The berserk drummer in his chest was still pounding out his frantic, nonstop beat. Ted was more afraid than he'd ever been before in his life.

Afraid for Ashley and Amanda.

Afraid of what would happen if he had to go up against a professional killer.

Ted was suddenly conscious of the service revolver in his belt. He had never even drawn the weapon on the job, much less having ever shot anyone. He was a trained law officer, a good shot on the pistol range, but he knew he could well be heading into a situation no amount of training or target practice could ever prepare him to handle.

Ashley stared into the darkness, seeing no sign of the man. He'd switched on a powerful flashlight when he left the car, its beam illuminating the bare trees and turning the snowflakes into thousands of whirling, glowing dots. The light had moved farther and farther away, and now it was gone.

Maybe he'll get lost in the blizzard, Ashley thought. Maybe he'll die. It was the first time in her life she had truly ever wished for the death of another human being. She did not feel guilty about it.

A gust of wind rocked the car. Ashley had been struggling with her bonds ever since the man had left, but the cords around her wrists and ankles were as tight as ever. She was fairly certain she could get out of the car. Although her hands were tied behind her, she could take hold of the handle by turning her back to it. She hadn't tried it because with her hands and legs bound, she really couldn't go anywhere, especially in a blizzard. And the man's warning hung ominously in the back of her mind. If she did try—and didn't freeze to death in the blizzard—the man would do something awful to her.

She shivered. Tears puddled in the corners of her eyes,

and then they spilled out, streaming down her face. There was a good chance she was going to die. Images flashed through her mind: her mom, her apartment back in Boston, her friends, her school, Eric Carlson. Would she ever see any of these people or places again? Frantically she fought with the cords encircling her ankles and wrists, desperately trying to loosen them, even just a little, enough to give her hope. With all the strength she had, Ashley attempted to pull her hand free, ignoring the pain as the cord bit into her flesh, telling herself it didn't matter if she stripped the skin right off, that only escape was important—freedom and survival. Finally the pain grew so intense, she was unable to ignore it. The cords were as tight as ever.

She screamed then, a cry of utter frustration and defeat, stomped her feet on the floor of the car, and went limp, tears dripping from her chin, making a *pit-pat-pat* sound as they landed on the vinyl upholstery.

"Oh, God," she sobbed. "I'm never going to see my mom again. Or Eric. Or anybody."

Instantly her mind was made up. Dying in a blizzard was better than dying at the hands of the man. If she could get far enough away from the car, maybe he wouldn't be able to find her; maybe help would come; maybe she'd be rescued. She turned around, trying to get numb fingers on the door handle. When she had it, she pulled it, at the same time pushing against the door with her body. It opened, spilling her into the snow.

Getting to her feet, she looked around quickly, seeing no wavering dot of light to indicate that the man was on his way back. Again she hoped he was lost, unable to find his way back to the car, but she knew that was something she could not count on.

With her feet bound, all she could do was hop. On her first attempt Ashley slipped and fell, landing on her back. She was lucky the snow broke her fall, because she was unable to use her hands, which made falling extremely dangerous. Struggling to her feet, she hopped again. This time she remained standing. Again she leapt forward, and this time she fell again, her face smacking into the snow. Stunned, she lay there a moment, then got to her feet once more. She was no more than a yard from the rear bumper of the car. It might take her hours to get away like this, and she was sure she didn't have hours before the man returned.

Unless he was lost in the snow. Please, God, she thought. Please.

And then she thought of a way she might be able to move a little faster and a lot more safely. Dropping to the ground, she lay on her stomach, pulling up her knees, then extending her torso forward, similar to the way a worm moved. It worked. It wasn't fast, but it was better than constantly falling.

Wormlike, she made her way forward, away from the direction in which the man had gone. It was hard work, and every time she reached forward with the upper portion of her body, her face hit the snow. The wind whistled through the trees, pelting her with snowflakes. Her hands, ungloved and with their circulation restricted, had gone numb, as if her arms stopped at the wrists, beyond which there was nothing. She tried to wiggle her fingers and had no idea whether she'd succeeded.

Exhausted, uncertain of how much farther she could go, Ashley rolled over and sat up to look behind her. Desperation and fear surged through her because she saw the flashlight, maybe thirty feet away. In the blizzard he might not have spotted her. Flopping over, Ashley began her stop-start belly crawl, pulling up her knees, pushing herself ahead, pulling up her knees, pushing herself ahead. The sight of the man's flashlight had given her a new burst of strength. Ahead was a tree, its trunk thick. Maybe she could hide behind it and the man wouldn't see her.

Ashley made it to the tree, rolled behind it, out of breath, her whole body quaking from the exertion. And then she realized how stupid she'd been. To find her, all the man had to do was follow her tracks. The snow and wind would obliterate them, given a few minutes. But not this quickly. Suddenly there was a light shining in her face.

The man grabbed her, dragged her toward the car, her feet leaving furrows in the snow. The distance it had taken her an enormous expenditure of energy to cover was a matter of twenty-five or thirty steps for the man. He dropped her in the snow by the rear of the car.

"You shouldn't have done that," he said, unlocking the trunk of the car.

Ashley just looked at him, trying not to show the terror that had settled like an icy glob in the pit of her stomach. Her attempt to escape had been a total failure. She was at his mercy now. He would do what he would do. There was no way Ashley could save herself.

The man began removing firewood from the trunk. On the way here, he'd stolen the wood from a house at which the people didn't seem to be home and filled the trunk with it. When the split logs were stacked beside the car, the man grabbed Ashley, picking her up as easily as she would pick up one of her old dolls, and dropped her none too gently into the trunk.

"I'll deal with you later," he said.

And then he slammed the lid.

Ashley heard the clank of firewood being gathered up, the crunch of footsteps in snow, and then there was nothing but the screaming of the wind. Tears formed in her eyes but didn't fall. Ashley was too numb, too exhausted and defeated to cry. She simply lay there in the cold, dark, cramped space, knowing that what would come would come. Crying wouldn't change it. Wishing wouldn't change it. Nothing would change it.

Someone will come, a part of her was saying. *Someone will rescue you.*

No, Ashley thought, *no one will rescue me*.

The voice of hope fell silent.

EIGHTEEN

TED Anderson stopped the car, rolled down the window, cold air and snow rushing into the cruiser. He was looking at a small notch in the top of the snowbank, along with some shallow dimples leading up to it, as if someone had recently climbed the bank at this spot and the snow hadn't quite covered up the evidence yet. If so, that someone could have been cutting through the trees to Amanda's cabin. Rolling up the window, Ted stepped on the gas.

The lights were on in the cabin, but Amanda's car was gone. Blizzard or no blizzard, Amanda probably would try to find out why her daughter hadn't arrived home. And then Ted realized there was one thing terribly wrong with this theory. He would have passed her on the way here.

Getting out of the car, Ted drew his service revolver. Although he'd carried the weapon for years, cleaned it, practiced with it, the gun suddenly seemed alien, as if it didn't belong in his hand. If someone had approached the house from the road, the intruder would have arrived at the north side. Climbing over the snow that had been cleared from the drive, Ted checked that side of the house. There were more dimples in the snow, possibly the remains of tracks, possibly nothing but ripples made by the wind. And then he saw something proving conclusively that someone had been here.

The telephone wire had been cut where it ran down the side of the house.

Whoever had done it had been a stranger because he hadn't known that the phones were already out. With a

253

storm coming on, they would quite likely remain inoperative for a few days. Cutting Amanda's line had been completely unnecessary.

Moving cautiously to the front door, Ted tried it, finding it unlocked. He went into the house, keeping low, holding his service revolver with both hands. The living room was empty. As were the kitchen, bedrooms, and bathroom. No one was here. Ted holstered his gun, and for a few moments he simply stood in the living room, trying to calm himself down. Excited by the adrenaline surging through his system, every nerve and fiber he owned seemed to be stretched piano-wire-taut.

Where was Amanda? If she wasn't here and he hadn't passed her on the road, there was only one way she could have gone. And then he thought he knew. Her phone was out, so she'd gone over to the Heikkinens' to see whether theirs was working, so she could call the Carlsons, ask about Ashley. The man had come here, cut the phone line, found no one home.

What, then? Would he have searched for her, waited nearby? Or would he have followed her tracks to the Heikkinens'? Ted hurried back to his car. As he drove, he could see brief straight depressions that might be the remains of tracks and might not. He came to a snowdrift so deep that he had to back up and get a run at it. The drift dipped in the center, as if someone else had pushed through it earlier. Then, as he sailed through the snow, throwing it in every direction, it occurred to Ted that this would be a good place to set up an ambush. He'd be an easy target as his car, barely moving by then, came out of the drift. No one ambushed him.

Ted fought with his nerves, tried to get them under control. To deal with this situation he had to be calm, had to think clearly. But coolness and levelheadedness were states that eluded him. He was too scared, too close to panic. All he could do was go on, hope Amanda was all right, hope he could deal with the situation if she wasn't.

He almost missed the Heikkinens' driveway. Hitting the brakes too quickly, he made the car slide, but it slowed enough to make the turn. Amanda's car wasn't here, but then it wasn't safe to assume that Amanda herself wasn't. If the killer had caught up with her here, he might have moved Amanda's car out of sight so no one would know she was in the house. Again Ted drew his gun as soon as he was out of the car.

The lights were on inside, but all the curtains were drawn, making it impossible for Ted to peek through a window. He considered his options, deciding he really didn't have any. He rang the doorbell. Barbara Heikkinen answered the door.

"Ted," she said, surprised. "What are you doing here in the middle of a blizzard? Come on in and get warm. Would you like some coffee? Some hot chocolate? Some hot mulled wine?"

Ted had been holding his service revolver at his side, out of sight. He holstered it as unobtrusively as possible and stepped inside. "No thanks," he said. "I don't have time to drink anything right now. Have you seen Amanda Price?"

"No," she said, "not for a couple of days."

John, who'd been sitting on the couch, reading a magazine, got up and joined them. "I think I saw her a little while ago, when I was out getting some firewood. It was either her or someone in a car a lot like hers. It was headed toward the Gustafsons'."

"The Gustafsons are in Hawaii," Ted said.

"I know. There's nothing out there, but the Gustafsons' place at the end of the road, but that's the direction she was going—if it was her."

"Is something wrong?" Barbara Heikkinen asked.

"I don't know," Ted said, shaking his head. "I hope not."

A moment later he was back in his cruiser, heading for the Gustafsons' place as fast as the slippery road and snowdrifts would allow. He figured the car John Heikkinen had seen had to be Amanda's. But why would she have gone out toward the end of Lakeshore Road in a blizzard? It was possible the man was holding her captive and he'd forced her to accompany him to the Gustafsons' house, because it was deserted and no one would find them there. But the man was a stranger. He wouldn't have known the Gustafsons even existed, much less where they lived and that they were out of town.

So why had Amanda come this way? Had she been lured in some manner? It was easy enough to pose these questions, but he had no answers for them. Another major question for which he had no answer was what had happened to Ashley. If she'd gone for help after the accident, she would have stayed on the road. Although she wasn't familiar with the rules of living in the north woods, she wasn't stupid, either. She wouldn't have wandered off the road with a snowstorm coming. Which had to mean that the man had her. Could Ashley have been the lure that got Amanda to drive out here where there was nothing but a vacant house and the end of the road?

He switched off his lights as he pulled into the Gustafsons' drive. The yellow clapboard house was slightly bigger than Amanda's. It had three bedrooms and a screened-in rear deck. The place was dark; there were no cars, no fresh tracks. Still, he had to be sure. Getting his flashlight, Ted climbed out of the car, drawing his revolver. He circled the house, checking every door and window for signs of a break-in. It was tough going. Near the house, the snow was incredibly deep because Matt Gustafson had shoveled off his roof, creating eight-foot-high mountains into which Ted sank every time he took a step.

He found no sign of a break-in at the Gustafsons' house, although someone recently might have stolen some of their firewood. The canvas cover had been removed and not replaced, allowing the pile to be covered with snow. Matt Gustafson always tied the canvas down well so the wind couldn't remove it. Looking at the chimney, Ted saw no smoke. Either Matt had failed to tie down the cover as well as usual or someone had stolen some of his wood. Thievery was rare here, except during the summer, when the city people were around. Perhaps the Gustafsons had given someone permission to borrow some firewood.

Had the man stopped here, raided the woodpile? It seemed unlikely. What would he want with it?

Back in his car, Ted headed for the end of the road. He was worried that he had overlooked something. Had the Heikkinens been acting strangely? Could there have been someone watching them, just out of sight, ready to shoot them if they betrayed his presence? Had the man found a key in the Gustafsons' mailbox, let himself in without leaving any evidence of a break-in? Ted shook his head. There was no place at the Gustafsons' to hide Amanda's car. He'd shined his flashlight into the window of their one-car garage, finding it empty. Amanda's car could have been concealed in the Heikkinens' barn, but John and Barbara hadn't been acting. At least he didn't think so.

But why would Amanda go to the end of the road? What would be the point?

Anxiety constricted his stomach, stretched his already taut nerves even tighter.

Two red dots appeared in the snowy darkness, brightening as Amanda's car drew closer to them. The reflectors in the taillights of a car. A blue car. Amanda had reached the end of the road.

She pulled to a stop but didn't switch off the engine or headlights. Taking in her surroundings, she saw that she was in a clear space where the snowplow turned around. Beyond the blue Chevrolet was a mountain of snow, apparently put there by the plow. As far as she could tell, the blue car was empty. Where was Ashley? Where was the man?

Leaving the engine running and the lights on, Amanda got out of the car, walked toward the Chevrolet, the wind pushing her to the side, snowflakes hitting her face like buckshot. The wind had packed snow on the Chevy's windows. Amanda tried to brush it off, but heat from the interior of the car had momentarily melted it, and now it was a solid layer of ice. She opened the door. The interior light came on. The car was empty. As she closed the door her own car's headlights went out and the engine stopped.

A flashlight was aimed at her.

Unable to see who was holding the light but certain who it was, Amanda watched as its brightness moved closer. The man was only about a dozen feet from her when he spoke, and even at that distance the wind distorted his words, tearing them from his mouth and trying to carry them away before the sound could reach her.

"Move away from the car," he said.

He moved the flashlight so it was no longer in her eyes, and Amanda saw two things. A narrow, bony face with peculiar dead-looking eyes. And a gun in the hand that wasn't holding the flashlight.

Amanda stood her ground. "Where's Ashley?" she demanded.

"In the car."

"I've looked in the car. What have you done with her?"

"If you want to see her, move away from the car."

This time Amanda obeyed. Slipping the gun into his coat pocket, the man unlocked the trunk, reached in, and pulled Ashley out, dropping her in the snow. Her hands and feet were bound. Looking bewildered, she simply sat there, apparently unaware of her mother's presence.

"Ashley!" Amanda cried, starting toward her.

"Stop!" the man commanded. The gun was back in his hand now, and it was aimed at Amanda. She stopped, something inside her chest shriveling because that's where the gun was aimed.

"Mom," Ashley said. "Mom." She still seemed dazed.

"It's okay," Amanda said. "Everything'll be okay."

The expression on the girl's face made it clear she knew

that everything was not okay, that, to use her expression, they were knee-deep in doo-doo. Again slipping the gun into his coat pocket, the man took out a pocketknife, squatted, and cut the cord around Ashley's ankles. He rose, pulling the girl to her feet. Though wobbly, she was able to stand.

Although Amanda desperately wanted to rush to her, hold her, comfort her, she knew the man would not allow it, so she just stood there, helpless, thinking about how awful it must have been to be locked in a cold trunk. How long had Ashley been in there? What had he done to her besides tie her up?

And what would he do now, to both of them?

This was the man who'd shot Bob Miller, terrorized his wife and children, tortured Dick Kilmer before killing him, murdered a security guard at the TV station. And for what? A scrap of information, a name. Was life so cheap, so ugly, that people could die so horribly just because a group of evil criminals wanted to find the one who'd broken their code of silence?

It wasn't revenge on Amanda herself; that was just a fringe benefit. It was the name, had to be the name. And this man, this monster who was holding her daughter captive, hadn't had to hurt Bob Miller or terrorize his family, hadn't had to cut off Dick Kilmer's fingers. These weren't acts designed just to acquire information. These were acts of unnecessary cruelty, acts of a deranged mind that took pleasure in the suffering of others.

"We're going over that way," the man said, pointing with the gun. Swinging it back to Amanda, he said, "You lead. Your daughter and I will follow."

Amanda did as instructed, walking to the edge of the cleared area, then into the deep snow surrounding it, where moving became slow and laborious. She tried not to think about what the man might do to them, for whatever he planned for them would be horrible beyond words. She clung desperately to the only thin hope she could find.

There were two of them, and they were alive. As his plan unfolded, he might make a mistake, give them a chance to do something. Amanda didn't know what. Just something. Anything.

And Amanda knew that given the chance, she would kill this man. She had always viewed unnatural death as an evil thing, the result of wars and violent crimes, humanity at its worst. But this was a life she would gladly take, for this man wasn't human. There was no way to rehabilitate him, teach him right from wrong, teach him to empathize with the suffering of others. This man was evil, as evil as the death he caused, evil personified.

Unbidden, the image of her shooting the man popped into her head, the weapon jumping in her hands as the bullets tore into him. And when the gun was empty, he grinned at her, apparently unharmed. Then he said, "You can't kill me. No one can kill evil." His normally lifeless eyes glowed red, becoming as bright as a pair of brake lights.

He directed them to a clearing surrounded by enormous spruce trees growing so close together that their branches intertwined at the bottom, making a wall that effectively blocked the wind. The snow blowing through the tops of the trees floated down, light and powdery.

"Stop," the man said.

Amanda did, and he pushed Ashley around her, taking the girl to the only non-coniferous tree in the clearing, a leafless stalk that stood alone among all the evergreens. He tied Ashley to the tree, and it wasn't until he was finished that Amanda saw what was piled up at the tree's base. Wood. Split firewood. Amanda's heart began to race. The icy wind that still howled beyond the protective evergreens suddenly seemed to be inside her, whipping the snow around her organs, piling it in drifts against her spine.

Reaching behind the trees, the man got a can of charcoal lighter and poured it on the wood at Ashley's feet. Turning to Amanda, he said, "Tell me the name of the guy whose face and voice were distorted in your New Shipton story."

"George Sprague," she said at once. It was a name she made up on the spur of the moment. She didn't know why she lied. She'd just opened her mouth, and that's the name that came out.

"And who's George Sprague?"

"He's an accountant . . . for Casperson."

Ashley was staring at them, her eyes wide, filled with terror. She glanced down at the wood, as if to make sure it was really saturated with the charcoal lighter. She was trembling, her mouth open, her lips quivering. Amanda thought the girl was beyond speech, so consumed by fright that she probably could do no more than squeak or grunt.

Powerful emotions welled up inside Amanda. Sympathy for the daughter she loved so much. Hatred, deep and intense, for the subhuman monster who was doing this to Ashley.

"You're lying," the man said. "I have a list of all the people who work for Casperson. We've gone over it several times, trying to identify suspects. There's no George Sprague." Putting the gun into his pocket, the man withdrew a disposable cigarette lighter. He flicked it, igniting a flame, which flickered in the breeze within the clearing but didn't go out. Quickly he leaned toward the wood at Ashley's feet, extending his arm.

"Ron Miner!" she screamed. "Ron Miner! Ron Miner! Ron Miner!"

"That's better," the man said, shutting off the flame and straightening. "Where does he work?"

"The . . . the police department. He's a computer operator in the records section."

"What does he look like?"

"Tall, but not as tall as you. Light hair. Late twenties, kind of a rough complexion, as if he had zits bad when he was younger and never quite recovered."

Amanda was trembling even more violently than Ashley. Cold sweat trickled down her back. Her breathing was ragged.

The man nodded, satisfied. Then he lit the butane flame again and leaned toward the wood.

For what seemed like an eternity, Amanda just stood there, unable to move, watching the flame get closer and closer to the fuel-saturated wood, something in her mind telling her that this wasn't really happening, couldn't possibly be happening. And then she snapped out of it, hurled herself at the man, her hand digging into her coat pocket, her fingers wrapping around the handle of the kitchen knife.

But the man was expecting this. He grinned, preparing to fend her off, make it look easy, maybe send her sprawling in the snow, then taunt her. He would play with her until he tired of it, and then Amanda and Ashley would die. But as Amanda was rushing toward him, her brain telling her that her charge would prove useless, a sound entered her consciousness—a loud, popping buzz—and apparently the man considered the noise a greater danger than Amanda because his eyes immediately shifted to its source.

As she closed in on him, Amanda pulled out the knife, raising it.

The man's eyes were still on the source of the noise.

Then she was within a few feet of him, her legs propelling her through the snow with all the strength she could get out of them.

The man glanced toward her, making sure he knew where she was, what she was doing.

The blade was arching downward, Amanda gritting her teeth.

The man saw the knife, tried to react, but he was too late, for Amanda, powered by her consuming hatred of this man, plunged the knife through his coat, the blade sinking deeply into his side. The man staggered backward, dropping the flashlight, his expression stunned, disbelieving.

Amanda heard someone shout, words that she was unable to understand. She turned, seeking their source, and spotted two teenage boys on a snowmobile. For some reason her initial reaction was to wonder how they could be so foolish as to go snowmobiling in a blizzard. Didn't they know they could get lost? And then she realized how ludicrous it was for her to think of things like that at a time like this.

"Help!" she hollered. "I need help."

The boys were staring at the scene, confused and wary. The man was sitting down now, clutching his side, still looking as though he was unable to believe what had happened. Ashley was tied to the tree, having come within a whisker of being burned at the stake. And Amanda held a bloody knife in her hand. She had been gripping it tightly, squeezing its handle with a strength that came from rage and terror and the need to protect her child, and apparently she hadn't released it even after stabbing the man.

"What's going on here?" one of the boys asked. He started to get off the snowmobile, then thought better of it, apparently reluctant to get too far away from his means of escape.

Amanda pointed at the man, who was still sitting in the snow, holding his side. "He kidnapped my daughter. He was going to kill us both."

The boys on the snowmobile said something to each other. Forgetting about them for a moment, Amanda hurried to Ashley and began cutting her bonds. The girl was shaking, still too terrified to speak. The man's butane lighter lay on the wood. It had shut itself off when he dropped it. Amanda thought, Thank God he didn't drop a lighted match.

When Ashley was free she collapsed against her mother, holding her, still shaking. Amanda squeezed her tightly. After a moment the girl's shaking began to subside. And then she was sobbing.

"Mom," she said. "I—" She was crying too hard to continue.

Suddenly the snowmobile's engine screamed. Amanda saw it roar toward the edge of the clearing. There were three loud pops, and it took Amanda a moment to figure out that the man was shooting at the boys on the snowmobile. He was still in the snow, holding his gun with both hands. He fired one last shot as the snowmobile disappeared between two spruce trees.

Amanda had Ashley's hand, pulling her away from the tree. The sound of the snowmobile's motor grew steadily fainter. Amanda thought the boys had escaped unharmed. She hoped they had enough sense to go as fast as possible for help. When she'd first surprised the man by stabbing him, she should have tried to take the gun away from him, she realized. But it was too late now. All she could do was try to get Ashley and herself away from him. As the two of them got closer to the edge of the clearing, Amanda kept expecting a shot to ring out, a bullet to penetrate her back, but no shots were fired.

As soon as they'd made it into the safety of the trees, Amanda stopped and looked behind her, seeing no sign of the man. Ashley was breathing raggedly. She was shivering again. Amanda hugged her.

"You have to get hold of yourself," she said gently but firmly. "He might come after us. Help's on the way, but until it gets here, we might have to keep moving, make sure he doesn't find us."

The girl nodded. "I'll be okay, Mom." But she didn't sound okay. She sounded as if the horror of nearly being burned alive had sucked the strength out of her, barely leaving her with enough energy to speak—as if half her mind had sought escape in catatonia and the other half was thinking about joining it.

Amanda saw movement in the clearing, and a moment later she saw the man himself. He was standing now. He'd picked up the flashlight and was holding it in one hand, the gun in the other.

And he was coming toward them.

"Come on," she whispered to Ashley. The girl let her guide her, moving blinding, listlessly. Amanda tried to make her move faster, but the girl wasn't capable of it. The deep snow was also slowing them down. And all the man had to do was follow their tracks. All Amanda could do was try to keep trees between the man and themselves so he couldn't shoot.

It would take all their strength just to keep moving from tree to tree. With the blizzard raging, it would be a long time before the snowmobilers got to town and help made it back out here.

Ashley stumbled and fell. Amanda pulled her to her feet. "We have to keep moving," she said. "We have to."

Removing her gloves, she slipped them on the girl's bare hands. Ashley didn't seem to notice.

A shot rang out, the bullet snapping into a tree trunk about three feet to Amanda's left. Grabbing Ashley's arm, she pulled the girl through the snow, forced her to move faster.

They were away from the protection of the clearing now, and the wind screamed as it battered them with snowflakes, tried to work its way under their clothes so it could steal their warmth. Amanda's face had gone from cold to numb. Although the snowflakes were still peppering her cheeks, she no longer felt them.

NINETEEN

TED plowed through a snowdrift and nearly collided with the snowmobile. Waving frantically for Ted to stop, two teenage boys leapt off the machine and rushed over to the cruiser. Ted rolled down his window.

Pointing back the way he had come, one of them said, "A man back there was shooting at us." Ted recognized him. Walt Franklin's boy, Keith. The other teenager was Ben Zimmerman.

"There was a woman and a girl there," Ben said. "The woman said they'd been kidnapped."

"The girl was all tied up with wood around her," Keith added.

"The woman and the man were struggling," Ben said. "I think she stabbed him."

"She had a knife. A bloody knife," Keith said.

"The woman cut the girl loose, and then the man started shooting at us, so we got the hell out of there."

The boys were talking so fast, Ted was having a hard time keeping up with them. "Where was this exactly?" he asked.

"Back at the end of the road."

"And there were three people there?" Ted asked.

"A man, a woman, and a girl."

"And the woman said she'd been kidnapped."

"The girl too."

"Okay," Ted said. "What kind of gun did the man have?"

"A handgun."

"A whatchamacallit—an automatic."

Ted said, "That's the only gun you saw?"

Simultaneously: "Yeah."

Ted nailed down a few more points, then told the boys to get into town and report to the substation. He got on the radio and asked Rachel to check with the state police, see how far away the officer sent to assist him was.

"They say it'll be a good fifteen or twenty minutes before he gets there," she reported. "Also, Hal Townsend has picked up Sue and Eric Carlson. They're on their way into town now. The only problem is that the road to Hibbing's closed. There's no way we can get them to the hospital till morning."

"Will they be okay till then?"

"Hal says so."

"Good." He filled Rachel in on what was happening, told her two boys would be showing up and that she should get statements from them. "I'm going on ahead," he told her. "Tell state police."

"Shouldn't you wait for backup?" Rachel said tensely.

"I don't have time. Amanda and Ashley could be dead before any help gets here."

"Ten four," Rachel said, but she clearly wasn't happy about the situation.

About three minutes later Ted reached the end of the road. Picking up the microphone, he said, "I'm ten ninety-seven, Rachel. I'll be going in from here on foot."

"Ten forty-eight, Ted. Please." It was the radio code for "use caution."

"Ten four," he said, and got out of the car.

Drawing his service revolver, he switched on his flashlight and began looking for tracks that led off to the right, toward the clearing the boys had described. He found them immediately, rapidly filling in with snow but still plainly visible. The danger to himself was no longer on his mind. Amanda and Ashley needed his help, needed it desperately, and he would do his best to rescue them.

Uncertain what he'd find, Ted followed the tracks in the snow, telling himself he was in time, he could still save them, knowing he would never forgive himself if he let anything happen to them. Some part of his brain was sending out a psychic message: *Amanda, I'm coming.*

But if a psychic link had been established, Ted was unaware of it. When he reached the clearing the boys had described, it was deserted.

Dexter Buchanan was having trouble keeping up with the woman and the girl. The pain in his side where the woman had stabbed him was growing more intense, and he could feel a sticky wetness beneath his coat. He was bleeding, maybe even worse on the inside, where he couldn't detect it. He was disgusted with himself for letting the woman use the knife on him. He was a professional who had handled other professionals—a killer's killer, you might say. That precise term had never occurred to him before, and he liked it. A killer's killer.

And yet, distracted by the snowmobile, he had let Amanda Price—a woman, a TV reporter—sink a blade into his side. He wasn't embarrassed about it, for embarrassment was unknown to him. But he was paying a price for his mistake. The weakness, the burning pain in his side. Moving through the deep snow was getting harder and harder.

Spotting movement ahead, Buchanan stopped, raised his automatic. The weapon was wobbling, impossible to hold steady in the wind, and all of a sudden the trees were fuzzy, out of focus. He squinted, tried harder to steady the gun, and could neither hold the automatic still nor focus on the spot where he'd seen movement.

He squeezed off a couple of rounds anyway, just in case. And then he wondered what was wrong with him. He never fired unless he had a sure target. Abruptly it occurred to him that he had no idea how many shots he'd fired. The automatic's clip could be empty. Sticking the flashlight in the snow with its beam aimed upward, he popped out the clip, intending to slip it into his pocket, but for some reason he dropped it. The clip disappeared into the snow. Although Buchanan thought he'd seen the spot at which it went into the white stuff, he was unable to locate it. After a few moments of digging around in the snow he gave up, got a fresh clip from his coat pocket, slipped it into the gun, and picked up the flashlight.

He started forward again, following the tracks in the snow, the beam of his flashlight putting yellow light on tree trunk after tree trunk, revealing no sign of the woman and the girl except for the holes in the snow that would eventually lead him to them, for they would have to tire before he did.

Suddenly feeling dizzy, Buchanan stopped. It was the damned knife wound, sapping his strength. And for the first time it occurred to him that the woman and the girl might not tire out before he did, that he might be losing so much blood internally, he'd eventually fall down in the snow and die. The thought stunned him. He'd never considered his own death before. Although life gave him few pleasures, Dexter Buchanan had no desire to leave this world. He did have a survival instinct.

The wind was adding to his problems. Although his hooded coat was well insulated, the exposed portion of his face felt like a block of ice, and the cold seemed able to use that opening to penetrate through the rest of him, drawing off his body heat faster than he could manufacture it. Despite his insulated shoes, his feet had gone from painfully cold to numb.

Buchanan wondered whether he should let the woman and girl go, get back to the warmth of the car, see if he could make it out of here, get to a phone, let Casperson know the name of the traitor. He was still trying to decide when he heard a man shout.

"Amanda! Ashley! It's me—Ted."

"We're here!" Amanda Price shouted back. "There's a man after us. He's got a gun!"

Forgetting about the woman and the girl, Buchanan

turned around and headed in the direction from which the man's voice had come. He switched off his flashlight, and in a few moments he was able to see the man's flashlight. There was only one light, so the man was alone. The guy had been stupid on two counts. He shouldn't have come alone, and he shouldn't have hollered, revealing not only his presence but his location as well.

The man was coming toward him. Buchanan moved to the left, away from the spot at which the man would pass closest to him, away from the man's light. When the man became clearly visible, Buchanan saw that it was a cop. The killer raised his gun. The cop passed behind a tree, and then he was visible again, a clear shot. A shiver passed through Buchanan, his vision blurring, his hands beginning to shake. Reaching deep down inside to find his last reserves of energy, Buchanan steadied the weapon in his hands, brought the scene in front of him back into focus, and squeezed the trigger.

The deputy cried out and fell. Buchanan started toward him.

Before Ted called out, Amanda had been frozen and exhausted, all but defeated, certain she and Ashley would collapse in the snow, unable to take another step, and the man would simply walk up and shoot them. Either that or they'd freeze to death, their bodies not discovered until spring, half eaten by animals. And then Ted had called their names. Suddenly there was hope.

With Ashley still moving mechanically, reluctantly, Amanda had pulled her toward the sound of Ted's voice, their pursuer all but forgotten. It was Ashley, abruptly snapping out of her stupor, who realized the mistake they were making. "Mom," she said urgently, "we don't know where the man is. We could be going right to him."

The girl was right. Amanda slowed down, tried to move more cautiously, quietly. She didn't want to step around a tree and find herself face-to-face with the killer. When a shot rang out, Amanda grabbed her daughter, pulling both of them down into the snow. And then she realized that no bullet had whistled past or thonked into a tree trunk. The shot had not been fired at them.

"Come on," she whispered, and the two of them got up, headed in the direction of the shot, still moving quietly.

Amanda saw the light. As they moved closer she saw the man standing over Ted.

Her heart seemed to flutter in her chest. She'd been afraid for Ashley and for herself, but it had never occurred to her that anything could happen to Ted. And despite all the confused thoughts swirling in her head, Amanda realized that she was looking at it as a personal loss, the loss of someone she loved. Her eyes filled with tears, blurring her vision.

"Mom," Ashley whispered, "he's still alive. Look."

Ted was struggling to sit up. But the man was standing over him, holding his gun. He would shoot Ted again at any moment. Amanda was sure of it. It was what the man did. He killed.

Amanda began moving forward again. Sticking out of the snow was a portion of a tree branch that had snapped off because of wind or snow or rot. Amanda pulled on it, and it came out easily, a piece of wood about three feet long and three inches in diameter. It was as good a weapon as she was likely to find.

"Stay here," Amanda whispered to Ashley.

The girl shook her head. "You'll need my help."

"No," Amanda whispered. "Stay here. Please."

Reluctantly the girl agreed.

Amanda crept forward as silently as the deep snow allowed. When she was about fifteen feet from the man, she heard his voice above the wind. "We'll just wait for Amanda Price to show up," he said. "Maybe she'll be brave, try to rescue you."

"What, then?" Ted asked, his voice weak, barely audible over the wind's shrieking. Amanda could tell by the look on his face that the deputy was in pain. And that he knew he was going to die.

"Then I leave three bodies here for the wolves or whatever wants them."

Ted, who was lying on his side now, spotted Amanda. His eyes quickly moved on so as not to give her away. "She won't come," Ted said.

"We'll wait a while and see. For you it'll work out the same either way."

It occurred to Amanda that this was her chance to try to get back to the car, get out of here with Ashley. But she didn't know where the car was; she was hopelessly turned around. Besides, there was no way she could abandon Ted. You want Amanda? she thought. Well, here she is.

Raising her club, Amanda charged forward, hoping the wind would mask the noise of her attack. But somehow the man knew, for he was instantly turning to face her, aiming the gun, and Amanda knew she would never get to swing the club, knew a bullet would sink into her body before she could take two more steps.

A shot was fired.

To her amazement Amanda didn't feel a thing. No bullet knocked her backward. No pain erupted within her as organs and muscles were torn apart. It just passes right through, she thought, and you don't even know it's happened until the pain catches up with you.

The man stared at her, wide-eyed, confused.

And then he collapsed.

Amanda's momentum carried her another step or two before she stopped, stood there looking at the killer stupidly. Had he passed out from the knife wound she'd inflicted, losing consciousness just as he fired, the shot going wild? Before Amanda could address that notion, Ashley rushed through the snow, almost knocking Amanda down as she collided with her, hugged her.

For a few moments the girl just cried. Finally she said, "I . . . I thought he shot you."

Amanda was shaking, trying to adjust to the notion that she'd just seen her own death, *felt* it inside, and yet she was standing there with her daughter, the killer lying at her feet. Abruptly it occurred to her that she'd better get his gun, find out whether he was still alive. And see to Ted.

The man's gun had fallen into the snow. Amanda was bending down to see whether she could find it when a man's voice said, "Hello, Amanda. How you doing?"

Quickly turning to see who was there, Amanda found herself staring at a man in a red parka. It took her a moment to recognize him. It was Ron Miner, the man whose image had been distorted in her reports on corruption in New Shipton. He was holding a revolver. "What are you doing here?" she asked, confused.

"I followed him," he replied, looking at the man who'd tried to burn Ashley alive.

"Why? I don't understand."

Without waiting for an answer Amanda moved to Ted, who was still lying in the snow. His flashlight was beside him, still shining, providing the light in which this bizarre scene had been played out. Ted's eyes were open, following her movements.

"How bad are you hurt?" she asked him.

"Shoulder wound," he said, his voice revealing the intense pain he was in. "I don't know how bad, but it hurts like hell." He shuddered. "I might be going into shock. I'm cold, light-headed. Have . . . have to get out of here."

Shifting her attention to Ron Miner, Amanda said, "We have to get him out of here. He's going into shock."

Miner shook his head. "You don't get it, do you?"

"Get what? I'm extremely grateful that you saved our lives, but we've got to get Ted out of here quickly."

Again Miner shook his head. "I wasn't saving you. I was taking advantage of the opportunity to kill him."

Amanda just stared at him, not understanding any of this.

"I didn't go to you with what I knew just because I'm a do-gooder. I wanted to get Casperson for a reason."

"What reason?" Amanda asked, the hope she'd felt a moment ago dissolving away, being replaced by the suspicion that all that had happened just now was the exchange of one executioner for another.

"The guy I told you about, Steen, the guy who wanted to build a restaurant and got stabbed to death because he wouldn't play the game by the rules, he was my half brother. No one in New Shipton knew, because we weren't from there. We grew up in Buffalo.

"I tried to tell him what it was like in New Shipton, but he wouldn't listen. He was too honest for that sort of thing. He would have taken on anybody before giving up his principles, and one of those principles was that he didn't like getting shaken down.

"I couldn't find out who did it, so I decided to get even the only way I could, by taking down Casperson and the whole damned town." He snorted. "And you know what? After I appeared in that series of reports you did, I found out who knifed my brother. Buchanan did it. So I followed him."

"Why?" Amanda asked. "Why follow him all the way out here?"

"Still don't get it, do you? I planned to kill him, sure. But I also needed him."

"For what?" Amanda demanded. "I don't understand any of this."

"To lead me to you."

"Me? Why me?"

"Because I have to kill you too. Casperson's never going to give up until he finds out who betrayed him. And you're the only one who knows. At the moment no one suspects me. I'm just a computer operator in the records office at the police station, nobody important."

"I'll never tell anyone. You know that."

"I bet you told him," Miner said, looking at Buchanan.

Amanda started to deny it, then stopped herself. There was no point.

"Casperson can hire hundreds of guys like him," Miner said. "And once you told one of them who I was, he'd find me. Wouldn't matter where I'd gone. He's got the money and contacts. He'd find me."

"Casperson's going to jail," Amanda said. "He can't hurt you from there."

"You are naïve, aren't you? Don't you know that guys like Casperson can arrange anything they want to from the pen?"

"So now you're going to become a killer, just like him." She looked at Buchanan.

Miner shrugged. "This way I get the best of everything. I kill the guy who murdered my brother, and I've messed up the people who ordered him hit. With you gone, no one can ever find out it was me. I quit my job in New Shipton, go to California or someplace else with a nice climate, and nobody ever knows it was me."

"But . . . but what about my daughter and Ted?"

"Breaks of the game," he said.

Amanda was still on the ground with Ted. He seemed to be trying to communicate something with his pain-filled eyes. But Amanda had no idea what. His gaze dropped slightly, and so did Amanda's. She saw the tree branch she'd tried to use as a weapon against the man whose name was apparently Buchanan. Amanda moved her hand closer to it. She noted that Ted's holster was empty. She assumed that his gun was somewhere in the snow.

The pain making him suck in a ragged breath, Ted pushed himself up on one elbow, looked beyond Miner, grinned. "Over here!" he yelled. "Over here!" And then he lay down again, wheezing, his face lined with the suffering he'd endured to do that.

Ashley caught on a second before Amanda did. The girl yelled, "He's got a gun!"

For a moment Miner looked confused, then he whirled around to see for himself, and Amanda realized this was her cue. Grabbing the broken tree limb, she lunged at Miner, swinging the makeshift club with all her strength. The snow caught her feet, and she was falling as the club made contact, so it hit his legs instead of his head, which had been her original target.

But it hit them hard, knocking him off his feet.

The gun flew from his hand.

Amanda scrambled after it on all fours, reaching into the depression in the snow that marked its location. From the corner of her eye she saw Miner, also on his hands and knees, trying to get to her before she could retrieve the weapon. Then Ashley was there, jumping on Miner's back, trying to keep him from reaching Amanda. But the girl weighed less then a hundred pounds, and Miner easily knocked her off him.

Amanda dug frantically in the snow, and then her fingers hit something hard. But it was too large and slippery to be the gun. Another fallen tree limb probably. She moved her search to the left, and again her fingers found something hard. Miner was on top of her now, his hands on her throat, squeezing off her air supply. The hard thing she'd found seemed to be the gun, but she was unable to get her hands around it.

Ashley came to her rescue again, attacking Miner with the tree branch. She was too light to do any serious damage, but she distracted him, and the grip on Amanda's neck loosened. At the same instant Amanda got a firm grip on the gun. Ashley swung the club at Miner, and he grabbed it, yanking it out of her grasp. And in so doing, he momentarily forgot about Amanda. She pressed the gun into his side.

But Miner was unaware of it. He had the club now, and he planned to use it on her. As he raised it over his head Amanda pulled the trigger.

Miner simply fell over. That was all.

For a moment Amanda just lay there, her heart thumping madly. Then she realized it wasn't over yet. She had to make sure Ashley wasn't hurt. She had to get help for Ted. Suddenly Ashley was beside her.

"Mom, you okay?" Her face was as white as the snow.

"Yes. How about you, kid? You okay?"

"Yeah."

"Let's see about Ted."

The deputy was lying where he had been, but now his eyes were shut, his breathing shallow. "We've got to get him out of here," Amanda said.

"How can we?"

They tried dragging him and gave up after ten feet. He was much too heavy for them. "We'll have to leave him," Amanda said. "We've got to get help."

Not knowing what else to do, they checked Buchanan, who was clearly dead. Amanda removed his parka and put it over Ted. Miner was still breathing, though raggedly, so she didn't take his. They followed Miner's tracks, assuming they would lead them out. Amanda was glad that jeans, insulated shoes, and hooded coats were standard wintertime apparel for this part of the country. They wouldn't have survived ten minutes dressed for winter in Boston.

Following the tracks worked. They emerged from the woods at the end of the road, where four cars were parked—Amanda's, Buchanan's, Miner's, and Ted's cruiser. They headed for the cruiser because it had a two-way radio. But before they got there, headlights appeared, grew brighter.

It was a state police car.

Amanda and Ashley rushed up to it, waving their arms.

EPILOGUE

AMANDA was sitting on the couch, doing her best to hold back a big grin when Ted came in. After giving her a quick kiss he stood there in his deputy's uniform, eyeing her curiously.

"Well?" he said.

"Well, what?"

"You're sitting there looking like you're about to bust."

"It's that obvious, huh?"

"It's that obvious."

"I got some really good news today," she said teasingly, not wanting to let it all out at once.

"There any chance you'll tell me what it is?"

"Guess."

"Give me a hint."

"Okay. I got a long-distance phone call about twenty minutes ago."

"You mean . . ."

"Uh-huh." She nodded, feeling the grin break out, spread across her face.

"Tell me."

"It's only a five-thousand-dollar advance, but I've sold my novel. My agent says the next advance will be bigger, but I have to start low to get my foot in the door."

"An extra five thousand bucks is five thousand bucks. Who's complaining?"

"It's going to be a paperback original," Amanda said.

She saw that Ted was grinning too. Suddenly he pulled her to her feet and hugged her.

After Ted had recovered from his bullet wound he asked

279

Amanda to marry him. Although she'd wanted desperately to accept him on the spot, she owed it to Ashley to talk it over with her first. To Amanda's relief Ashley thought it was a marvelous idea, but then Ashley always had been and always would be a great kid.

To Amanda's immense relief Bob Miller had pulled through. The bullet that had put him in a coma had grazed his skull but caused no permanent damage. The other bullet hit him in the chest, managing to miss everything that was vital—by a sixteenth of an inch in some cases.

Bob had told Amanda she could come back to the TV station whenever she wanted, but she'd decided even before Ted proposed that her career in journalism was over. Because of the New Shipton story, three people had died, including Buchanan himself. And the total had nearly been seven, she and Ashley and Ted and Bob Miller being the other four victims. Amanda was soured on TV news. In her mind it would always be linked to what had happened to Bob Miller and Dick Kilmer—and what had nearly happened to her and Ted and Ashley.

She was happy living out here in the country with Ted. She loved him completely. He was thoughtful, kind, caring, generous, and hundreds—if not thousands—of other adjectives, all of them complimentary. If he had a fault, she was unaware of it—or maybe just too much in love with him to care.

Although she was Amanda Anderson now, Ashley was still Price. They'd left it up to her, and Ashley had said she had nothing against Ted or the name Anderson, but she was used to being Price; besides, she said, learning a new name would be confusing enough when she got married, and at thirteen she simply didn't need the hassle.

Her crush on Eric Carlson had ended after about six months. Apparently Eric's crush on her was over as well, because he'd become interested in a girl named Jennifer, with whom he'd put together a joint project for the state science fair. Ashley, meanwhile, had been talking about a boy named Nathan. It seemed like only yesterday that she'd considered boys a subhuman life form.

"Damn, I'm proud of you," Ted said. He took her hands and they began jumping around in a circle, like a pair of kids imitating a square dance.

After a few months of being a housewife Amanda had become restless and decided she needed something to do. Ted suggested she try writing a novel. Amanda had resisted the idea at first, thinking her TV background hadn't really prepared her for book writing, but she'd finally tried it—a novel about a woman TV reporter investigating corruption in a medium-size northeastern city. At first she'd become caught up in the project because it was a way of getting it all out of her system, but eventually she'd fallen into the story, the telling of it, the use of words, the manipulation of sentence structure.

When the book was finished, she sent query letters to agents, asking whether they'd like to see the manuscript. The second one to read it said he'd like to represent the book.

"The second publisher to see it bought it," she said to Ted, who was still swirling her around.

"The one that passed it up will regret its error," Ted said, and she could tell that he truly believed it. His confidence in her ability was absolute.

"The publisher wants another book from me as soon as possible—one similar to the first one."

Ted stopped dancing with her and went back to hugging her. He was almost happier than she was. "Let's go into Hibbing and have a celebratory dinner," he said. "As soon as Ashley gets home from school."

"Sounds good to me. Who's going to protect the people in Fiddlehead Lake?"

"I'll ask the state police to cover for me. I figure I'm entitled to a night off every six months or so."

They sat down on the couch. Ted said, "While we're waiting for Ashley, tell me everything your agent said."

She did.

They were living in a small rented house, while workmen put the finishing touches on the one being built for them. The new place was on the other side of the lake from Bob Miller's cabin. They'd be moving into it in a few weeks. It was a log house, which Ted had always wanted. Three bedrooms, a big kitchen, a spacious living room. Amanda was sure she'd love it.

Bob Miller had sold his cabin to some people from the Cities. He'd offered it to Ted and Amanda at a good price, but they'd declined. Ted wanted his log house, and for Amanda the place was a constant reminder of what had happened. A new house was a new beginning.

Edward Casperson and at least a dozen officials of the city of New Shipton, Massachusetts, had been indicted, tried, convicted—on numerous charges—and were serving long prison terms. Ron Miner had worked a deal with the Minnesota and Massachusetts authorities, agreeing to testify against Casperson and the others if charges against him were dropped in Minnesota. Persuading Minnesota authorities to go along hadn't been too difficult because the medical examiner had been unable to say which had killed Buchanan, the bullet wound inflicted by Miner or the knife wound inflicted by Amanda.

Amanda had learned to live with the knowledge that she might have killed him. After what he'd done to Dick Kilmer and Bob Miller—and what he'd tried to do to Ashley—she knew the world was better off without Dexter Buchanan. The knowledge left her with a clear conscience, and she saw no reason to do any heavy-duty soul-searching.

About a month ago, Bob called to inform her that her New Shipton series had won three awards. She told him the station could keep them; she didn't want them. Bob said he understood.

She heard the school bus pull up out front, and a moment later Ashley hurried in, stopped when she saw Amanda and Ted sitting there. After studying them a moment the girl said, "There's a name for the grins you guys have on your faces, but you'd get mad at me if I said it."

Ted and Amanda laughed. "I sold the book," Amanda said.

"Wow! My mom's an author!"

For the second time that day Amanda was pulled to her feet and hugged.